"I fell in love with TWO ACROSS twenty seconds into the first page, and I swear—with my right hand raised and my left on a Jane Austen novel—that with this book you'll meet your new favorite author. His warmth and wit remind me of Laurie Colwin and the other best practitioners of smart romantic comedy. I wish I'd written this wonderful novel. Well, first I'd have to be as good as Jeff Bartsch."

—Elinor Lipman, author of *The View from Penthouse B*
and *The Inn at Lake Devine*

"What a quirky, witty, wonderful read. I ignored my family for the better part of a beach vacation because I couldn't bear to put down this gem of a book. Jeff Bartsch is an immensely talented writer, and I plan to be first in line to buy whatever it is he publishes next."

—Cristina Alger, author of *The Darlings*

"Hard to resist."

—*Library Journal*

T
W
ACROSS

a novel

Jeff Bartsch

GRAND CENTRAL
PUBLISHING

NEW YORK   BOSTON

Grand Central Publishing
Hachette Book Group
1290 Avenue of the Americas
New York, NY 10104

HachetteBookGroup.com

Printed in the United States of America

RRD-C

First Edition: August 2015

10 9 8 7 6 5 4 3 2 1

Grand Central Publishing is a division of Hachette Book Group, Inc.
The Grand Central Publishing name and logo is a trademark of Hachette Book Group, Inc.

The Hachette Speakers Bureau provides a wide range of authors for speaking events. To find out more, go to www.hachettespeakersbureau.com or call (866) 376-6591.

The publisher is not responsible for websites (or their content) that are not owned by the publisher.

Library of Congress Cataloging-in-Publication Data
Bartsh, Jeffrey.
    Two across / Jeffrey Bartsch.
        pages cm
    ISBN 978-1-4555-5462-1 (hardback) — ISBN 978-1-4555-9015-5 (international trade paperback) — ISBN 978-1-4789-0446-5 (audio download) — ISBN 978-1-4555-5460-7 (ebook) 1. Teenagers—Fiction I. Title.
    PS3602.A7785T96 2015
    813'.6—dc23
                                                            2015010958

For my parents, and for Zoe

Wisdom comes to us when it can
no longer do any good.

—Gabriel García Márquez,
Love in the Time of Cholera

T
W
ACROSS

CHAPTER ONE

1960

C harlatan."

Vera took a step forward, put one hand on her hip, touched the microphone stand with the other, and said, "Excuse me?"

"Charlatan," said the official pronouncer, Mr. King, exactly as he had the first time, with Old Testament rectitude.

The overhead lights, as well as those pointing up at her from the edge of the stage, bubbled with heat. She could feel the eyes of the eight remaining contestants seated behind her penetrating her back, their little hearts thumping in unison. She gripped the microphone stand. *Charlatan.* How did they know?

"C-H..." she began. She felt so light-headed that it seemed as if the entire ballroom in the belly of the great Hawthorne Hotel lifted slightly, and the crimson curtains lining the stage seemed to sway. There was no escape. Yes, she was a charlatan. She didn't belong here, little nobody Vera. There was her mother in the front row, hands in her lap, encouraging her with furtive lifts of the eyebrows. Of course she knew this word. It was a freebie, a stroke of luck. The previous word had been *dhurrie*, and after the atro-ciously peppy California girl with the long braid running down her back misspelled it, omitting the "h," the bell tolled with all the mercy of a scythe's blade.

Charlatan. She had been feeling like one all week, ever since the first day in DC when the kids got a view of bullet-shaped President Eisenhower waving from across the White House lawn. She didn't belong here. In fact, she didn't belong anywhere in that hotel, where a team of maids placed your toothbrush in a little porcelain stand, and room service arrived on fine china un-der silver domes delivered by a pair of men wearing white gloves. No, Vera was only really comfortable in her little nest of red leather and auto fumes, windows that roll up and down, roadside billboards drifting by. She had gotten used to spending quite a lot of time in the backseat of her mother Vivian's red-and-white 1955 Ford Fairlane Crown Victoria. That is, when she wasn't at their apartment in New York, where they'd been spending less and less time lately, and which felt as if it were their residence in name only. More and more now, she found herself biding her time in musty hotels settled into the crotches of crumbling East Coast towns, hotels that were made of cinder block and smelled of wet clay, or rickety wooden motels that smelled of attic and peeling paint, perched on the shoulders of lonely highways. The Hawthorne Hotel, however, had delightful odors floating nose-high on the air: lavender and rose and mint, fragrances that Vera associated in her mind with Paris, although she had only read about it, fantasizing a *jolie* existence there during her French lan-guage studies.

"I'd like to begin again," she said. Starting over was permit-ted, as long as the speller repeated the letters she had already spoken. "But first, may I have the definition?" She told herself that it was a good tactic to ask as many questions as she could, especially when feeling uncomfortable—even if she knew the answers. At the age of fifteen, Vera had already developed a coquettish, sly attitude toward adults, who, she found, could be surprisingly easy to fool.

"Charlatan. One making especially noisy or showy pretenses to knowledge or ability; fraud." Mr. King's careful voice seemed disembodied from the solid bald head that glistened in the haze behind the lights.

Vera took a deep breath. She was ready. She was alert. She had been preparing all her life to face the challenges of a merciless world. This is nothing, she reminded herself, compared to what's coming. If you're a charlatan, then be a good one. She stated the letters with pride. "Charlatan: C-H-A-R-L-A-T-A-N. Charlatan."

She turned to take her seat before the head judge even began to say, "That is correct." Applause lifted her like a wave and deposited her in her folding chair. She liked applause. Most charlatans do.

A small boy, Arthur Ito, who had all along seemed undefeatable, handling *daguerreotype* and *incunabula* easily, approached the microphone, pushed up his glasses, and clasped his hands behind his back.

"Aretalogy," stated Mr. King.

The boy squinted. "May I have the language of origin please?"

"The word comes from the Greek," answered Mr. King.

Arthur closed his eyes, and proceeded without pause. "Aretalogy: A-R-A-T-A-L-O-G-Y."

The brief, devastating chime of the misspell bell preceded a few groans from the audience, which, despite lasting mistrust of the Japanese still lingering from the war, was very much on Arthur's side. He pushed up his glasses and walked off with the same blankness of expression he possessed when he spelled correctly, only dropping his head into his hands once he passed into the wings.

Vera, motionless and defiant in her folding chair at the back of the stage, allowed herself to look side to side. Only seven of them left now. She still had a chance, a 14.29 percent chance. But they were in the final rounds, where the words get treacherous, and the pitfalls were much more sinister than the simple "e" that had felled Arthur.

As she awaited her turn, Vera tried to imagine what life was like for these kids who lived in permanent homes in Minneapolis, San Francisco, Denver. She was both jealous of and curious about the solidity of their lives but, at the same time, assumed that they were exceedingly dull. What were their houses made of? Were they fancy or plain? Did they have long straight driveways and dogs resting on the living room rugs?

Vera sighed in a dismissive way and said to herself, "Tedious children." She spelled the words in her head that felled two more contestants—*katharometer*, *crepitant*—until it came around to a handsome, slender boy, fifteen years old like herself, who she'd heard lived in a hotel too. Only he lived in *one* hotel, this hotel, the palatial Hawthorne in Washington, DC, only blocks from the White House.

His name was Stanley. A strange boy. She didn't know quite what to make of him. He seemed languid and self-effacing, nearly melting into his chair when he sat down, but at the same time his manner was unbearably aloof and much too confident for a boy his age. The way he loped up to the microphone in his tweed jacket and oversized wing tips, took hold of the microphone, cleared his throat, and leaned down into it as if it wasn't at all an awkward thing to be doing—like he was a professor at a lectern, or a magician.

Exactly right, Vera thought. Incorrigible. That's exactly what that boy is. And maybe a little conceited too. Incorrigiceited. There's a word for him.

"Incorrigible," Stanley repeated. He spelled it gently, pronouncing each letter as if it were a tender thing—a puppy or a seedling—waited politely for the head judge to affirm that he was correct, although he clearly knew it, said "Thank you, sir," and turned and walked soundlessly back to his seat. For an instant, his eyes settled on Vera with apparent disinterest and then moved on. I will beat him, thought Vera. By the end of this day, he'll have Vera Baxter burned into his memory.

When Stanley settled into his folding chair, he felt a bit exhausted by it all for the first time. He had spent his entire life pretending to be somebody he wasn't—somebody ambitious, hardworking, responsible—when in fact he was just naturally gifted, with a mind that never let go of a fact. The truth was, he had no ambition besides lying on his back on his bed, looking at the ceiling, and thinking about things. He would have liked having a girl by his side now and then, but that was about all he really wanted out of life. To be left alone. Now here he was on the stage, pretending once again to be somebody he wasn't. The words themselves hadn't become very challenging just yet, but the strain of having to compose himself and walk all the way to the microphone, spell his word under all of that crushing attention, in particular the pressure of his mother's gaze, and then walk carefully all the way back to his seat was taking its toll. When Arthur Ito went out Stanley started to feel that he had a real chance. Sitting calmly in his chair he had tried to tell himself that he wasn't interested in winning, but now, as he turned to look at the trophy that flashed distractingly on a table at the edge of the stage, he had to admit that he was eager to take it back to his room.

Up next was a blond boy from a farm in Indiana, with whom Stanley had chatted in the hotel lobby, the place where Stanley spent most of his time. For as long as he could remember, he had made it his living room. He talked to senators there, generals and admirals, members of the diplomatic corps from pages to ambassadors, political speechwriters, lobbyists, reporters from the *Post* and the *New York Times*, Douglas Edwards from the TV news. Very seldom did he have the chance to talk to another boy, and never a farm boy from the Midwest. When he arrived, Stanley and this boy sat in the plush leather chairs between the marble pillars of the lobby and quizzed each other on word lists. Stanley silently wished him luck, hoping that if he weren't the winner, this boy would be.

His word was *bioluminescence*. There's one he'll know, having seen plenty of fireflies in real life, Stanley thought.

"Definition, please?" the boy asked, his voice amplified and cracking.

There was a pause as Mr. King placed his fat finger upon the word in question in Webster's 2nd Unabridged. "The emission of light from living organisms as the result of internal oxidative changes."

The bell chimed when he spelled the end of the word as "essence," a careless mistake. Stanley could see the frustration register on the boy's face as he quickly wheeled about to leave the stage, his long journey over. It was clear that he knew he should have gotten it, but he was tired or anxious or both.

Then came the quiet, nervous girl in the blue dress, Vera, and he suddenly felt that he had figured out what it was that struck him about her. Bioluminescence. Her pale, almost bluish skin seemed to soak up the light from the stage and glow with it. It was enchanting, but something about her also repelled him— her reticence, her ferocious concentration, maybe. She was good. She was a threat. He didn't know why he wanted to win—this whole thing was his mother's idea—but he did want to win, and he hoped for a wickedly difficult word.

"Brujo," said Mr. King, his finger on the page as if he were ordering a rare bottle of wine.

"May I have the definition please?" Despite how delicate she looked, the girl's tone was strong, almost challenging.

"Sorcerer, witch doctor; especially one who works black magic."

Stanley found himself staring with fascination as she dispatched it in a burst of letters and seemed to make a show of walking slowly back to her seat.

He saw his mother in the front row, wide-eyed and recoiling like a trapped animal. With the help of their friend Sonny Jones, one of the hotel's managers and jack-of-all-trades, she had pried herself out of her reading chair and made her way down from their room to watch the bee. This pilgrimage was a testament to Sonny's abilities, because Stanley's mother was deathly afraid of people—anthropophobia was what it was called—and this was one of her rare appearances outside Suite 512, the William Henry Harrison Suite. The hotel gave the suite to his mother after the death of his father, who had been the hotel's concierge and whom Stanley never knew, in the Second World War. Ever since then, Stanley and his mother lived there for the token rent of one dollar a month. It was the least desirable suite in the hotel, and Stanley assumed that factored into the hotel management's largesse. The sort of people who could afford a suite wouldn't be pleased with this cramped one named for a president who died after serving only one month in office.

Stanley's mother, who'd sat fixed in her chair by the suite's window overlooking Vermont Avenue since the early 1950s, had learned about a local spelling bee in the *Washington Post*. What caught her eye was not the bee itself, but the fact that the winner, if he or she went on to win the regionals, could then compete in the National Spelling Bee, which was to be held that year right there in their very own Hawthorne Hotel.

"How about that!" she said to Stanley, smacking the paper with the back of her hand, an unusually enthusiastic gesture for her. "Right here in our very own ballroom."

Children would travel from all over the country to compete, but her Stanley, her senator-in-training, could simply walk the crimson carpet down the hall to the elevator and ride the golden car down to the ballroom. It was this nifty convenience, rather than a strong interest in spelling, that started her off on a course that eventually saw her son become a master speller, win regionals, make it to nationals, become one of four spellers out of an original 103 still on stage, and lope up to the microphone to await his next challenge.

Mr. King examined the word he held in captivity beneath his forefinger.

"Brummagem."

*   *   *

Vera's feeling about Stanley had gone from curiosity to strong dislike. He was too arrogant, too self-assured. She could sense something duplicitous about him from the start. And now she was disappointed with his word. She had hoped for something more difficult, a real assassin.

"Brummagem," Stanley repeated. "May I have the definition please, sir?"

"Spurious," said Mr. King. "Especially in a cheap and showy way; phony, sham."

Vera tucked a hand under her thigh and scrutinized Stanley as he spoke.

"Does it originate from the city of Birmingham, England?"

"Yes, it does," said Mr. King.

Vera pulled her hand from under her leg and quickly covered her mouth. What a showoff, she thought.

"And does its meaning come from the fact that counterfeit coins and other cheap and flimsy things were manufactured there?" Stanley asked.

Mr. King, whose emotions played out clearly on his face, looked down at his tome and said, "Why, yes, it does."

Soft laughter rippled through the audience. Stanley waltzed through the word with ease, spelling it in a careful cadence, and returned to his seat in an insufferably dignified manner. Maybe I'm not the only charlatan here, Vera thought.

Vera found herself searching the audience, wondering which of the faces belonged to his parents, and she missed hearing the next word. Donna Walker, the very brainy-looking thirteen-year-old from Seattle with spectacles thick as security glass, was beginning to spell. She tested the letters as if stepping out on a frozen lake.

"P . . . U . . ."

What was the word?

"I . . . S . . . A . . ."

Vera knew she'd misspelled. Automatically she covered her eyes with her hands.

"N . . . T."

The bell rang. Mr. King delivered the correct spelling of *puissant*, and the quietly sobbing girl was led offstage by one of the bee coordinators.

Only three of them were left. Vera cocked her head and stole a glance at Stanley.

Up stepped the only other remaining girl, Agatha, who lived in Alaska with her parents, her grandparents, and several dozen malamutes. Her father was a chemist and her mother bred dogs. She was an outgoing kid who had befriended Vera on their very first day in DC. Vera had met her parents, and spotted them in the audience now, straining forward in their seats like the very dogs they harnessed to sleds.

"Thurible."

Agatha asked for the definition and got it: a censer used in religious services.

Agatha asked for the language of origin and got it: Middle English, from Middle French, from Latin, from Greek.

Vera spelled it in her head and waited. She knew she was next. A tremor of nerves ran through her and she tried to squelch it. She crossed her arms and knitted her forehead, willing Agatha to succeed even though they were competitors. Agatha's allotted time of ninety seconds ran out.

"T-H-U-R-A . . ."

* * *

Stanley knew then who his final challenger would be. He watched her sashay up to the microphone, looking utterly in control of all those judges and spectators. She was virtually glowing in all of her bioluminescent splendor.

As she stood there awaiting her word, Mr. King announced that because there were only two spellers remaining, they would move on to the championship words. They were taken from a fearsome list of twenty-five of the most difficult words in the English language, devilishly selected from the remote depths of Webster's 2nd Unabridged. If one of the two remaining spellers were to make a mistake, the other would get a final word, and if he or she spelled it correctly—victory.

Vera tightened her grip on the microphone stand. Mr. King cleared his throat. The thickness of the air was visible in the dusty beams of the stage lights. A chair creaked in the audience. With the utmost gravity, King delivered *oligopsony*, and Vera crumpled to the floor.

The audience got to its feet in a great wave from front to back. Stagehands rushed from the wings and the judges' table cleared as they surrounded the girl. A figure cut through them all with the purpose and authority of a doctor. She cradled Vera in her arms and the others made room. With practiced efficiency the woman administered raisins from her handbag to Vera as she regained consciousness.

"Low blood sugar levels," the woman said to the judges, the stagehands, and Stanley Owens, who craned his neck to get a view over the others. "She's..."

"Hypoglycemic," Vera said flatly, lying on her back and staring up at the insectile underbelly of the stage ceiling.

The woman was apparently known by Mr. King and the other

judges, but she introduced herself to those standing nearby—"I'm Vera's mother, Vivian Baxter"—and briefly described how she'd been unable to coax her stubborn daughter to eat her oatmeal that morning, when Vera's voice broke in.

"Oligopsony," she said, still lying on her back and staring at the ceiling. "O-L-I-G-O-P-S-O-N-Y."

Mr. King leaned over so Vera could see up into his fleshy face and said with delicious bemusement, "That is correct, young lady."

Back in her seat, among the empty chairs of all the departed spellers, Vera ferociously chewed raisins and watched Stanley ruffle his hair. She couldn't forgive herself for losing control. She would have liked nothing more than to sneak outside and puff furiously on one of the Chesterfields that she hid from her mother, not necessarily because she needed a cigarette, but because she enjoyed the image of herself doing risqué things that were beyond her years and forbidden.

His word was *seigneur*. She knew he didn't have to ask the origin; of course it was French. The ending was easy. She knew he knew it. It was the first syllable he was considering. But in French there aren't a lot of possibilities for the spelling of a sound like that. It wasn't that difficult. Was he stalling to give her time to recover? She hoped he wasn't patronizing her. Finally, he sighed, spelled the word correctly, and returned to his seat. As he passed he looked down at her and smiled. Suspicious, she couldn't decide if the smile was genuine or smug.

Stanley tried not to look at his mother. Sonny sat with his hands on Martha's shoulders as if holding down a wet cat in a bathtub.

Sonny, the avuncular figure in Stanley's life, was forty going on eighteen and somewhat the opposite of Stanley. Sonny smiled all the time. He had fabulous teeth and was as lean as a bundle of sticks, even though he was always helping himself to a bit of whatever food passed by his nostrils. He had the metabolism of a lion and a squirrel's appetite for the busywork of life. In the absence of a father, Sonny watched over Stanley as he grew up, administered fatherly advice, and taught Stanley how to serve a tennis ball in the indoor court and how to throw a pitch on the hotel roof. Now he was helping out with Stanley's mother, whom Stanley couldn't look at without fearing what would happen if he didn't win. At the back of the room he saw a few men enter: senators from Virginia, Maryland, and Delaware, with whom he was particularly friendly. The watchful eyes of these men didn't give him anxiety, yet his mother did, motionless in her seat with her chin on her fist.

Vera's word was *Thucydidean*. Vera was the caretaker of a small collection of nervous ticks: the eye rub, the elbow flex, the neck crack, the finger extension, the hair flip, developed under the pressure of her own expectations for herself. She ran through them all as *Thucydidean* waited. Vera asked if the word was related to the Greek historian Thucydides. Then she spelled it correctly. Stanley's mother sat back, removed her glasses, and polished them with her handkerchief.

Vera watched her mother watch Stanley. Her mother was a smart competitor, and Vera imagined her wishing to climb up onto the stage and finish off the bee herself. During their years together living part of the time in New York City and part of the time in hotels as Vivian sought a husband and traveled for her work as a secretary to a sales executive, sometimes with the hope of the latter leading to the former, Vera escaped into her books and fashioned herself into a sharp instrument of learning. She grew to love learning, especially math. She was perplexed by the common perception of math as a dry subject. To her it was a playground of the imagination, rich with ideas and fascinating magic. Vera also loved languages, finding pleasure in French novels that could transport her out of her mother's car and into entirely different worlds of adventure and passion.

Stanley got *scopperil*. Vera knew her mother couldn't spell it. She could see her trying to work it out, anticipating a Stanley stumble, but she also sensed that her mother was fascinated by that precocious kid. Stanley made a little wave to the important-looking men at the back of the room and proceeded to spell. Every eye in the place was on him as he pronounced each letter as an honored member of the alphabet. The men at the back applauded as Mr. King declared his spelling of *scopperil* correct, and Stanley gave a nod and thanked Mr. King.

The competition moved along briskly without either fifteen-year-old showing any sign of weakening. Vera spelled *mycetismus*.

Stanley spelled *pyrrhic*.

Vera spelled *ageusia*.

Stanley spelled *chopine*.

Vera got *piscivorous*. She ran through the eye rub, the elbow flex, the neck crack, the finger extension. She stumbled and gripped the microphone, and the audience briefly rose from its seats. "I'm okay," she said, and a nervous laugh ran through the room. With composure, she asked the judges if it came from the Latin root *pisci*, meaning "fish." Once that was confirmed, she cleared her throat and with impeccable posture laid out the word with ease. When Mr. King pronounced her spelling correct, she performed a celebratory hop before taking her seat.

When Stanley spelled *inessores* after a moment's contemplation, his only show of joy was a smile and a slight lift up onto his toes before walking back to his chair near Vera. His world had tightened to a small triangle containing his mother, the judges, and his seat near the enigmatic Vera. All else was a haze. Behind Vera's static exterior Stanley sensed a tiger pacing in its cage.

"Damascene," said Mr. King.

"Damascene," repeated Vera. "D-A-M-A-S-C-E-N-E. Damascene." She spelled without a single question or show of emotion, singeing Stanley with the blaze of her concentration as she passed on to her seat.

Mr. King himself seemed exhausted. He took a handkerchief from his pocket and wiped his brow. Silence in the audience. Silence in the ballroom, save for the hum of the ceiling fans and the amplified crackle of papers on the judges' table. Stanley approached the giant microphone in its mesh cage.

"Exsiccosis," said Mr. King rather grandly.

Vera watched the movement of Stanley's jaw and his shoulders as he asked for the definition and language of origin. She couldn't take her eyes off him. His shoulder blades made marks on the back of his jacket.

Mentally she took a stab at the word just before Stanley began to spell it.

"E-X-S-I-C-O-S-I-S," he said.

The bell rang. Disaster. The judges at the table couldn't seem to look at him. His mother gazed up at a distant corner of the ceiling, and Sonny held on to her tightly. Stanley's legs carried him back to his seat.

"If the next word is spelled correctly," said Mr. King, although everyone knew the rule, "we will have a champion."

Vera approached the microphone.

"Dioscuric," he said.

"Dioscuric," she repeated. "Is its origin Greek?"

"It is."

There was a long pause, during which Vera's mother crossed and uncrossed her legs several times, adjusting her skirt, adjusting, adjusting.

"D..."

The audience collectively inhaled.

"I-A-S-C-U-R-I-C. Dioscuric?"

Ding. The audience flared up with chatter and motion. Stanley was back in.

"We have six words left," said Susan Nestor, the director of the bee. "If you two spell those correctly, that's the end of the championship list. We would have only the second tie ever in the history of the National Spelling Bee."

Vera seethed, feeling suddenly claustrophobic and in love with the idea of rushing off the stage and out of the building, but she floated along on the moment, lost in a fog of letters and prefixes and suffixes. Stanley got *flammulated* and spelled it. She hated him. *Hated* him.

Vera spelled *oecus*.

Stanley spelled *salaam*.

* * *

"Appoggiatura."

Stanley watched her narrow form swaying slightly as she went through her routine. He closed his eyes and wished for her to omit the second "p" or the second "g" or to do something stupid like add a second "r."

"Appoggiatura," he heard her say. "A-P-P-O-G-G-I-A-T-U-R-A. Appoggiatura."

"Eudaemonic."

Vera imagined a car sailing through a guardrail on a mountain pass, the guardrail weak as aluminum foil, Stanley's profile in the backseat, Stanley finally losing his annoying composure as the car dropped out of sight and a big, cartoon-like explosion rose from the valley below.

"Eudaemonic," he said calmly. "E-U-D-A-E-M-O-N-I-C. Eudaemonic."

"We've now arrived at the final word on our championship words list. Our last chance for a sole victor," said Susan Nestor. The audience murmured softly. Vera stood at the microphone.

Mr. King said, "The word is ornithorhynchous. Ornithorhynchous."

After getting the definition, Vera fell silent. No neck crack. No finger manipulations. No hair flip. She dropped her head as if conceding. Stanley looked out at the audience and saw his mother packing her purse. For her there could be no other outcome but victory for her son. She got up and Sonny guided her out of the ballroom.

Vera's mother, Vivian, in her black dress, waited nervously on the edge of her seat, forming a crisp L shape with her perfect posture. The room was silent. A sense of something gone wrong swept through. What was going on? Had she given up? Stanley simply sat with his hands in his pockets. This didn't feel like victory.

As Stanley's mother left through the double doors at the back of the ballroom, a rush of air swept all the way up to the stage and seemed to rouse Vera.

"Ornithorhynchous," she said, as if in a trance. "O-R-N-I-T-H-O-R-H-Y-N-C-H-O-U-S." Then, as she repronounced the word, she knew she had it and her voice rose up with triumph. The audience cheered wildly and Susan climbed up onto the stage to unite the hands of Stanley and Vera.

"We have a tie! Two very deserving winners, who spelled their way through the entire champions word list."

Vera hopped up and down with excitement. Even though she hadn't gotten the sole victory she was trying for, she couldn't contain herself. Stanley looked calmly happy. This was a result his mother could live with.

Together Vera and Stanley drifted through a speckled world of mandatory ogling, dreamy with light—flashbulbs, TV lighting, still photo lights under umbrellas, city lights—leaving an overall impression of pixie dust spilling across the days. Their mutual detestation was swept under the rug, and they found themselves paraded about like a royal couple, obligingly posing together, set up in mock spelling competitions, and rudely poked and prodded like sideshow freaks. The whole thing was covered in a paralytic haze, which may have explained why an exhausted Vera returned to her hotel room one evening and doodled on a pad, "You are cordially invited." In elaborate script she added "to the marriage of

Vera Baxter and Stanley Owens." She looked at the words blankly, then in a fit of disgust tore the sheet from the pad, crumpled it, and threw it in the trash.

*   *   *

June 1962

"It doesn't look like much, does it?" Vera said.

"No. It looks like a smashed penny," Stanley replied.

"Or a rusted bottle cap."

It was two years after their tie. The previous June, their first year back as visiting alumni, they were interviewed by a reporter from the *Washington Post* for an article on their joint victory titled "Fit to Bee Tied." During that interview, it emerged that Vera had never done any proper DC sightseeing. So there they were, in an area of the Medical Museum of the Armed Forces Institute of Pathology that dealt with Lincoln, and the thing they were looking at, under a glass sphere like a snow globe, was identified with a small brass plate that read, "The bullet that took the president's life."

"Gives me the heebie-jeebies," Vera said.

"Me too. Yet it's one of the least creepy things we've seen here." Stanley was referring to the plaster cast of Lincoln's face, with hollow divots for eyes and, below the face, hands that seemed to be reaching out to them. And the gruesome Civil War–era amputation kit. And most disturbing of all, the fetus floating in a glass jar, pale as candle wax, featuring cyclopia, with one eyehole above the mouth and a proboscis above that.

"Let's get out of here," she said. "Where to next, my guide?"

Stanley led her out past halls of historical prostheses, antiquated microscopes, and curious specimen jars. They hailed a taxi and got in.

"Fifteen twenty-nine Eighteenth Street Northwest, please," Stanley said. "I think you might like this next stop."

The cab pulled up to a light brown brick town house with a metal gate in front. Vera got out and said, "This place looks familiar. Where are we?"

"Mathematical Association of America, HQ. Don't know if there's anything to see here, but I figured it's more interesting than sculptures of dead presidents."

"Agreed," she said, opened the gate and stepped right up to the front door.

On a side table in the lobby was an easel holding a board that read, "Today's Problem." The two of them paused to read it: "Al gets the disease algebritis and must take one green pill and one pink pill each day for two weeks. A green pill costs ten cents more than a pink pill, and Al's pills cost a total of $54.60 for the two weeks. How much does one green pill cost?"

"Expensive pills," Stanley said.

"Piece of cake," Vera said, and walked on. Stanley stood there puzzling for a moment longer and then caught up to her.

They spoke to the receptionist, who informed them that they just missed the president, Albert Tucker, who returned to Princeton the day before, but that they were welcome to poke around. Vera introduced herself to some of the mathematicians wandering about, and boldly proclaimed that someday she would be a member, "maybe even president. If my future husband doesn't mind me being a career woman," she added with a facetious grin. Two shaggy-haired gentlemen gave her a problem to take with her. On the way out, the receptionist handed Vera a complimentary copy of their journal, the *American Mathematical Monthly*. As she flipped through it, she saw a photograph of the building and said to Stanley, "Ah, that's how I recognized this place." Whispering to him, she said, "I already subscribe. Didn't want to burst her bubble."

"One last stop," Stanley said to her as he closed the iron gate outside the MAA headquarters. They walked the half mile to the corner of Fifteenth and L Streets in introspective silence. Lifting his hand toward the building as they approached, Stanley said, "The *Washington Post*," as if it were the finest destination in the capital. They took the company tour, and while they were in the stifling room where the printing presses banged away at rolls of newsprint, Stanley said loudly over the noise, "That math problem—the answer is two dollars." Vera turned to face him and held out her hand for him to shake. She nodded and smiled.

Back at the hotel, they parted in the lobby, with an awkwardness that was typical of brainy teenagers. But something additional sputtered and sparked around them with algebraic depth. Stanley stood rigidly and Vera did too as they arranged to accompany each other to the bee over the next few days. "See you tomorrow," she said. "Be a good boy, now," she added as she twisted a strand of hair around a finger, and slipped coyly between the closing doors of the elevator.

CHAPTER TWO

O n a quiet evening in the fall of 1962, two and a half years after the bee, Stanley sat in his chair in the lobby of the
Hawthorne Hotel and turned his notebook to a fresh page. On it
he drew sixteen vertical lines and crossed them with sixteen horizontal lines, making a grid of boxes. Below the grid he made a list
of his theme words and phrases, and sketched in some ideas for
clues.

Stanley's pencil scratched on the paper as he began by filling
in his longest theme entries. BLITZENKRIEG, he wrote in the
boxes running vertically along the upper right side of the grid.
The clue sketched below was "Swift attack by a reindeer."

A cardinal rule of crossword construction, as Stanley figured
out during his years of solving them, is that each puzzle must
have diagonal symmetry. So his twelve-letter theme word in the
upper right had to be matched with a theme word using the same
number of letters in the lower left of the grid. MASTERRACERS,
he penciled in. He already had his clue for that entry: "Aryan
NASCAR drivers." He tilted back his head and looked apprais-

ingly at the puzzle, assessing the quality of the theme, one that skewered the Nazis who were responsible for taking away his father.

At eighteen years of age, Stanley was five feet ten and arguably as intelligent as anyone in Washington. He had a mind ravenous with curiosity, almost dangerously so, but at this point in his life, zero wisdom. Stanley's brain ached with the knowledge crammed into it, and yet everything felt wrong. His father was dead, had died before Stanley was even born, and without him, everything—every report he wrote, every book he read, every puzzle he made or solved, every look from his mother, every tennis game he played, even lunch—everything felt wrong.

Everything, that is, but the newsstand in the Hawthorne Hotel. The newsstand was positioned in the grand lobby like a sailing ship moored in a bay. It was the ten-ton flagship of news vendors everywhere. With pillars at its four corners and a canopy where heraldic cherubs trumpeted the latest happenings, it reminded him of the baldachin in St. Peter's Basilica. Stanley saw a picture of it while reading the *Encyclopaedia Britannica*, under the entry for "Vatican." From there, he sailed on through the Wyomings and Xerxeses and Yellow Fevers and Zambias, and presented his Summary Encyclopedic Report to his mother, ending the task she had set him at the age of ten—reading the entire twenty-four-volume set, Aachen to Zymurgy.

The newsstand was a freestanding autonomous territory of polished mahogany and marble and fittings that could declare itself at any time, secede from the hotel, unmoor itself, and sail away. There were papers hung from clips, papers stacked for sale, and papers stretched on wooden rods, to be borrowed like in a library, and the guests in their overstuffed chairs holding up their long broadsheets looked like so many independent dinghies luffing out upon the windless lobby. Every morning, the trucks rumbled up to the loading dock at the back of the hotel. Then Charlie, the morning attendant in waistcoat and bow tie, snapped the twine on the bundles and set the sails of the great flagship. Up went the *Washington Post*, the *New York Times*, the *Philadelphia Inquirer*, the *Boston Globe*, the *Chicago Tribune*, the *Los Angeles Times*, the *Charlotte Observer*, and all the minor papers from coast to coast. Charlie raised them all up and the voyage of discovery began, powered by great gusts of local, national, and international events.

Stanley looked back at the puzzle he was constructing and filled in more theme words. HEALHITLER, he wrote, for which the clue would be "Fix the Führer." For the clue "Fork's role at breakfast," he filled in the answer LIFTWAFFLE, hoping that solvers would get the connection to *Luftwaffe*. He placed them carefully around the grid and, based on the architecture established by the theme entries, began to think about the black spaces and the pattern they might make.

Stanley looked up and saw Albert, Charlie's evening counterpart, with his hands flat on the marble and his bifocals perched on the very outermost molecule of his nose. Albert gave him a smile and a wave, and Stanley walked over to say hello.

"Good evening, professor," Albert said.

"A fine evening to you as well," Stanley replied, with the panache of a Hollywood gangster.

Maybe it was only Stanley's imagination, but Albert seemed to be examining him with a curatorial eye, looking for small changes. In the years since his spelling bee tie, Stanley found himself increasingly disgusted by his books, a new attitude that was partly a natural change brought on by the pressures of his life and by the fact that he considered it pretty much finished. His entire existence was one of academic slavery, performing like a trained monkey for the satisfaction of his neurotic mother, and the future she laid out for him was more of the same. To be fair, he loved learning. He had a junkie's craving for knowledge, a need for information of all kinds, from atomic structure to the haiku masters of Japan. But he did not love forced learning, the hours of study measured by the kitchen timer, the monthly IQ tests. Enough was enough. His mother, on the other hand, already had a very grand and kingly future planned for him: Harvard, Harvard Law, a job in Washington, an ascent to district attorney, a move to Virginia where he could run for senator, then a long and noteworthy career in the Senate and a retirement on the golf course. Maybe she'd watch him Sunday mornings on *Meet the Press* when her bones were brittle as breadsticks.

"I won't do it, Albert," Stanley said softly. "I don't know what I'll do, where I'll go, or how I'll survive, but I won't do it. I may as well climb into my coffin." But Albert had already walked away to help a customer before Stanley even started speaking.

Stanley returned to the comfort of his chair to finish entering theme words. His play on *Third Reich* was penciled in near the center: THIRDREEK. The clue would be "Stink after second." GUESTAPO (clue: Invited secret police) and NOTSEE (clue: To be blinded by ideology) finished out the theme. Now it was a matter of creating a pattern of black squares and filling in the remaining spaces around the established entries. He appraised the grid so far, closed his notebook, and returned to the William Henry Harrison Suite.

*   *   *

Stanley's mother, Martha, worked for the Honeythorne Publishing Company as a proofreader. They sent her manuscripts wrapped in brown paper, and she carved them up with a red pencil, as focused as a medical examiner, clucking her tongue in disbelief at the grammatical crimes perpetrated there. Occasionally she would gasp, jolting Stanley from, say, the essays of John Stuart Mill. Stanley used to wonder what shocking subject matter she had come across, but when he asked, it always turned out to be nothing more scandalous than subject-verb disagreement, or a wayward apostrophe lodged between two letters like a poppy seed in the teeth.

Three months ago, just as the summer was winding down, Stanley came into the suite from his weekly indoor tennis match with Sonny to find his mother waiting for him at the little table in the main room of their suite. Instead of his usual language books, she had arrayed in front of her, fanned out like a fortune-teller's deck, an assortment of brochures from all the Ivy League colleges.

"Well, Stanley," she said. "I think it's time we bestow upon Harvard the gift of a brilliant new student." She looked up with her usual intensity, eyeballing her son with the mastery of a lion tamer. "These other applications we'll use for practice."

"I don't think I want to go to college after all," Stanley said, fiddling with the racquet. He liked to test his mother's ever-positive attitude, beneath which he knew lay a deep pessimism.

She gave an exasperated sigh, as if to say, "Your humor does not amuse me."

"I've been thinking about becoming a crossword puzzle creator," he said truthfully, but in a way that suggested he was teasing.

Martha looked down and unclipped the application from the

Harvard brochure. "Harvard, Stanley. Pay attention. You'll write the essays for the other schools first so you'll be in form."

Stanley knew that she knew, despite her refusal to admit it, that there was a chance, minute though it might be, that he would not be admitted to Harvard. It was *possible*, the way a volcano erupting on the Washington Mall was possible. So she armed herself with the other applications just in case. Yale, Princeton, Cornell, Dartmouth...all the Ivy League schools. Not cooperating was not an option, because Martha Owens could brook no disappointment. Not since the horror of that day in 1945 when a certain Sergeant Promise, of the United States Army Air Forces, knocked on the door of their apartment. Martha answered, newborn Stanley lay drowsily cupped in her arm, and Sergeant Promise took off his hat.

Martha had loved her husband deeply, and from that day forward she would not stand for disappointment, bad news, or negativity of any kind. Up would go her hand and out would come the words Stanley learned to detest: "I don't want to hear about it. I've had enough for one lifetime." So in this way a gloss of sham happiness was brushed over everything and he was forbidden from talking about his doubts, his nightmares about war, the frightening thoughts that came to him about his future, the deep pangs of yearning for the grinning man in the photograph by the door. Forbidden from asking the questions he longed to ask about his father: Did he like his job? Was he smart? Was he curious about everything like his son? Did he do crossword puzzles too?

Stanley could talk to his mother about what he was reading, or about the happenings around the hotel; he could tell her about the pigeons on the roof and whom he'd seen in the lobby and whether or not he was hungry and what he wanted to eat. But he couldn't talk to her about anything that really mattered to him. So he went to the desk in his room, took a paper and pen from a drawer, and began writing.

Dear Dad,

I don't want to study anymore. I want to retire from it. To be totally honest, I want to retire from life. I'm trapped in this hotel while Mom's becoming more and more disfigured by her own self-imposed imprisonment. She's embraced her aloneness and turned away from the world. There's surrender and decay everywhere in this stifling suite, and life's only hope and salvation is college, college, college. I hate the thought of it, and of law school and a life of work without passion. My hatred of it is equal and opposite to Mom's yearning for it. For every action there is an equal and opposite reaction. Do you know Sir Isaac Newton's Third Law of Motion? Can you believe he formulated those thoughts way back in 1687?

Better question: Why am I asking things of you when you no longer exist? It's crazy. I guess I just want to believe that you can help me find some kind of solution. Dad, put a message in a newspaper headline. Send an idea in a song lyric. Help me think of a way to escape.

Love,

Stanley

He carefully folded his letter, slid it into an envelope, licked it, sealed it, and affixed a four-cent Camp Fire Girls stamp. On the envelope he wrote in big capital letters, one word: DAD. He stuffed the envelope in his back pocket and left the suite while his mother napped in the chair she permanently occupied, as if she had been stitched into it. This chair in which she interred herself over the years had a deep indentation in the cushion, bearing a facsimile of her backside, and the velvet armrest on the right was worn to a reflective sheen. He walked three blocks to the mailbox positioned on a corner like a small blue soldier and dropped in his letter. He stopped for a moment with his hands thrust in his pockets, gave the mailbox a longing glance, then sighed and turned back toward the hotel.

Feeling ridiculous about the letter, he rationalized that people do things all the time that don't make any sense, just because they have an itch to do them. Like it or not, people are driven by whims, hopes, superstitions, commemorations, dreams, and why-nots. He knew what would happen to the letter. It would be picked up and taken to the post office, where it would be handled by the mail sorter, who would frown and toss it into the dead letter cart. The cart would sit there until it filled up with rejected mail that could not be returned for any number of reasons, then be wheeled away and its contents tipped into the Dumpster beside the loading dock. Even so, he still could imagine a scenario in which somehow his father's spirit was united with the thoughts and wishes in the letter, just as children imagine their wishes in letters to Santa being received and given very careful consideration by a man who does not exist.

That was a few months ago. Now it was time to do something. In his room with the door closed, he concentrated so deeply on his Nazi-themed puzzle that it felt as if he might tip headfirst into the notebook page and disappear through it. Tight fists of interlocking letters twined together almost too easily, as if the words themselves had their own will. Some of the longer words flopped into their places with great cordiality but later presented intractable problems and had to be exhumed and new, more agreeable words were knitted into the lattice. Where MAPLE didn't work, MABLE did. Where OPERATIC presented a problematic ending, OPERATOR sufficed. If a word wasn't interesting, the entry could be made so by the clue. "One who performs an aria?" for example, for OPERATOR. The pencil flipped from lead to eraser and back again. With a sharp "Fff!" he blew the erasure scraps away and almost as quickly filled in another section. He flew along with the speed and precision of a surgeon involved in a time-sensitive operation. Then suddenly he was surprised to find that the grid was complete. He sat up and looked around to see that the world of his room was just as he had left it some time ago. He stretched, stood up, and sat back down to check his work. Many of the clues had already suggested themselves as he filled in the grid, and so it was a fairly simple and enjoyable matter to write the remaining ones as the frenzy and euphoria of creation settled and all that was left was a gentle bouncing of one leg.

When he had finished writing the clues, he slid a sheet of paper into his typewriter and began typing up the puzzle. When he was done with that, he drew in the grid lines with a black pen and a ruler. With the puzzle spiffed up and formalized, he opened another drawer and took out his legal pad. It still brought a quick smile to a corner of his mouth—his solution to what he called The College Problem. The page was divided into two columns. On the left, a list of newspapers to which he planned to submit his crossword puzzles. On the right, a list of colleges to which Martha expected him to apply. His plan was this: Each time he sent out a new puzzle, he would address it to the paper in the left column and write the name of the college in the right column as the return address on his stamped self-addressed return envelope. This way, he reasoned, he could send out his puzzles, and when the responses came back, they would appear to be acceptances of his college applications (for there was no possibility, in his mother's mind, of any rejections). He hadn't yet figured out how to handle her wanting to see the letters of acceptance, but he'd cross that bridge when he came to it.

Stanley put a check mark beside the two items on the first line: the *Washington Post* and Princeton University. Then he slipped his freshly made puzzle into an envelope, along with a cover letter to the puzzle editor. He added his self-addressed stamped envelope, with Princeton's admissions office as the return address. If the editor was confused by that, so be it. He licked the seal, folded it over, and pressed it closed very thoroughly from end to end. As for the colleges, Stanley didn't apply to a single one.

And so began the first big deception Stanley practiced upon his mother, designed to put an end to his life of study. For an hour or two each day during the few months leading up to the new year of 1963, Stanley sat at the little table with a notepad in his lap, seemingly hard at work on the applications and the essays while Martha sat in her chair by the window, wearing her robe and slashing her way through a heap of manuscripts. Every week or so, he found himself especially satisfied with one of his crossword creations. He took that puzzle, paired it with a university he was instructed to apply to, and sent it off to the next newspaper on his list. Day after day, Stanley waited for the mailman to bring the replies. Weeks went by. The mailman was a short, lively little fellow of fifty or so with tidy habits and a slight limp that caused him to rock side to side as he sped into the lobby of the

Hawthorne. He traded his brimming cart for an empty one, and whoever happened to be working at the desk sleepily distributed the mail into slots with little clicks.

Finally, the first response came in an impossibly thin wisp of an envelope.

No, said the *Washington Post*.

The wording was maddeningly brief and evasive:

"Thank you for your fine puzzle submission. However, we regret that we are unable to accept it at this time."

If it was so "fine," then why were they "unable" to accept it? His legal pad reminded him that the Nazi puzzle was the one he sent to the *Post*, and even though he tried to put a little humor into it, he was convinced that the gloomy theme was his mistake. Or maybe the puzzle just wasn't very good.

One early-winter day, he started work on a grid whose theme was words ending in "-some." He began by listing all the words he could think of in that category. Winsome, awesome, toothsome, wholesome, burdensome, darksome, fearsome, frolicsome, quarrelsome, twosome, threesome, venturesome. He thought about what he might title it. "Try Some"? Martha's Point-O-Matic electric pencil sharpener emitted a viperous hissing.

"Irksome," he mumbled.

"Pardon me, Stanley?" His mother looked up.

"I said I'm lonesome." He didn't know where it came from but it was true.

"Oh, Stanley. You have me."

"I know, Mom."

"And you have all your friends here at the hotel."

It was true he couldn't leave the suite without running into some maid, porter, or frequent guest who would quickly engage him in conversation. He was easygoing despite the brokenness within, knowledgeable about most any topic, and always enjoyed talking. But his mother set such a demanding study schedule that, until recently, he naturally found it imperative to do what was asked of him, which was to study. Alone.

"And you've got your tennis friends," Martha added.

That, Stanley knew, was also true. His teammates admired him because he was an excellent player—slim and limber and quick—with a serve turbocharged by bottled-up frustration. He was good enough to be the team captain, if only his school attendance record were better.

"It's all right, Mom. That just slipped out. I'm fine."

Martha went back to her work. She was inhospitable to negativity, and it slid off her like facts off a politician.

Stanley's thoughts returned to the tennis team. He wasn't close with those boys largely because he didn't see them often enough. Mainly due to the fact that most of his schooling was done at home. Martha didn't trust the schools to teach her son, not *her* son, and she couldn't afford private school. So to avoid sending him to "that place with all the hoodlums," the two of them established a lie.

He didn't like school much as a young boy, because he was such a foreign specimen that the kids made fun of him and left him by himself. He knew that in addition to his bookishness, his keen hunger for a father and the frozenness of his mother lent him a sort of stunned maturity that didn't mesh at all with the free-form energy of his classmates. So he started going only sporadically.

Then, when he was in fourth grade, as Martha struggled for an excuse to keep him at home, Stanley took it upon himself to come up with a solution. He thought that he might convince the school that his mother was an invalid who needed his vigilant attention. He studied diseases and long-term illnesses. Testing them out in his imagination, he cast her in the role of paraplegic, narcoleptic, stroke victim, parasite host, cripplingly obese, colon lacker, malaria victim, basket case, leprosy sufferer. That is not to say that he didn't love his mother. Despite all her flaws, she wanted nothing but the best for him, as far as she was capable of understanding what that meant. But, as a simple matter of fact, and as a consequence of her being constantly underfoot yet controlling him from above, her omnipresence had a kind of Chinese water torture effect.

"Mom, I think the best solution to this conundrum is for you to write a note to the principal telling him that you've had a stroke, and you're partially paralyzed, and you need my help at home," the precocious boy said after much thought.

"That just may do the trick," she replied.

So that was the story they created. It helped that she really was paralyzed, in a way—paralyzed by fear of calamity, fear of the life that lay beyond the hotel room door. Through a doctor acquaintance who worked directly for the Surgeon General, and who Stanley knew was stashing his rather horsey-looking mistress in a room at the Hawthorne, Stanley procured, by way of a very delicately phrased understanding, a genuine signed statement of Martha's condition. He didn't have to worry about her being spotted by someone from the school at, say, the grocer's reaching up on her tiptoes for a jar of pickles, because she almost never left the suite, and absolutely never left the hotel. She was so hermitic, in fact, that the hotel doctor pleaded with her to sit by the south-facing window on sunny days to get her vitamin D.

Upon receipt of the note, Stanley's school let him do his work at home, assigning a teacher—dopey, confused Mr. Platt—to monitor him. Stanley blasted through his flimsy homework assignments on the bus on the way home from the one or two days a week he spent at school.

Now, Martha tried again to put a positive spin on Stanley's claim that he was lonesome.

"You know, you have Vera's spring visit to look forward to," she said.

Yes, Vera. That diamond-sharp character in a blue dress with a hand on her hip and one eyebrow raised, as if to say, "And in what way will you fail to impress me now?" Despite his intent to remain aloof from attachments, he looked forward to seeing her.

"Hey, partner," she said when he saw her again last year, their second year at the bee as previous winners, surprising him from behind with a bump on the shoulder.

"Hey there," he said. "How have you been?"

"How have I been?" She thought for a second and said, "Itinerant." Bouncing her head with each letter, she said, "I-T-I-N-E-R-A-N-T, itinerant," and laughed, touching his forearm and leaving her hand there for a long moment. "Feels like Mom's been dragging me around the East Coast since the Truman Administration."

In the days after he took her on their unconventional sightseeing tour, he waved to her wherever they happened to come across each other in the Hawthorne, and she waved to him, and they sat contentedly side by side not saying much to each other, like foreign dignitaries who didn't speak each other's language. Or longtime spouses who thought they already said everything there was to say.

There was something very capable about Vera. She had an appearance of lost nobility. And she was bold, though the results were mixed. One day she walked up to him in the hotel, cocked her head, and studied him, squinting a bit, and said, "Hey there, brown-eyed handsome man," apparently in reference to the Chuck Berry song. It came out of nowhere and felt more clumsy than sweet. He said, "Thanks, I guess," and tried to relax his features.

There was something else that was odd about her. It felt as if some important signal meant specifically for him lay within her. He suspected she had a crush on him. He got enough glances from girls at the hotel to know what an admiring look felt like. Almost a bit too frequently it seemed, he and Vera came across each other passing through the hotel on their separate ways somewhere, and Stanley would steal a glance at her—simply out of curiosity, of course—and catch her stealing a glance at him.

"By then you'll be admitted to Harvard," said Martha, interrupting Stanley's thoughts and bringing him back to the conversation about Vera's upcoming visit. Martha aimed her pencil at the sharpener and said, "You'll be all set, and you can share the good news with her." She smiled the smile of a girl who is abruptly crossing the street on a summer's day to meet a friend she has just spotted, and is about to be flattened by a truck. *Grrr* went the Point-O-Matic.

Stanley left the suite for the hotel lobby, where he searched for a stray paper. He found a *New York Times* and instantly folded his way to the puzzle page. He took a seat and pulled out his pocket watch and set it on the arm of the chair.

The Air Force had never sent any effects from his father. The details of his death were never explained to Stanley, and asking his mother would have been to poke into her deep, infected wound.

So one summer when he was a boy, Stanley bought a cheap pocket watch that he saw hanging in an overlit display case in the hotel sundries shop, and ever since then, he pretended that the watch was sent to him along with the rest of his father's imaginary effects. The folded and pressed uniform that he visualized with a frayed hole right through the "O" in Owens. The crinkled photo of his mother, looking girlish and beautiful and not the least bit reclusive. Maybe a medal of some kind, stone-heavy with rococo brass and inlaid porcelain—like something pinned directly into the bosom of a czar.

Stanley glanced at the watch, containing within it not only tiny gears and springs but also intricate dreams of a man he never knew. He noted the time and began to work the crossword.

Eskimo woman's knife: ULU
Bird shot by the Ancient Mariner: ALBATROSS
Moslem prince: EMEER

Stanley's fingers raced to keep up with the answers his brain was sending. He finished and looked down at the watch. Three minutes ten seconds. Acceptable. One of the problems with crosswords, Stanley felt, was the lack of consistency from puzzle to puzzle, the lack of any guiding principle aside from a rigid love of the arcane fact: minor characters of myth, long-forgotten vaudeville performers. Later, Stanley would notice that puzzles were changing, establishing a pattern of increasing difficulty as the week wore on—first in the *New York Times*, then other papers. But back then it was random. Three minutes ten. He took a notebook out of his pocket and wrote down the date, the name of the newspaper, and the time.

Across the lobby he spotted a round smudge of blue. As Stanley's eyes adjusted from the close scrutiny of the puzzle, he recognized Charles Greaper, the owner of the Hawthorne. He was a bloated puffball of a man with a confused expression and a tuft of white hair sticking up from the top of his head. He was constantly hurrying somewhere and poking his nose into things, so it seemed like he was permanently perched on his tiptoes. Stanley bristled at the thought that he should feel grateful for the man's generosity. In his assessment, Greaper was so benevolent only because he coveted Stanley's mother. "How are you enjoying the suite, son?" was Greaper's standard absentminded hello to Stanley, forever reminding Stanley that he and his mother were under the thumb of their debt to him. He stopped by their suite just a touch too often, at just the wrong hours, just to say a shy hello to Martha, while he seemed to eat her up with his eyes. The man was married and had a family. Stanley stood straight and tall near the door at those times, waiting to escort him out. Now, the sight of him ruined the fun of doing puzzles in the lobby. Stanley folded his newspaper and got up to return to the suite.

The next morning, Stanley sat on the floor of his room with his back against the door, bouncing a tennis ball against the wall and catching it with an oven mitt, in imitation of Steve McQueen in *The Great Escape*. Stanley sighed and stood up, left his room and went to the door of the suite, hesitated a moment above the white rectangle on the blue carpet, and then scooped up his prey.

The letters had been coming in from the newspapers. The puzzle page editors didn't seem to be concerned about the return addresses of Ivy League colleges on the envelopes he enclosed for their responses, and Martha didn't seem to notice that the envelopes his replies came in were all stamped and not metered. She also didn't seem to notice that they were all typed in the same style and not printed with each college's unique graphic identity, as the stationery of an Ivy League college would be. Martha's hopes for him soared in blissful ignorance over all such trivial detail.

He walked into the kitchenette, where she was seated in front of a piece of wheat toast and a hard-boiled egg in an eggcup. He shredded the edge of the envelope and unfolded the white petals of the letter. The sound caused Martha to look up, her eyebrows delicately elevated.

"Congratulations," he pretended to read. There was no other possible outcome.

His mother was impressed by his lack of egotism, the modest forbearance with which he seemed to accept his acceptances.

He let the envelope drop onto the table where she could see the return address: Brown University. He was very careful not to let her see the letter, and was worried that if she asked he would have to abruptly change the subject and try to distract her. But she didn't ask. He then folded the letter and returned to his darkened room, where he imagined all the nasty things that might one day happen to the paper that just rejected him: the *Wall Street Journal*. He'd sent them his puzzle featuring words ending in "-some," and the fact that this puzzle, one he was so proud of, was passed over left him feeling, as he mumbled to himself, "gruesome."

Five mornings later he loped into the kitchenette, where his mother huddled in front of a steaming cup, cradling it in her delicate hands as if it were the sole source of heat remaining in the universe.

An envelope appeared in her field of vision.

"Another one!" she said, meaning another acceptance, sitting up and extending her neck like a goose after a slice of bread.

"Yes," Stanley replied, gravely analyzing the letter in his hand.

The goose got a peek at the torn envelope. "Penn?"

"Yes, the U of Penn," he said absently, looking at the letter from the *Philadelphia Inquirer*.

"Congratulations, Stanley!" She shivered with positivity as he puzzled over the rejection notice—a form letter. Not even a personal note suggesting he try this or try that next time. And it was a damn good puzzle. Stanley had started tailoring some of his puzzles to the cities he sent them to. For Philadelphia, he used the theme of famous Phils: Phil Spector, Phil Silvers, Philip Johnson, Punxsutawney Phil, Philip the Bold, Philip of Macedon. He titled the puzzle "Phil It In." It had taken him a week to construct, because he had to engineer it around "Punxsutawney," and because he wanted it to be exactly perfect. He even planted a little gimmick just for his own satisfaction. In the four corners of the puzzle he placed the first, sixth, eighth, and second letters of the alphabet, forming 1682, the date Philadelphia was founded. What a shame.

Only two of his puzzles remained in circulation, the ones he'd sent to the *Chicago Tribune* and the *New York Times*, still carrying out their marching orders or possibly making their beleaguered way back from the battlefield in shame. What if these puzzles failed? What then?

He imagined winding up in some end-of-the-line flophouse somewhere in America, populated by old men whose parts were falling off, with a stained cot and a dripping tap, that he would pay for with some dreadful job washing dishes or bagging groceries, and maybe selling his blood. If only there were some kind of freak show he could join—The Amazing Brainiac! Ask him any question and he'll answer it! How many protons does a uranium atom have? 92! Who was Charlemagne's successor? Louis the Pious! What is the capital of Jan Mayen? Olonkinbyen! Step right up and try to stump the champ!

March 12. Martha sat at the table, gently tapping the shell of her egg with the side of her spoon the way a doctor taps a patient's knee with his mallet. Stanley tore into the envelope with a sound like the biting of toast.

The physician looked up.

He almost blurted it out in his frustration—the *Chicago Tribune*, and no. He thought they would have been tickled by his "Windy City" theme. He'd arranged synonyms for wind throughout the puzzle: breeze, gust, puff, blast, gale, draft, squall, bluster, tempest. Zephyr was particularly hard to fit in, but he'd made it work. He placed the envelope very gently, very sadly onto the table, as if lowering a body into a grave. The return address of Yale made itself visible to his mother, as Stanley made a quick association then between the university and the maker of locks.

"How *wonderful* darling!"

Yes, how wonderful.

A week crept by. Then another. On Saturday, March 28, the mail was late. Stanley was too impatient to wait for Steven or Jesus, the friendly porters who usually slipped the envelopes under the door, so he went down to the lobby to watch for the mailman. He observed a formally dressed elderly gentleman escorting his wife into the hotel with his hand on the small of her back. Maybe it was Stanley's state of mind, but there seemed to be much more activity than usual. A group of excitable young women clutched each other and hopped up and down. Then one of the managers came out of the office to greet them. Stanley recognized immediately that it was a wedding.

Weddings at the hotel had been a part of Stanley's life for as long as he could remember. The swooshing silk of a bridesmaid rushing by with pins in her hand, or the sight of a caterer fretfully transporting a wedding cake, were as common to Stanley as a man tending his lawn was to a suburban kid.

By late afternoon, Stanley had given up waiting for the mailman and found himself wandering around the hotel in a state of agitation. The Hawthorne had been stormed by the wedding party. Through open doors he saw sheets and blankets torn from beds, empty pants collapsed on the floor showing the white flashes of their pockets, wallets clam-shelled open and cast aside, gnawed bones on china plates, gossamer dresses on hangers waiting to be occupied. Every open door offered a glimpse into worlds not meant to be seen, revealing the private, messy transitions from one self to another, with a maid at work quietly resetting the order of the universe. Esther, one of the older maids whose husband had also been killed in the war, turned and saw him and gave him a look of exasperated futility. "What you going to do?" she said. "Big day. It's okay," referring to the mess all around her. She too was in thrall to the theater of the wedding party, herself a part of its stagecraft.

After leafing through all the major dailies at the newsstand until well past sundown, Stanley finally wandered into the ballroom where the reception was being held, and found Sonny flattening himself before the wonder of womanhood. He was penned in behind one of the crepe paper–covered bars set up along the sides of the ballroom, faintly whimpering with desire, and when he was visited by cautious female customers, his teeth sparkled as he filled their glasses to within a hair's width of the brim. He filled them so full that they couldn't walk off with them and had to bring them to their lips ever so carefully as he inquired whether perhaps they would like a cigarette, a fresh rose, a taste of the world's finest caviar, a foolproof method for removing wine stains, tickets to a show for a fraction of their face value. The wedding reception was at full tilt, the men reddening, the women exalted, the dance floor heaving, and livers in full throttle. In a far corner stood the table holding gifts—piled high with a metropolis of shiny, beribboned boxes, silver and white and blue and gold. A stack of envelopes spilled from under a cloud of baby's breath. Stanley had a vision of the checks and cash they contained releasing a hazy array of dollar signs. A speeding idea passed through his mind, but just as quickly, he started thinking that it might actually be quite pleasant to be Esther, just going about her work with no expectations of greatness overshadowing her, and by the time he turned his attention back to the idea it was gone, and his memory couldn't catch it.

He returned to the suite and went straight to his room and was immersed in a book about the making of porcelain when Martha tap-tapped on the door.

He opened it. She stood there in her threadbare pajamas, holding a letter in front of her and grinning like an asylum escapee.

"Harvard," she breathed heavily.

Finally. Stanley had arranged it so that the return address from the college that was most important to his mother coincided with the paper that was most important to him: the *New York Times*. She delivered the precious object from her fingertips to his. He made her wait while he went to his desk and retrieved a letter opener, carefully lanced the envelope, unfolded the letter and read the contents as Martha suffered greatly.

"Oh for God's sake!" she said.

He looked up. A genuine smile spread across his face, reflecting the breaking news of a joy greater than any he had ever felt.

"Oh, Stanley!" She hugged him tightly, wrinkling the letter they had taken such care with.

Late that night, she did something extremely rare. She cooked. In their tiny kitchenette, which folded out from a vestibule like a magician's kit, she boiled two lobsters, delivered by a room service waiter from the hotel's walk-in cooler. The ever-present classical music of WGMS was turned up just a little bit louder for the occasion, and as steam filled the suite and made the windows opaque, it felt a bit like New Year's Eve. Stanley found himself naturally searching his mind for someone to tell his good news to: He was going to have a crossword puzzle of his own making published in the nation's greatest newspaper, the *New York Times*. And in the Sunday edition, at that. Exclamation points danced in his head.

The puzzle's theme was the neighborhoods and boroughs of New York City. Not only had he worked the city's neighborhoods into the puzzle, he had arranged them geographically around the square. The Bronx was at the very top, and below that, Harlem. Queens was at the right, above Brooklyn, Staten Island was at the bottom. Midtown was dead center, and below that, Chelsea and then Greenwich Village. The Upper West Side was on the left, the Upper East Side on the right. It had taken him two weeks, three pencils, and four erasers, but he'd done it. And now, thousands of people would solve his creation in their living rooms, on subway trains, at kitchen tables, in parks, in Pennsylvania Station, at lonely diners, in secret at their desks. He wished the paper would identify him as the puzzle's creator so everyone would know, but the fact that crosswords weren't published with bylines was actually a good thing for now, in that Martha wouldn't know what he'd been up to. In any case, he wasn't doing it for fame. For the first time in a long, long time, he had something to care about and treasure. He repeated the name of the paper to himself in a whisper, the *New York Times*, as Martha in the kitchenette was no doubt whispering to herself, *Harvard*.

He had an urge to share the good news in a letter to his dad, and drop it into the swinging jaw of the mailbox, simply for the comfort of knowing that a message to his father was out there in the universe, giving him permission to imagine an impossible delivery. But he rejected that in favor of telling someone living, someone whose reaction he could enjoy. Of all the people he knew, there was one in particular he felt an impulse—for no logical reason—to tell. Vera Baxter. As his mother poked the red lobsters in the pot of boiling water, he asked her to remind him of the exact date of Vera's arrival, less than two months away. Then he went to the calendar hanging near the picture of carefree Nick Owens and marked on that date a small V, for Vera, and for Victory.

CHAPTER THREE

Vera Baxter was one of those girls who was in love and didn't have anyone to talk to about it. Further complicating matters, she wasn't quite sure whom she was in love with, or even if the urgent feeling she had inside really was love. She could speak fluent French; she could understand and be thrilled by Gödel's incompleteness theorem, running her finger over the lines that thrilled her; she could tell you everything that was known at the time about subatomic particles; but she couldn't make sense of the seemingly obvious lamentations of her own heart.

Vera and her mother, Vivian, had been holed up at the Nitee-Nite Motel on Route 7 east of the Adirondacks for almost the entire month of May. It was a low, decrepit row of doors and windows with a thin covered walkway dividing the line of dank, pine-paneled rooms from the gravel parking lot out front and the interstate beyond that. It smelled of dry cedar and musty linen, and even in May, enormous weeds breathed forth their vivid scents like a sigh. Its creaking porch of weatherworn planks was an invitation to bad decision-making. It was crawling with boys—marvelous-looking cretins.

The Nitee-Nite Motel was roughly equidistant to Burlington, Albany, and Concord, New Hampshire, towns into which Vivian made her sorties while Vera lay on the bed reading book after book and going loopy with the mildew and the time and the lust that swirled all about. She often went out onto the porch to stretch and watch the cars blow by. The wretched family that owned the motel had a son who was about Vera's age and had a thing for T-shirts with the sleeves cut off. He had a couple friends who came around in a Cadillac convertible and sometimes could be seen shirtless in their wet cutoff jeans after swimming in the river behind the motel. It was hard to concentrate on the articles in *Nature*—a stack of which she had stored in her mother's trunk—while through the open bathroom window she could hear the whoops of the boys whose abdomens rippled like the Vermont hills. And then there was that feeling restlessly moving within her, something she compared to the turmoil of a werewolf during a waxing moon. She couldn't sit still and moved with her books from the bed to the Naugahyde chair to the linoleum floor and back to the bed again. She couldn't stop pulling back the curtain and spying on the boys, and every now and then Stanley made a chance appearance in her fantasies, like a professor shuffling absentmindedly into the wrong classroom.

The last time she set eyes on that young man was almost a year ago, their second year at the bee as alumni, when they did their sightseeing. She remembered that as she walked up to him in the hotel, a porter passed by with a transistor radio that was playing "Brown Eyed Handsome Man," and she blurted out, "Hey there, brown-eyed handsome man." The idea was to make him blush, but instead it was she who got all flustered and tripped over the next thing she tried to say. What was it about that boy that had gotten under her skin? He was the smartest person she knew, that was a fact. He had an attractive physique and she supposed he would look rather interesting without his shirt on, but that was merely conjecture. No matter, she thought, it's only because chance tied us together as winners that he stumbles into my thoughts in the most impertinent way. She forced a yawn.

She grew frustrated and bored. She was sophisticated; she was urbane; she was brilliant. She was stuck in this shithole in the middle of nowheresville. Vera leafed through the stack of *American Mathematical Monthly* journals that she last collected from their post office box in Manhattan. Open on the bed was *The Book of One Thousand Nights and a Night*, with which she identified because she felt a little like that captive who had to sustain her existence by making up things in her head. She put a hand on her hip, struck a match on the wall, and lit up a Chesterfield. She puffed on an extraordinary amount of Chesterfields in the Nitee-Nite Motel, and with her usual resourcefulness and improvisational mastery, she managed to hide pack, matches, butts, ashes, and odors from her mother.

Vera hadn't been able to work up the courage to talk to her mother about the strange feelings that were expanding inside of her. Vivian was a good mother, and a quick, competent secretary to a traveling salesman at IBM. Perhaps it was her determined attitude toward life that scared Vera off. Perhaps she was a little too ambitious for Vera's good, on the road more than she should have been, working hard taking dictation and putting together presentations so that someday maybe she might be given the opportunity to try her own hand at sales. And always on the lookout for husband material, always hoping that she might remarry and provide a "real home" to Vera. While it seemed to unnerve Vivian that her daughter at eighteen was the smartest person she would ever know, Vivian's determination alarmed Vera in turn. Sometimes it seemed that Vivian, with her perfect posture, had a warden-like way of closing the passenger door on Vera every time they motored on, scrutinizing her daughter for a split second through the car window.

So Vera never mentioned the crush she had on a boy named Doug. He was the motel owners' son and she thought she was in love with him. She imagined staying right there with him for the rest of her life and becoming a world-famous thinker from her remote location in a back room of the motel office. Douglas—she would call him Douglas, that would help—Douglas would run the show after his moronic parents shriveled and dried up and conveniently blew away somewhere. After a hard day's labor of the mind, she would lie with her hand on his chest and his supremely smooth body would flow and ripple darkly beside her, and she would feel gloriously sinful for a change. It was improbable. Doug was no genius. Doug probably wasn't going to college. He probably couldn't even spell *chrysanthemum*. Doug wore shirts without sleeves and his arms looked like rockets.

Vera wrote in her journal. When she wrote things that gave her an illicit thrill, she used a disappearing-ink pen with a skull on it that she'd found in a professional magician's shop in New York City on her twelfth birthday. The shop was an oddly disappointing place for such an art, sloppy and dreary, excessively revealing for a practice that depended wholly on concealment. Vera felt a deep kinship with magicians—so secretive and then, all at once, astonishing!—that she took this sloppiness as a personal insult. But the pen was a small miracle that she liked so much that when she left the shop, and the bell on the door jingled, she stopped, turned around, and went back in. She bought a box of refills. "One ought to last years," the theatrical man behind the counter said, one of his nails long and filthy. "No, I want two dozen," she said. She had plans; she had to provide for her future self, a shadowy figure slipping through obstacles to dazzle the world.

The day she bought it, she tested her new pen as the sun was warming her room. *With this pen I can write the saddest lines*, she wrote, paraphrasing Pablo Neruda. For long moments thereafter, the line looked so sturdy, the letters firm on their haunches and the ink rich and black. She watched carefully and nothing happened. Later that evening, when her mother was massaging her face with cold cream, Vera opened the journal to visit what she'd written and already the phrase was beginning to slip away. Next morning, faint traces prevailed: a trail drawn by a finger dipped in tea. By the following afternoon, only a phantom remained. The words surely were there if she wanted to believe they were there, and if she didn't want to believe, they just as surely were not.

With the disappearing-ink pen, which she had named Socrates, Vera wrote about how she was looking for someone to tell her that she was head and shoulders above all others. How she wanted to be chosen from among all the billions of people on the planet as the exceptional one. She wrote about how she was looking for a boy to be absolutely obsessed with her. *That* was the kind of love she wanted. She wanted a man to spend his life solving her and proving her like a theorem. She wrote about what she wanted on the floor of the Nitee-Nite Motel with her feet kicking furiously back and forth, and then what she wanted began its long disappearance.

During her time in the Nitee-Nite Motel, Vera feasted not only on the stack of *Nature* journals, but also *Fantasia Mathematica*, Arthur Rimbaud's *Une saison en enfer*, and *Euclid's Elements*, blending the romantic swirl of French literature with the fantastic machinery of math. The whole mélange left her feeling tumbled about, then afterward, blue, cool, and relaxed. Now she used the disappearing ink to describe how she had dreamed more than once of climbing a thick rope. To write about how she felt sexual whatever she was doing: peeling an orange, licking her middle finger to turn a page. She wrote freely of these things because she knew that after twenty-four hours, any trace of her confessions to herself would be gone.

Doug was washing the Cadillac with two friends when Vera came out to stretch, and surreptitiously advertise her figure to these boys who looked downright wolflike. "Candy Girl" was playing on the radio, and the sponges in the boys' hands swept big soapy arcs across the robin's-egg blue surfaces. At the moment, however, she didn't feel like a piece of candy in front of these boys. She felt like a math geek. She tried to relax her shoulders and then turned to retreat to her cave.

"Hey!" said one of them, a red-haired kid with a flattop.

She squinted into the glare of the sunlight throwing sparks off the car's chrome.

Then Doug said, "You look like you could use some sun."

She was pale as a snail, but privately vain about her Victorian skin that, in her reflection in the mirror, shone like the moon.

"Ever ride in a convertible?" asked the boy with red hair, his head cocked.

"Sure," she lied.

Doug said, "Vera, right?"

She wished she had some kind of title to resort to, something to throw in their faces that would show them how different she really was. "Vera Baxter, recipient of the Fields Medal in Mathematics," she would like to say, applying her sunglasses to her face and anchoring her hands to her hips. But then of course they wouldn't know what that was, or even care. Same with telling them she had won the National Spelling Bee. It would either have the opposite of the intended effect or none at all. What impressed these sculptures?

Her mother was in Albany assisting her boss with the sale of the 7080 to the government of New York State. She had brought Vera with her because, well, what else was she to do? She had no family to leave her with and didn't want to leave her alone. So Vera got the schoolwork for the weeks she would be away from her teachers, blasted through it before the car tires came to a rest at the motel, and carried on with her own independent inquiries of math and French and the peculiar ways of rural boys. There behind Vera, the motel door with ROOM ONE hand-lettered on it stood open. They'd spelled that right, at least.

"Care to take a little jaunt along the river?" Doug asked.

She liked the way he put that.

"Have you back in fifteen minutes."

Her mother was expected to return soon. Then they would pack to leave for New York the next morning, where the responses to Vera's college applications would be waiting for her in their PO box (Radcliffe, her number one; Barnard, her number two; and her safety, Pembroke College in Brown University). Then it would be on to Washington for their annual trip to the bee. It was her last chance to get to know Doug, maybe slip him her address in New York, perhaps written with disappearing ink, or perhaps not.

He opened the passenger door. "You can ride shotgun."

Also known as the suicide seat, she thought as she took it.

"So you like to read," Doug said as he inserted the key. It wasn't a question. He was puzzling her out and she liked that too.

"I read a book once," said the redhead.

Off they sped, white gravel pitching into the eastern dusk. She wished she had a scarf to tie around her head. Now it was "He's So Fine" by the Chiffons on the radio. It got lost in the air as the wind that fumbled frantically with her hair also snatched away the song.

What the hell was she doing? Vera had always been a creature of the mind. She had read about hormones, and long after she had gotten her period and her perfectly normal breasts and the hormones that came along with puberty, she was still bracing herself for their effect. The change they brought was slow in coming; maybe her defenses were too strong, because she still regarded most boys as fools. But this strange spring heat and sudden fascination with her buzzing body, this motel in its pocket of timelessness, this odd feeling at the back of her mind, had her all mixed up.

The forest whipped by on both sides, a green-and-black fantasia. Doug caressed the steering wheel. She saw a deer poke its way out of the dreamscape. An electrical storm began its attack off to the west, though it hadn't yet begun to rain. A little more driving and Doug pulled onto a dirt road to put the top up as enormous round clouds the color of grapes rolled overhead.

Doug let the car roll down a slope and under the branches of a pine tree. The branches scraped the roof of the car and made snapping sounds and then he braked and shut off the engine. The two boys who were not Doug went off to the river, as if they were running a play that had been called against Vera's defense. It felt wildly daring to just sit there in the seat next to Doug, as if she were standing on the ledge of a tall building, feeling the sensations of attraction and repulsion at play. She could think all sorts of wonderful thoughts that were almost as good as the physical experiences. A part of her mind was thinking about Sir Richard Burton traveling through Arabia in disguise. She had an urge to talk about *A Thousand and One Nights*, but these assorted boys in these forgettable towns knew no references. They'd heard of nothing. She had tried in the past to make a polite comment as she stood waiting at some grocery store or filling station with her mother, but they never understood. No. None. Nothing. She looked at beautiful Doug. He was a VACANCY sign dimly aglow, but it didn't matter.

He slung an arm around her, as simple as that. She felt confused—maybe those damn hormones were having some effect after all—and subject to wild swings of emotion. On one hand she was overcome with an amorous feeling, but then at the same time, did she really even like this guy? One thing she felt certain of was that she had courage. In fact, sometimes when she was huddled in motel rooms alone in the dark of night, her mother taking notes at a dinner meeting in some far-off town, with the wolves in the woods and the crickets laying siege in their hordes, she thought she was one of the bravest girls ever, learning to face her anxieties on her own.

On the radio the Miracles sang "You've Really Got a Hold on Me," rain clobbered the roof—it had started without her noticing—and the other two boys were still not back at the car. Here she was, with a boy, life-sized, with an epidermis and everything. He was going to kiss her, she knew. She waited for it like a special meal you've just ordered at a fancy restaurant—that notorious first kiss a dish she'd heard praised and moaned over but never tasted. Fortunately, her hypoglycemia did not present itself and leave her swooning ridiculously in the seat next to him. She was acutely aware of what she was doing. The part of her that watched herself was more alive than the one being watched.

Thunder. A percussionist warming up on the kettledrums. She had a question for him. She was going to try to put it to him kittenishly. Her plan was that after he gave her the obvious answer, she would open the door for him by saying, "Good boy. Now you can kiss me." It didn't feel natural to her, but she could imagine being impressed by some screen actress doing it, Grace Kelly for instance, and she steeled herself to pull it off.

"Say, what's the square root of four?"

He opened his eyes wide—*"Are you kidding?"* they said.

"What's the square root of four?" she asked, as incredulous as he. She couldn't believe it.

He couldn't believe it.

They sat there huffing in disbelief of each other, a standoff. His slack-jawed confusion appalled her.

"TWO!" she yelled at him.

He grabbed her by the wrist and pulled her toward him. Vera was startled; it happened so quickly. With her other arm she reached for the handle of the door but he was too strong for her. He pushed her down onto the long front seat and immediately was on top of her. He still had her by the wrist, and his other hand was up her shirt. That hand quickly came out when she started yanking his hair. Then she started screaming. That insipid "Lollipop" song came on the radio. It seemed to give him renewed vigor....*Lollipop, you make my heart go giddyup.* Her heart was going giddyup all right. The spurs of her adrenaline were tearing right into it. She scratched his face. He straddled her in his anger and ripped her shirt, which made a shocking noise.

Vivian had taught Vera the lessons contained in a brochure she had picked up at the YWCA called "Three Foolproof Ways to Disable a Man." They practiced them at rest stops for exercise, along with calisthenics. Vivian expected to need them someday; Vera never did.

Although Vivian's longing for a romantic partner was acute, her default strategy toward men was acutely defensive. Whether it was due to some flaw within her or simply bad luck, she tended to find herself all too often running the gauntlet of some very unsavory characters, initially disguised as quite ordinary men. This Vera knew from many monologues on the dangers of men that her mother delivered to her over the years. And although Vivian would allude to it only in the most vague of terms, Vera knew her own father had been one of these characters. The only thing she remembered of him was a scene that she may or may not have merely imagined: a man she somehow knew to be her father showing up at their door with a duffel bag that he dropped on the floor and out spilled a pack of cigarettes and a vial of prescription pills that made a sound like a rattlesnake. That sound was echoed in Vera's memory by the clicking of the rotary dial as Vivian calmly picked up the phone and dialed the cops, filling in the menacing silence between them. That was all Vera remembered, and as far as Vivian was concerned, the less she knew, the better.

And so as a girl, Vera was made to practice the Three Foolproof Ways at rest stops across the Northeast. At the time, Vera wondered, "If they're foolproof, why do you need three of them? Why not just one?" Nevertheless, having this arsenal she never thought she would need at her command was proving to be useful after all.

Doug was on his knees, straddling hers, and digging below the waist of her pants. She gave him a number one, the "Knee to the Acorns," and as it turned out, it *was* foolproof. Spectacularly, wincingly foolproof. He crumpled like an imploded building, all of him gathered in toward his groin. She rolled him off her, reached over her head for the door handle, pushed the door open, and clawed her way out.

Then she ran.

It had stopped raining but every leaf was shimmering and dripping, and now and then the wind caused the trees to shudder and throw down a shower. She ran to stay alive, her dove-gray brassiere switching side to side between her arms, her legs springing high like a doe's to clear the underbrush. The boys regrouped and were following her, whooping and shouting terrifying, obscene things at her and crashing and slipping not far behind. The effect of it all was enough that she believed if they caught her it would be the end for her. She ran until she couldn't distinguish the thrashing of the boys through the forest from the dry rustling at the back of her fear.

The boys were faster than Vera and came within spitting range, but she had more stamina because she had the ultimate motivation of survival. She ran like the gazelles on *Mutual of Omaha's Wild Kingdom*, cutting and banking. Her predators stumbled. Absurdly, that horrid "Lollipop" song kept pace with her effortlessly until the force of her panting scrubbed it away.

She ran with indignation at the failure of the world to come to her rescue. Shadows in the dusk were the forms of people she knew in life. She passed her friend from her school in New York, the smart girl with the big glasses obscuring her face whom she saw only every third week or so, clutching her books to her chest. She passed the principal of that school with his square haircut and the look of anguished concern for his students that he always wore, standing waist-deep in ferns. She passed Judith from the spelling bee, with whom she kept up a correspondence, proudly scribbling on a pad. Her mother, wanting to help but trapped in a wrapping of thornbush. Danya from the apartment next door to theirs, who had survived the Holocaust and now stood there in the ivy, touchingly confident about leaving Vera to survive her own terror as she rolled out rugelach.

And then, at last, over the crest of a moraine, came the motel. The boys had vanished. Her mother's car was parked in front of ROOM ONE as indifferent as could be, and Vera walked across the gravel while her chest heaved with the force of her panting and her repressed sobs.

"Where's your shirt?" Vivian asked. "What happened to you?"

Vera ran straight to her mother and planted her head on her shoulder and cried and didn't say a word about what happened because she couldn't bear to and because she knew Vivian would surmise the truth. Vera was already working to bury that incident within the unvisited deep reaches of her memory.

"Give me that pen of yours," Vivian said to Vera the next morning in the motel office.

Vera was reluctant, but dug out Socrates from her bag and handed it to her mother. Vivian looked the father of Doug directly in the eyes as she removed its cap. The father of Doug presided over Vivian's writing of the check with both of his filthy hands on the filthy front desk. Vera did a quick calculation in her head. Twenty-two days' stay amounted to a hundred and four dollars and ninety-four cents with tax, which is exactly the amount that Vivian wrote on the check. However, by nine o'clock the following Monday morning, when the father of Doug stood in line at the bank, inching closer and closer to the person in front of him, every number on that check had disappeared entirely, along with the date, name, and signature of its writer.

Sprawled across the red leather backseat of the Ford Fairlane Crown Victoria with her arm thrown over her face and the engine thundering under the direction of her furious mother, Vera cast herself into a very dramatic state. She was being rescued. The car was an ambulance. Her mother was the EMT. Down the road lay the emergency room, her bedroom in the New York apartment.

Amid the turmoil of the day, it became crystal clear to Vera that Doug had not been at all the one her restless emotions were calling for. She had a sudden vision of Stanley as an ER doc, coming to her rescue. She sat bolt upright in the backseat, wondering where that thought came from, and as the scenery went by it felt as if the world was being pulled away and something important was being taken from her.

CHAPTER FOUR

Stanley sat slumped in the lobby of the Hawthorne Hotel in his favorite chair, the one that felt like a throne. For the past three days, he had been building a crossword around the theme of anxiety. It wasn't the most promising theme for a puzzle, a bit macabre for the average Joe, but he didn't care. He sat in the chair with his notebook on his lap, fiddling with the hair that he was letting grow and twiddling his pencil so fast it resembled a hummingbird in flight. On the grid was one word: CONCERN.

The day before, Stanley overheard a businessman, stuffed tightly into his suit, say to another man, "... he runs a concern that handles insurance for the coal and gas industry." Stanley was struck by this other meaning of the word. Concern was on his mind lately. Concern for a life that was about to change radically. Concern for how he might support himself. Concern about the wild far ends of lies that had to be tidied up. So he started a puzzle whose theme was words that are synonymous with anxiety, but that also have another meaning, and then used that other meaning in the clues. "Concern" was a business. "Apprehension" was the catching of a suspect, and so on.

He was waiting for Vera. She had sent him a postcard, with only the words "Coming soon—May 26th!" on it, and her elaborate signature, and half a thumbprint in her red lipstick. The bee that she came back for every year was due to begin the next day. It would be their third year as returning winners, and he was genuinely looking forward to seeing her. He liked the little jokes she came out with and the way she tried to dress herself in an aura of sophistication. He caught himself daydreaming about how she might walk through the doors in front of him, then shifted in his chair and tried to focus.

Stanley fitted in a theme word near the lower right of his grid: AGITATION. Clue: Stirring.

He would have to move out of the hotel, naturally, because his mother would expect him to be going to school. He had typed up and actually mailed to himself a fictitious letter from Harvard, awarding himself a full scholarship. He showed it to Martha as a means of dealing with the tuition question, and she reacted happily and with relief, as that had been her hope all along. She didn't want to borrow money from Greaper, but she would have if it had been necessary. Stanley thought he might as well move up to Cambridge, where she expected him to be, in case hell froze over and she made a visit up to see him. He would have to make a living in Massachusetts, and he knew nothing about that. He knew so very many facts about the world outside the Hawthorne Hotel, at times his head felt congested with the burden of it, but all his knowledge came from things he read in books and newspapers, not from experience. He was scared of what experience might bring. He filled in another word: FEAR. Clue: Old Testament term for respect.

Stanley was eager to tell Vera about his crossword being published in the *New York Times*. Waiting there for her in the lobby, it amused him to think of himself as a lobbyist, a term that had actually originated in that very hotel, when certain opportunistic characters with business interests would lie in wait for politicians as they passed from their rooms to the carriages that took them to the Capitol building, and would buttonhole them in the lobby and make their cases. Then suddenly he saw her, swishing through the doors that Willis held open for her and her mother. The way she came through so breezily in a print dress, it seemed as if she were bringing in spring itself with her.

His mind presented him with another theme word: TENSION. Clue: Degree of tightness. He couldn't ignore the interruption and paused to jot it down. When he looked up she was walking toward him.

He stood and gave her a wave. "Miss Baxter," he said.

"Mr. Owens."

"Welcome back. I'm glad you're staying here again."

This year, the bee would be taking place at the Marriott, a newer hotel in another part of town, but staying at the Hawthorne was a special treat for Vera, who endured so much on her mother's travels.

"The Marriott? Nooo, no, no. We wouldn't stay anywhere but here," she said, and smiled.

"Did you have a good trip?" He tried to affect a rakish pose.

"Let's just say I'm just glad to have someone else to talk to. God, I need a break from her." She looked back over her shoulder and made a quick series of gestures to her mother, indicating that she wanted to stay there and talk to Stanley. Her mother tapped her wristwatch as a way of telling her not to take too long, finished checking in, and went up to their room.

"*Mon Dieu!*" Vera said with high drama, dropping into a chair and letting out a heavy sigh. "Does your mom hover over you every second?"

Stanley sat down and replied, "Unfortunately, yes. But she's terrified of leaving the suite, so I can escape."

Still unwrapping herself mentally from the confinement of the car, Vera let his comment pass, and said, "For the past hour she had me list the pros and cons of every college I was accepted into. Oh, I wanted to tell you—I got into Harvard!"

"Congratulations."

"So," she said, prodding him for news, but he was lost in thoughts of his own overbearing mother and said, "My mom times me on everything."

"Stopwatch?" Vera asked.

"Alarm clock. One hour per subject. Eight hours a day. Five days a week."

"Only five," Vera said challengingly. "I do seven. Half days on weekends."

"It may be only five, but I start at six a.m. With a test," he said, looking at her to gauge her reaction. "You know, to see how much I retained from the day before."

Vera flopped back in her chair, then lit a Chesterfield and blew smoke at the ceiling.

He lay back in his chair as well, and they stared at the ceiling together in silence.

After a while, Vera softly said, "I'm tired of always being the good girl," apropos of nothing.

Stanley turned his head and looked over at her.

"Vera, do this. Vera, do that. Study. Get in the car. Read these books."

Stanley cut in. "Write a report on the political dynamics of prerevolutionary France."

"In French." Vera blew out a long stream of smoke. "I'm tired of always doing what my mother tells me to do. I'd like to run away. Would you like to run away?"

"Yes, very much. I've thought about it. I don't have much money though."

"Let's be hobos," she said, sitting up. "Let's ride the rails and sleep in boxcars and eat beans from a can by a campfire."

"Sounds groovy," he said. Then after a pause, added, "Do you like beans?'

"No."

"Me neither."

They watched the people in the lobby shuffle about, all of them seemingly impressed with themselves as they made requests of the staff or struck poses.

"How about something scandalous," she said, with excitement in her voice and a sly lift of the eyebrow. "Let's impersonate some-body famous and live like royalty for a day."

"Yeah," he said, without much enthusiasm.

"Oh, I know! Let's steal some car keys from the valet stand and go for a joyride."

They were quiet for a while, and then Stanley said, "We could rob banks."

"Oh, that would be excellent," she said, and laughed. "I'd probably drop the gun. Or shoot myself in the foot."

"Who said anything about a gun? I'd poke my finger into the

lining of my coat, like they do in the movies. 'See here now, pal,'"
he said, imitating James Cagney. "'This here's a gun, see? No
funny stuff, see?'"

She laughed. "We'd be a great team. Jailed in five seconds
flat." After a moment, she sighed and said, "I guess it'll have to
be Harvard for the both of us." She looked warily at him and said,
"You...you did get in, yes?"

"Hm? Oh, yes, of course," he said and then quickly got to his
feet. "Well, I think I'd better go back up."

Vera stood and together they went up the crimson and
gold–carpeted stairs.

Vera joined her mother, and Stanley returned to Martha in the
birdcage that was the William Henry Harrison Suite. He slipped
quietly in and tiptoed toward his room. Then he paused, and
turned and crept into her room. He had a question he wanted answered. He walked past the white dressing table with its shrine
to Nick, made of photos, including one of Nick shaking hands
with Bing Crosby in front of the hotel. Stanley opened her closet.
Bathrobe. Cotton pajamas. Five-foot-long nightshirt. Unwearable
dress from the forties, black with yellow polka dots. Another
bathrobe. More pajamas. When had this happened to her? When
had she started wearing only housecoats and sleepwear? Then the
voice of his mother signaled her catlike detection.

"Stan-ley?"

He scurried quietly out and went to the living room, where
she was embedded as usual within the cushions of her armchair.

"I hope you're not coming to bring me some horrible story
from downstairs."

"No, I'm not," he said.

"Whatever's in those papers you're always reading..." She paused to give a little shudder, but didn't give Stanley time to answer. "I don't want to hear about it. I prefer to look at the positive," she said with an unconvincing smile. "Like your first year at Harvard."

He thought about what a piece of really bad news might do to her, like the fact that he would not be going to college. Without saying a word, Stanley turned and retreated to his room. He picked a book up and opened to the marked page. Then he looked up and dropped it on the bed: Stanley had an idea.

Unfortunately, he was not an ideas guy. He was a facts guy, a memory guy, a thinking guy and a connector of thoughts, but not an originator of ideas. His brain had no room left for that. It was stacked floor to ceiling with facts. Or perhaps there was room in his head to accommodate a sound idea, but his inability to conceive of one had to do with the fact that he was cheated out of his childhood and never had the chance to grow up emotionally. Perhaps he never really learned common sense, or the difference between what one does and what one doesn't do.

In any case, Stanley's idea was a big one. He had no one to discuss it with so he just went with his gut. He had read that that was the way great ideas happened. Products of inspiration and whatnot, pushed forward despite logic to the contrary. He silenced his rational mind and set to work on his spectacularly bad idea.

It required a bit of financing, so he went to his dresser, where he stored his cash in a sock. It was money he'd been given over years of birthdays and holidays, silver dollars plucked from behind his ear by congressmen when he was a boy, tips from guests when he used to help the porters. He took out the bankroll and counted it. One hundred and sixty-one dollars. He'd hoped for more, but it would have to do.

Stanley put on his jacket and went down to Woodson's Jewelers on New York Avenue. He'd passed it a thousand times, but never imagined going in, and so it had lived a shadow existence. Now it was as real as a house on fire.

Stanley wasn't the kind of person who was easily embarrassed. Bent over the warm illuminated glass, in conference with Mr. Woodson, he gently nudged the old man toward the cheapest diamond in the store. Several times he had to affirm that yes, *that* was the diamond he was referring to, and yes, he did indeed want *that* diamond mounted on a ring.

"Oh!" said the drowsy old man, pushing up his spectacles on his nose. "Oh, I don't know if...Oh, I suppose that might be possible. I've never..." He collected the item in question with a pair of tweezers and placed it on a square of black velvet to prevent it from vanishing. Studying it, he seemed to be mulling over how he might attach such a wee thing to a band of gold.

"It *is* a diamond?" Stanley asked.

"Yes. That I can confirm. It is a diamond."

The next morning, Stanley wandered the halls of the Hawthorne Hotel, but Vera was nowhere to be found. So he took the bus across town to the Marriott and saw her immediately in the crowded hall outside the theater, jam-packed with jabbering young eggheads whose nerves combined with the usual trembling psychoses of extraordinarily smart and socially inept kids to form a sort of hair-raising voltage. Vera was a bit of a star, because she had tied with him in '60, so wherever she went in the halls of the Marriott, she was followed by a group of awkward girls. The same applied to Stanley, so that when he finally approached her, it was two groups coming together—he with a group of starstruck boys and she with her group of girls.

"Vera," he said, "may I speak to you alone for a minute? I have something to ask you."

Her eyebrows shot up. "How intriguing."

"It is. It certainly won't bore you—what I have to say."

"I thought it was a question," Vera said, twirling a strand of hair around her finger and giving him a sidewise, teasing look.

"It's a question and a statement. A questment."

She flipped her hair over one shoulder and sighed, somewhat dramatically. "I suppose we have a little time before the bee starts."

Their respective groupies took the cue and shuffled off with their intellects virtually leaping from their brains in the pressure cooker of the pre-bee throng.

Stanley led her down a hallway and tried the door of an unused conference room. Finding it open, they slipped in and stood in the gloom.

"Vera, guess what?"

"What? You seem very excited."

"I am: A crossword puzzle I made got accepted by the *New York Times*." He said the name of the paper as if it were the most revered entity in the universe.

"Extraordinary, Stanley. Quite an achievement," she said, with the same playfully aloof attitude as before. But then, unable to hide her excitement for him any longer she smiled broadly and said, "That's absolutely fantastic news. I know how long and hard you've been working on this, and I'm so happy for you."

He gripped her shoulders and said, "Thank you."

"Well, *my* big news is not only did I get into Harvard—okay, fine, Radcliffe," she said, with some disdain for the separate women's college, "I was offered a partial scholarship."

"That's wonderful, Vera."

"So . . . I'll see you there, I suppose."

"I'm hoping you'll see me again before that."

"Pardon?"

"Vera, I have something to ask you."

"Oh, right. Your questment."

"My questment. It has something to do with what we were talking about yesterday."

With a confused look, she said, "You mean running away?"

"Sort of, yes." He cleared his throat and rubbed his hands together. "Okay, here we go." He thrust one hand into his jacket pocket and felt the faux velvet on the tiny box there. "Do you know what a con is?"

"Short for 'confidence game'?"

"Yes. But wait. Never mind. That's a bad way to start. Vera, I have a plan to make some money and leave this place with a bang. But I need your help. It's a little crazy . . . Okay, it's a lot crazy. But you and I—we can pull it off. It's an *idea*," he said, as if that explained it all. "A big idea."

She put a hand on her hip and raised an eyebrow. "I'm intrigued."

Stanley got down on one knee. "Vera. I'd like to marry you. But not for real," he was quick to add. "It'll be a fake wedding. For the gifts. I know a lot of wealthy people, and I know they'll give us sizable cash gifts. Any other gifts we get, we return or sell and split the take. Then we go off to Harvard and no one's the wiser."

She stood there frantically twisting a finger in her hair. He pulled out the small black box from his pocket and opened it.

"Vera Baxter, will you be my accomplice?"

She suddenly felt as if all the substance was drained from her head, but she'd be damned if she was going to pass out again like she did at the bee. "I'm going to sit down now," she said, exactly at the moment she did so. She lay back on the floor and closed her eyes. She opened her mouth while her eyes were still closed and said, "My bag. Raisins."

Stanley fumbled through her purse until he felt the box. He opened it with one hand and lifted her head higher with the other. She opened her eyes, took the box, and chewed. "Low blood sugar," she explained as she began to recover. "You know I'm hypoglycemic, silly boy. Don't shock me like that."

"I'm sorry, I didn't mean to startle you. I guess there's no casual way to ask that question."

"Startled, stunned, and stupefied. Give me a minute."

"Certainly."

Vera lay on her back in the dim conference room, the only sound the hum of the ventilation system, and stared at the drop ceiling, white with a million tiny black dots on it, the inverse of stars. She sat up and went through the routine of nervous ticks that Stanley remembered from the bee: She rubbed her eye, flexed an elbow, cracked her neck, twisted a strand of hair around a finger. A song began to play in the room next door, with a hauntingly slow, sweet melody. He tried to make out the lyrics but the song was too muffled for him to understand.

"Tell me about that crossword puzzle," she said.

"Well, let's see. It has a theme. Every good puzzle does. The theme is the neighborhoods of New York City. I managed to arrange them geographically around the grid. It also contains words that relate to New York, like subway, Stuyvesant, knickerbocker..."

"Maybe."

"Maybe?"

"My answer to your questment. It's *maybe*."

"Oh. Well, that's great. Maybe isn't no."

"It isn't yes either."

Stanley thought of holding her hand, but he wanted to keep it a business relationship. After a while, she said, "You had a box."

"Oh, right."

He held out the box for her. She took it and cracked it open apprehensively, one eyebrow raised. She squinted at the molecule inside, throwing off a single photon of light.

"It's a diamond," he said.

"Thanks for clarifying that." She squinted again at it. Then, raising the eyebrow again, she said, "I know you're not exactly a Vanderbilt, but this is, um..." She stopped and looked at him.

"Small," he said.

"That's the word I was looking for," she said, and laughed.

She put one hand on the ground behind her and held the ring in the other, keeping it at a distance. "How come you didn't mention this yesterday? After all, it beats robbing banks."

Nervous and unaware he was wringing his hands, he said, "I thought of it after our conversation."

She screwed up her mouth and studied him. "Weddings are expensive, to state the obvious. Who's going to pay for this shindig?"

"I have a strong feeling the owner of the hotel will insist. You know, the man who provides my mom and me with the suite for a dollar a month."

"I've been meaning to ask you about that. Excuse me if I'm being impertinent, but it seems a little odd to me."

"Well, with my father gone all my life, he sort of thinks of himself as my substitute dad. I'm not happy about it, but what can I do?"

Vera gave him a comforting half smile and touched his shoulder.

"Anyway," he said, "he'd probably consider it his duty to pay for it."

"Hmm. Generous man."

Stanley didn't respond, didn't want to darken the moment with his thoughts and suspicions about Greaper, or his worries about what would happen if the man didn't offer to pay for the wedding. He would have to move on to plan B: becoming a vagrant or joining the circus. Getting Greaper's cooperation was a *concern*.

"What if he doesn't offer?" Vera asked, as if reading his thoughts.

"Then it's off," he said, perking himself up. "Simple as that. Thank you kindly, see you around." Stanley stood and gave Vera a hand to help her up.

"I cannot believe you're really serious about this," Vera said as she got to her feet. She shrugged her shoulders. She laughed and said, "It's the stupidest thing I've ever heard. But, to be fair, it kind of sounds like fun. I like fun." Then she added softly, "I think." Stanley was about to hug her when she put up a hand. "But... If I decide to go along with this—and I haven't decided I will, but if I do—then my mother can't know about it. She cannot be involved and must never know. Understood?"

"Understood," he said.

"At least not until..." She stopped. She was going to say, "At least not until it's real." Peeking around the inconvenient moment and looking down the road, she saw it becoming real somehow, some way. Instead, she said, "You'll have to solve that on your own. This is your baby." Then she opened her arms and let him have his hug.

As they left the conference room to watch the bee, she straightened her dress and hurried on ahead of him. When Stanley reached the ballroom where the bee was taking place he caught up to her and approached Vera as if he'd never met her before. "Pardon me," he said, affecting a caricature of nonchalance. "Is this seat taken?"

"Why, no, I don't believe it is," she replied.

He sat down next to her and said, "My name's Stanley."

"I'm Vera. Delighted to make your acquaintance."

The lights went down, and together they watched the spellers, who looked impossibly young and fragile to Stanley now. During a moment of great intensity, when a very serious young speller was suffering through the personal Gethsemane of *synecdoche*, he leaned over and whispered in Vera's ear, "Bosoms," and she couldn't help but let out a sharp little splinter of laughter before she clapped her hand over her mouth and all the parents in the two or three rows ahead of her turned back to glare. Stanley gave her a look of disgust as well, and she pinched him.

Stanley made a gesture with his head and they got up, and he led her back to the very last row. "Want me to show you how to make a crossword puzzle?" he whispered. Vera nodded vigorously, with a look that implied more than just acquiescence to puzzle making.

Stanley began a whispered tutorial on crosswords, and Vera

tried to serve two masters—the demands of what Stanley was trying to teach her and the demands of her imagination with their bodies so close together.

Stanley took a legal pad from his satchel and drew a grid of boxes. "This is a standard fifteen-by-fifteen grid. You can also do a twenty-one by twenty-one or even nineteen by nineteen or twenty-three by twenty-three, but this is the most common."

"Where are the black spaces?" she whispered, leaning in to him.

"Those come later. Now, we need a theme," he said softly. "Ice cream flavors, for example, although that's not a good one."

"Oh, how about Ivy League schools?"

"Great idea. There are eight of them, a good number of theme words for a fifteen by fifteen. So you begin with your theme words or your longer phrases. Make a list. Then scatter them evenly around the grid. Look for opportunities to use common words that you can write unexpected clues for. Oh, and the pattern of the grid should be diagonally symmetrical, so keep that in mind when placing your theme words or phrases."

She wanted to impress him and show him she could do this too. How hard could it be? So she listened the best she could, and when he cast about for words to fill the spaces she was quick with suggestions.

"Try to use words that are interesting or quirky," he said. "Words with a lot of vowels come in handy too."

Her mathematical mind engaged the problems in the grid. They leaned close together over the page.

"Chicane," she heard a young voice say over the PA system. "C-H-I..."

When Stanley seemed a little too impressed by how she was

doing, she pretended to be insulted by his low expectations, gave him a shove and laughed. The woman in front of them turned violently and shushed them.

At the end of that day's competition, they took the bus back to the Hawthorne together, looking the part of two sharp characters among the pedestrians of DC. Vera had been so completely lost in the joy of whispering and conspiring on the puzzle with him that she was unable to recall many of the finer details of the day, and that night she lay on her bed and tried to bring back those moments from the hold of her memory. She was looking to catch a recollection of something he said that contained a clue, some hint that he felt something deeper for her. She was certain he did.

Vera could pull off the wedding con without telling her mother, but Stanley certainly couldn't do it without telling his. For all her isolation, she lived in the hotel, and the fact of her own son being wed five floors below would not escape her attention, limited as it was. With half an eye on his puzzle, he filled in the word for anxiety's effect on the stomach: BUTTERFLIES. Clue: Winged insects. Then he tossed the puzzle onto his bed and went into the other room, where he found his mother, who, as usual, was being swallowed and digested by her chair.

"Mother."

"Yes, dear," she said, without looking up from the manuscript she was examining.

"You know Vera Baxter?"

"Of course I do, dear." She scratched over something with her red pencil.

"She's pretty great."

Martha looked up, as if she might take up her pencil and make a correction mark on him as well.

"We've been seeing each other a lot since she's been here."

She stared at him and cocked her head. "When did she get here?"

"Two days ago."

Again, she scrutinized him with a touch of dismay. He couldn't take it, and decided to jump right in.

"I asked her to marry me."

This moment was a bit of a test. For as long as he could remember, Martha Owens had been perched like a delicate knick-knack on the edge of life itself, ready to topple and smash into shards at the slightest tremor in her fragile little world. For his part, Stanley was never really sure if this frailness was real. He suspected it was mostly an act, a trick of emotional hypochondria. If it was an act, she put on a masterful performance.

The pencil fell to the floor and she clutched her chest. Stanley jumped up.

"Mom?"

She lifted herself half out of her seat, with incredible effort, as if tearing herself from decades of captivity by that beast, spilling the manuscript pages across the floor and then collapsing onto them. Stanley knelt beside her and lifted her head and torso into his lap. He called to his mother, but she was out cold. He blew on her face, but to no effect. He gently tapped the side of her face, slapping it a bit harder and harder until finally she opened her eyes and cried out, "Stop it, Stanley, that hurts!" Then she asked him to fetch her a glass of water.

When he returned with the glass, she was already restored to her customary seat as if the chair itself had simply reabsorbed her.

"Stanley," she said, still catching her breath. "You don't waltz into the room and tell me you just asked a girl you barely know to marry you. For goodness' sake, you're going to Harvard in the fall," she said, as if that obviated all other activity.

"Mom," Stanley said. "If you think about it and give it a chance, you might see that this could actually benefit my studies. She's going up to Cambridge too—she's got into Radcliffe. I won't be distracted by girls. I won't have any incentive to stay out late in bars."

"Stay out late in bars!" She gasped and clutched her chest.

"Mom, please, don't excite yourself," he said with concern.

Her hand sought out the Point-O-Matic as a source of comfort. Stanley pulled over a chair and sat facing her. For a long moment the room was silent. Martha looked as if she was locked in a conversation with herself.

"I'm...concerned," she said. "Yes, that's it, concerned," she repeated, taking a gentle approach. "I'm a little anxious, Stanley, to be honest. I'm uneasy."

Unease. He made a mental note to go back and edit his anxiety puzzle—that was one he'd forgotten. He had just the clue for it: "To make difficult." Like springing an engagement on your paranoid mother out of the blue at the age of eighteen.

"I trust you, as always," she said. "But isn't this a little rash? You're only eighteen. Why not wait until you've completed your undergraduate degree? I don't want anything getting in the way of your academic career. You can see Vera. You'll be together. Why this rush to marry?"

"Because..." Not for the first time, his mother had cast her spell of reason upon him. There was no tolerance for impulse in the William Henry Harrison Suite. "Mom. Haven't you ever wanted something so badly you had to put rational argument aside for a moment and just seize it?"

"That's not how I raised you. I raised a son who thinks before he acts."

"What was it like for you and Dad?" There, he said it. He knew how tender that part of her still was, even after all these years, but he had to say it. She sat back, lost within herself.

"Nick and I were different. There was never anyone like him..." Her eyes reddened and glistened, and then came the tears. She reached for a tissue.

"Well, believe it or not, I understand how you feel. Lightning can strike more than once. There's also no one like Vera." Saying that came easily, and it surprised him to discover that he was getting the hang of his role.

Stanley stood and pondered the carpet; his mother sat and pondered the pencil sharpener. A tear bigger than the diamond he purchased formed itself in the corner of her eye and tumbled down her cheek. Finally she said, "I've taught you the best I can. I'm going to trust you to make the right decision." Stanley bent down and hugged her. And that was the way they left it.

Stanley retreated to his room and closed the door. He sat on the edge of the bed and thought back on his proposal to Vera earlier that day, which seemed preposterous in hindsight. Odd, he thought. Why was Vera even considering his ridiculous proposal? Was she just like him—an adventurous soul who didn't care for society's norms? Or was it in fact society's norms—specifically, the expectation of a young woman to find a man and marry—that made it feel okay? He told himself that it was all in good fun, and she wouldn't do it if she didn't also get an illicit thrill out of it. After all, she was the one who suggested they do something scandalous together. Plus he'd give her half the take from the cash and the gifts he'd sell off afterward. Being bad together would be fun. But the web of emotions confused him. He lay down on his bed and stared at the ceiling and tested out her full name in the quiet. "Vera Bernice Baxter."

CHAPTER FIVE

"Am I, Vera Baxter, after everything is considered and added up, a crazy person? Am I a fallacy?" Vera asked herself as she sat at the little table on the balcony of the room at the Hawthorne, with a stack of books in front of her. "Am I one of those people you hear about," she wondered, "who do the most illogical things but seem stunningly oblivious to their nonsense?"

"Yes," she said out loud. "Yes, I think it must be true." She turned her journal to a fresh page and wrote with Socrates, "I am a little bit crazy."

Vera was accepted by each of the schools to which she applied. They all promised her everything the average female student could possibly want: academics on a par with men's colleges or nearly so, professors who were the envy of lesser institutions, athletic and sporting groups to offer respite from cerebral exertions, extracurricular activities for her to participate in if she so chose, and adjacent or nearby men's colleges where one might perchance meet one's future husband. They promised her everything but the thing that mattered most, the one thing they could not promise:

his presence. With his evasiveness on the question of Harvard and this elaborate scheme, she suspected he wouldn't really be going.

She thought about the word *smitten*. "Smitten," she said to herself. "What an odd little word." She looked it up in her ten-pound dictionary and saw that in an archaic form it meant "to be defeated or conquered." "I've been smote. How interesting."

After sitting motionless for a moment, she turned to the L tab and looked up "love." She scanned the definition and then quickly slammed the book shut.

She coughed softly, then snuffed out the cigarette and tossed the butt from the balcony, fanned herself, and popped a mint in her mouth. "Stanley Owens," she whispered to herself. "Stanley Owens, my accomplice." Her general mood was like an ugly fraction or an untidy proof, but in a way she was also delighting in this fog of melancholy. One thing was for sure: She was alive. She was no longer her mother's captive, pacing the floor with a math journal in one hand and hypothesizing to herself that this was as exciting as life would ever get for her. She had a real, honest-to-God situation on her hands, involving an interesting boy, a boy who most certainly knew the square root of four. And he was offering her a genuine, here-and-now opportunity to do something adventurous and a little bad, which she often dreamed of in the warm, sleepy afternoons when her books were overheated by use and in her exhaustion she lay her head on her arms and set loose her fantasies. Also, paradoxically, getting married—"Okay, fine, pretend married," she said to herself—would offer her a way of finally feeling like she fit in. Even if she never told anyone, being "married" would simultaneously make her feel somehow less of an oddball and also make her feel wildly interesting and forever outside the grip of society. Out of the confusion of these thoughts, she knew one thing for certain: Something, finally, was going to happen.

She was going to marry Stanley Owens. But not for real, as he put it. "So *charmingly*," she added. "However, I ask you," she posed to an imaginary Stanley, "what is real? Is it the certification of the thing that makes it real, or the process of going through the ceremony? In my mind, I just might choose to consider the bond real. Or perhaps not."

"Over time," she thought, striking a match and then blowing it out, "he'll like me just as much as I like him. More so," she told herself in a burst of confidence.

The day after Stanley's proposition, while her mother was flipping through the Radcliffe course catalogue, Vera abruptly changed her mind and decided to tell her about the wedding. So, while Vivian was reading the description of a course Vera had circled, "Math 210: Survey of Pure Mathematics," Vera left the suite and went to fetch Stanley. He was immediately opposed to the idea. "What if she objects?"

"In that case," Vera answered, a new boldness in her tone, "the solution is simple. We do it anyway, while she's off in some godforsaken East Coast town helping her company sell its computer junk. We'll just tell everyone she came down with shingles at the last minute and couldn't make the trip. By then it will be too late to reschedule. If she somehow hears about the wedding later, well then, que sera, sera."

Vera flattered herself that she knew him well enough now that she could read the mixed emotions playing on his face. He was clearly delighted that she finally agreed to go along with his scheme. But she could also see that he was still worried about telling her mother. He opened his mouth and said, "Vera, telling her might..." Vera put her finger to his lips and shook her head.

As Stanley escorted Vera down the hall to her room, to speak to Vivian, she stopped and clutched his arm.

"Oh, one thing," she said, looking him dead in the eye. "What's the square root of four?"

"It's the cube root of eight."

Vera smiled. "Good boy."

The two of them stood in front of Vivian with their arms around each other. Stanley spoke up right away in his confident collegiate voice. "Mrs. Baxter, we have some great news. I've asked your daughter to marry me, and she said yes. We're excited to tell you and we hope you approve."

Vivian was not one to be shocked by anything. She approached the news as if it were one of her many secretarial tasks requiring attention. She looked stiff in her navy jacket and skirt, and held a white teacup that released a curl of steam like a question mark.

"Why?" she asked.

Why? Stanley didn't have an answer at first, but then he thought, Of course:

"Because we're in love."

Vera cracked her neck and twisted a strand of hair around her finger.

"I see. Love." Vivian handled the word as if it were something stuck to the bottom of her shoe. "That's a tricky one." She took her time setting down her teacup on a table cluttered with contracts, invoices, and binders. "You just never know. And when you start to get comfortable, it changes."

"Ours won't," he said right away.

"Won't it?"

"Mom! That's enough," Vera said. "You should be happy for us."

"It's just so sudden, my dear. You barely know each other."

"It doesn't take a lot of knowledge to love someone," Stanley said.

Both mother and daughter raised their eyebrows at that.

"Believe me, I know a lot of things," he said. "I've spent my whole life gathering knowledge. Knowledge is nothing to love."

Vivian looked like she was at a loss. Then she said, "Tell me some of these things you know so much about."

"Ask me. Anything."

Vivian thought for a moment. "What's an indemnity clause?"

"An indemnity clause is a stipulation in a contract whereby party A compensates party B for any losses suffered by party B," Stanley said.

"What's the roller called on a typewriter, the thing the keys strike against?"

"A platen."

Playfully, as if to put an end to the game, Vivian said, "Who was the first emperor of China?"

"This is stupid," Vera said. "Mom, we're getting married. That's it. Do you want us to do it without you, or would you like to be invited? A simple yes or no will do."

Vivian took a sip of her tea. Vera knew better than to give her stubborn mother an ultimatum.

"I'm all for you being married, but why don't you wait, sweetheart? Until you graduate."

"I've waited long enough already."

Vivian looked pensive, as if she were sincerely trying to reason out a way to accommodate her daughter, who never failed to make things interesting. "On one hand," Vivian said, "I'm happy for the two of you."

Vivian took another sip of her tea and began arranging her papers, as if the conversation was over. Then she said, "But on the other hand, you're only eighteen." She stopped her fussing and turned to face Vera. "You know who gets married at eighteen? Girls who are soft in the head and girls who are knocked up, that's who. Now, I know you're not soft in the head. You're not knocked up, are you?" she asked sarcastically.

"Jesus, Mom."

"Well...are you?"

"Of course not."

"All right, I'm sorry. That wasn't fair. But I was too young when I married your..."—she paused as if the word was difficult to get out—"father. I was young and I made a mistake. And I was older than you. Look, you have my permission to marry Stanley. But please, after you've gotten your college degree."

Vera looked at Stanley and bit her lower lip. She flexed her fingers. After a moment's hesitation, she said, "Lots of perfectly sensible girls get married at eighteen. Besides, what if I don't want to get my degree?" she added, knowing full well how ridiculous that sounded coming from her.

"What if the earth is flat?"

"What if we just get married anyway?" Vera said. "I'm old enough to do what I want."

"You're absolutely right about that." After a moment, Vivian sighed and put her hand on her hip. Cocking her head, she said, "So how do two people who are accustomed to being right resolve a situation in which one of them has to be wrong?"

There was no answer in the room for that somewhat rhetorical question.

"We have to go talk to Stanley's mom," Vera said.

"Come back and have lunch with me," Vivian said. "We'll talk this through."

Vera didn't bother to respond, grabbing Stanley's hand and heading for the door.

"Ying Zheng," Stanley said over his shoulder as they left.

If the conversation with Vera's mother was contentious, the one with Stanley's mother was anything but. She had a lost look in her eyes as they had their audience with her, and Stanley suspected that, as she often did, she had gone off into a romantic swoon reminiscing about his father. She awoke from her dreamy state to ask a practical question—how they planned to pay for the wedding. Stanley told her it would be a small affair. Like a cocktail party. He would ask favors of his hotel buddies. She offered to contribute five hundred dollars, then said, "At least you'll be together in Cambridge. That gives me peace of mind." She gave them her blessing in a misty-eyed way, and that was the end of the conversation. She sank back into her chair and was enveloped in its anesthesium the way a breaching whale is enveloped by the sea.

When Stanley saw Vera out, she took his hands and looked him in the eyes and said, "Yes, we'll be together at Harvard."

"Well, not exactly," he said. "I'll be living there, but I actually won't be attending in an official capacity. I'd like to sneak into lectures now and then..." Vera couldn't hide her disappointment. "Vera. Listen. I can't study anymore. It's what she wants, but it's not what I want. I'm going to live my life the way I want to live it. Of course, my mom doesn't know that yet. I'm not quite

sure how to tell her." He chewed a fingernail. "I'll think of something."

"Oh," she said, and looked at the floor. They stood for a moment in silence. Vera looked up and said, "I'm glad you'll be in
Cambridge, anyway," and left him at the door.

Later that day, at lunch with her mother, Vera could see right
away that Vivian hadn't changed her mind.

"Get engaged, Vera," her mother said with empathy, like the
saleswoman she was determined to become. "Just don't get married. Girls do extended engagements, you know. Let that be
enough for now. You have a long life ahead of you. Who knows,
you might just meet a nice rich Harvard boy. Now, would you
like to split the crab cakes?"

Vera declined the crab cakes, but as she perused the menu, she
was already working out the combination of lies she would have
to employ to make a credible excuse for Vivian's absence at such
an important occasion as her daughter's wedding.

The very moment the bee crowned its winner, Vivian packed her
daughter and headed off on another one of her business sorties.
She was so eager to meet her boss and be once again showing him
how promotable she was that the whitewalls of her Ford Fairlane
Crown Victoria made a sharp squealing sound as she pulled out of
the hotel drive, and the valet clutched his hat with a white-gloved
hand. A few days later, after they arrived at their hotel in Syra-
cuse, Vera received a letter from Stanley detailing his conversation
with Greaper.

Stanley wrote that the man had heard about the wedding and
called him into his office for a chat. After some awkward con-

gratulations, he said, "Now, I know you and your mother aren't rich. So in light of your situation, and your father's service to our country"—he quickly crossed himself—"I would like to take care of the wedding for you." He shyly lowered his gaze and tapped the blotter on his desk with a thick finger. The clack-clacking of his secretary's typewriter penetrated the wall from the adjacent room. "I heard something about a small cocktail party, but Stanley, I want to make it a real celebration. I have all the facilities here at my disposal—the ballroom, the kitchen, the chefs, the waiters. It's easily done," he said with a wave of the hand. "Not only do I feel it's my duty, it would be my pleasure." Greaper was far more generous and human in this little encounter than ever before. And yet, Stanley couldn't forget all those times as a boy when he was ordered to do work around the hotel without compensation. Washing dishes, pushing luggage carts, and cleaning mirrors with an industrial window cleaner that had to be poured from a jug into a spray bottle.

"Thank you so much, sir. I really appreciate your generosity. We'll keep it reasonable. In fact, neither of us has much family, so it ought to be a small gathering. Mostly friends from the hotel, actually."

"That's fine, Stanley," Greaper said with his hospitality professional's smile. They shook hands and Stanley made his escape.

Vera spent the month of June on the road with her mother. She sent Stanley postcards from places like Chicopee, Schenectady, Woonsocket. She wrote short greetings on them that were intended to drive home the illusion of the marriage to Stanley's mother, should she see the postcards. It gave Vera a thrill to communicate her true feelings for him under the pretense of their game. She wrote things like, "Soon we'll be together for good, my love."

Vera was beginning to consider herself a bit of a deviant. She was keeping so many secrets, not least of which was the fact that, although her mother thought she had won the argument and the ring on Vera's finger was only symbolic of a hazy future commitment, Stanley was planning their wedding at that very moment. She slumped in the backseat of her mother's Ford Fairlane Crown Victoria as they motored on to the next crappy roadside motel whose windows in the night presented the creeping illuminations of passing headlights that always made her feel watched and hunted. She yawned and curled up like a cat and felt sly and catlike in her mischievous new role. With one eye she caught a glimpse of her mother looking back at her in the rearview mirror.

At the end of July, Vivian left on an important trip to Boston to close a huge deal with a pharmaceutical company. Instead of accompanying her, Vera had fixed it with her to go visit Stanley for several days in DC. Initially, Vivian balked at the idea, but Vera looked her dead in the eyes, crossed her arms, thrust out a hip, and said, "He's my fiancé. I should be permitted to visit him."

When Stanley met her at the station, she didn't know what to do at first so she kissed him on the cheek, in case anyone was watching. "I missed you," she said, and laughed. She had a ring on her finger, and despite the minuscule size of its diamond, she made sure as many people as possible saw it.

"I missed you too," he said, and gave her what felt like a significant hug, a hug she needed very much.

She was tempted to let her feelings show and smother him

with affection, but knew she should continue to occupy the role of clever cinema coquette that played in her head, and had difficulty dividing her attention between what her heart was screaming and what he was saying.

"Pardon me, I missed that last part," she said.

"The wedding. I don't want to put any of the burden of planning it on you. I'm taking care of everything. Actually, Sonny is. You remember him, right?"

"Of course I remember Sonny." That was a disappointment. How would Stanley get to know her intimately if they didn't get to spend time together planning the wedding? "I know I told you this is your game, but promise you'll at least let me help a little?" she asked.

"Of course," he said with a smile.

They got in a cab, and as they rode she stared out the window, thinking of how different the passing scenery seemed when she was in the car with him than it did from the window of her mother's car, where it struck her as harsh and brittle, like pages in the microfilm reader at the library zipping by. When they arrived at the hotel, Sonny was the first to greet them. He gathered them together and pulled them both into an embrace, smelling of cigarettes, lavender, and Lavoris. Sonny immediately began making her feel incredibly special. He kissed her hand and smiled with his eyes the whole time he was with them, but kept a level of respect verging on awe.

"This is my boy," he said, putting his arm around Stanley. "I'd do anything for him. Likewise, I'd do anything for you, since you're his girl."

His girl. She smiled and steadied herself on her feet.

"I still remember your performance at the bee," he said. "How could I forget? G-E-N-I-U-S. I'm honored to help with your wedding."

Performance. Her mind was stuck on that word. She was putting on another performance now.

"Help?" Stanley said. "You're doing everything."

"Just the way I like it," Sonny said. "I don't want you to lift a finger. Only a few last details to finish up," he said, touching Vera's arm. It was his nature to reassure, to put people at ease, to remove burdens, and he was very good at it.

"Where's your mother?" he asked.

Vera sighed and did her best. "Oh, you won't believe it. The day before we were getting ready to go, she came down with shingles. The doctor advised her to stay in bed, and absolutely forbade her from traveling."

Sonny's face registered shock, and then he went into action mode, his specialty. "I'll put a stop to everything," he said. "Don't worry, I can postpone this thing..."

Vera felt Stanley squeeze her hand, as if to say, "Quick, think of something."

"No, no, no! She wouldn't hear of it," Vera said. "The show must go on, right?"

Sonny was about to insist, but thought better of it. "If you're sure," he said. "But if you change your mind..." He shook his head. "What luck, huh?"

Stanley and Vera glanced at each other. "Yeah, what luck," she said.

They parted and Stanley took Vera to her room. "He is just the sweetest man I have ever met," she said.

"Yes, he's a good friend."

"What's his job here?"

"No one really knows, to be honest." Stanley laughed. "Well, technically he's a manager of some sort, but he does a little bit of everything. Sometimes you see him helping guests with their bags, sometimes he's receiving shipments at the loading dock, sometimes you'll even see him in the kitchen with a sauté pan in his hand."

Vera smiled. "Ah, interesting fella."

"He has a funny way around women. Sonny Jones in the presence of a woman can be embarrassingly servile." Indeed, if a woman happened to want a marigold from the gardens at Versailles, he was the man who would lay it at her feet. If she wanted a poem etched into a grain of sand, all she had to do was ask. "He told me once that he's on a quest for his queen, and though he hasn't yet discovered her, I think he's convinced that someday she'll come to him. He said he believes there's one and only one true love out there for everybody."

"Do you agree?" she asked. She flipped her hair back and cracked her neck.

"I think...I think I do. And I told him so." Stanley shook his head. "A man who loves and respects women as much as he does without a woman of his own is a sad thing."

Before Stanley left her at the door of her room, Vera sighed and cocked her head. She couldn't help herself. "Don't you feel just a little bit guilty about all of this? Deceiving all these people who care about you and taking their money? It doesn't really seem like you."

Stanley looked at the floor and put his hands in his pockets. "You're right," he said. "It isn't me. But you know something? I don't really see the harm in this. These people I know, congressmen, lobbyists, judges, they'll be happy to give us the money. And what does it matter if it's for buying china together or for starting out life in our own unique way? Also, it's not like we have any family, really. So there won't be many guests who are close to us. And to be frank, ninety percent of these people I know are outright criminals. For God's sake, do you know what it means to be a politician in Washington these days?"

"I read the papers," she said.

"I'd say there might be three or four good eggs at the wedding, and I'll donate any money I get from those people back to their campaigns or causes," Stanley said. "Does that make you feel better?"

"I feel fine. I was talking about you. I'm just an actress here, remember?" She squeezed him playfully and slipped through her door with a wave of the fingers.

How desperate he was, she thought. But his situation wasn't her problem. Rather, his existence was her problem. His eyes, his mouth, his way of moving. Marrying him without marrying him. Those were the problems. "So he's coming up to Cambridge regardless," she said out loud alone in the room. "Good." She looked around. She spotted the complimentary *Washington Post* sitting on the desk, picked it up, found the crossword puzzle, and sat down with a pencil in her hand.

The prelude to the wedding was jackrabbit fast—a stride or two in time and they were there. Sonny was a one-man stampede of forward momentum, handling everything solo, gratis, a cigarette constantly burning in the corner of his mouth. Martha watched from the safety of the William Henry Harrison Suite, quizzing the maids and porters who stopped by, and once or twice venturing, warily as a soldier carrying an unpinned hand grenade, down the hall to Vera's room in her robe and slippers to see if there was anything she could do via telephone from her suite.

On Thursday afternoon, two days before the wedding was to take place, Vera opened the door of her suite on her way to Stanley's, and there was Vivian with her fist in the air, about to knock.

It took Vera a moment to reconcile the apparent fact of her mother standing in front of her with the known fact that she was supposed to be in Boston. "Mom! I..."

"All better," she said with a smile. Sonny was standing next to her with her bag in his hand.

"Can you believe it?" he asked. "I tracked her down and gave her a call on behalf of everyone here at the Hawthorne, to wish her a speedy recovery, and it seems it worked," he said, lit up ear to ear with joy. "Here she is!" He could barely stand still.

"You're just the sweetest man," Vivian said to him, and thanked him as he slowly backed away, bowing as he went, with a grin that could've spanned the Mississippi.

Vivian was furious with Vera. Quite a storm brewed in Suite 505, the Abraham Lincoln Suite, until at last mother and daughter exhausted each other, and Vera apologized several times to the tenth power for lying about the wedding, and finally Vivian admitted that, yes, she did like Stanley and, no, there was no real harm in her getting married if that's what she really wanted. A lot of girls went to college to find husbands; Vera had already found hers and would be going to college to make something of herself. There was comfort in that.

Later that day, Martha did make one contribution to the proceedings, and that was to order the tuxedos for Stanley and for Sonny, who would be the best man. The tailor came to the suite and fitted the two of them while the ladies kept out of the way. For the mothers' dresses and shoes, which they would not allow Sonny to misappropriate or acquire by dubious means, Vivian wrote a check with a pen that did not contain disappearing ink. Vera had glimpsed her mother's savings account passbook one day as it missed its trajectory into her purse and flopped open on the car seat, and although they often seemed to live a gypsy's life, she knew that Vivian had been scrupulously squirreling away her paychecks and was far from poor.

On Friday morning, the day before the ceremony, Vera lay on her bed going over Russell and Whitehead's infamous 378-page proof that $1 + 1 = 2$. It was a knotty nebula of a problem, venturing far into the nether regions of human thought, and the lengths to which they had to go in proof of such a seemingly simple union raised doubts about the immediate prospect of couplehood. A knock on her door interrupted her. It was Stanley, asking her to join him for breakfast in the hotel restaurant.

"Wait," she said. "Before we go, I want you to hear something. Remember when you 'proposed' to me? There was a song playing in the next room. I heard it again since then and bought a forty-five. Every wedding couple needs their song, right? Well, this can be ours," she said as she slipped the 45 from its sleeve.

"Great, let's hear it."

She put it on the record player in the room. After a moment of crackle and static it began, a sweet voice, soft and slow over a gentle beat.

> *I love how your eyes close whenever you kiss me*
> *And when I'm away from you I love how you miss me...*

She moved close to him and he put his arms around her, and they slow danced with the door of the suite open. He felt warm and strong and smelled wonderful. After the second verse, Stanley let go of her and went to the record player and lifted the needle. He picked up the 45 and read the label. "'I Love How You Love Me.' The Paris Sisters." He looked over at her standing there in the middle of the room. "Vera, this is fantastic! Great contribution, thank you. I love how it helps with the verisimilitude."

That boy sure knows how to deflate a situation, she thought as he took her hand and they made their way down to the restaurant.

On the first of August, 1963, Vera Baxter stood in a simple white dress at the entrance to the Jefferson Room of the Hawthorne Hotel, which was done up like a small chapel. General Walter Bremer, an assistant secretary of defense and a commander in the Pacific theater during World War II, stood at the other end of the aisle, in front of the audience, prepared to marry the couple with great solemnity. Stanley once had a regular backgammon game with him in the Hawthorne's lobby, a game he learned from a staff member of the Shah of Iran; they played every Thursday at 1400 hours until the general, frustrated by his losses, scheduled another activity at that time.

The ceremony was small, top-heavy with dignitaries, and peppered with secret service officers who could be identified by their crew cuts and the bulges in their breast pockets. Vivian was too toughened up by her life and her character to cry tears of anything. Martha had used up her lifetime's allotment of tears when she learned of Nick's death in '44, but her lower lip was seen to quiver with emotion, whether joy or sorrow no one knew, and she looked magnificent in her Coco Chanel dress. This was the first dress Martha had put on since the bee, and as she waited with Stanley and Vera outside the chapel, she squirmed as if it were made of horsehair and occasionally glanced toward the elevator that could deliver her back to the safety of her suite. Finally, the ceremony began.

Stanley made his way down the aisle with his mother clenching his arm as if he were leading her to the electric chair. She walked at a slightly backward-tilted angle, braking with her feet while Stanley virtually pushed her through the gauntlet of staring eyes and deposited her safely in her seat beside Mr. Greaper and family. The organist played "Here Comes the Bride" at a peppy pace, per Stanley's instructions. He knew he would feel like a thief in a bank vault all the while the deed was being done, and he had tried to ensure that the whole thing went down briskly.

Stanley turned and watched Vera enter amid the swan-white nimbus of her gown. It had been suggested that, in the absence of a father, Stanley's friend Senator Rodgers of Virginia could walk her down the aisle, but Vivian gave one disapproving look, put her arm around her only child, and the suggestion was dead on arrival. Vivian walked proudly beside her daughter and passed her to Stanley after waiting an uncomfortably long time to remove her arm from the bride. In fact, Vera had to whisper, "Mom, really," before Vivian let go and took her seat across the aisle from Martha.

The hotel chaplain began the proceedings, and after a couple hymns and a short homily, he deferred to the command of General Bremer. The general asked the theoretically happy couple to stand in front of him, and as they did so, Vera noticed that Stanley was squeezing her hand so tightly in his nervousness that she stroked the back of his hand with her thumb to try to soothe him. When Bremer asked whether anyone had any objections, Vivian straightened slightly. Stanley and Vera looked over at her and a cough echoed in the long, quiet moment. Vivian ran her hands under her rear to adjust her dress, sat back down, and the ceremony continued.

As she stood there holding Stanley's hand, Vera felt like the queen of the world in her elegant dress. But she also felt like a charlatan—there was that word again. A fake, a phony, a fraud. The veil tickled her ear so she pulled it away. She couldn't believe what she was doing. The implausibility of it brought to mind other great implausibilities that had come to her attention, like the fact that a set of all sets must by definition contain itself and therefore cannot be a set of all sets, or that a solid can have an infinite surface area but finite volume. We do sometimes witness occurrences of the seemingly impossible.

As Bremer began the vows, Vera thought: Last chance to call it off. Stanley looked at her anxiously. She was determined to be strong and conquer her nerves, even though she hadn't been able to eat much of a breakfast because her stomach was in a state. The vows were the traditional kind, slightly abridged.

"Do you, Vera Bernice Baxter, take this man to be..." As these words rumbled out of the general, Vera indulged in a fantasy of rapid-fire images: she and Stanley side by side in wealth and in poverty; him tending to her as she lay sick in bed; the two of them flying a kite in full health, and then withering away together in old age as they held each other's hands.

"I do."

"Do you, Stanley Carl Owens, take this woman..."

Vera looked into his eyes and he looked into hers. "Take me," she beamed from pupil to pupil, optic nerve to optic nerve, brain to brain, her soul to his. She saw herself reflected in him. "Take me."

"I do."

The reception took place in the grand ballroom, a massive space that was puffed out as if a giant balloon had been inserted into the center of the hotel and inflated. The hotel staff had outdone itself, transforming the place over two days of secretive activity into a palace court fit for a coronation. Sonny was possessed by a smile that seemed to threaten the structural integrity of his face. A military band played popular jazz numbers in a very diligent style. Everyone was overwhelmed by the ferocious love of the young couple, for they played their roles with inspiration, and the people who weren't talking about the coincidence—child geniuses who tied in the National Spelling Bee tying the knot in the very same room—were talking about the suddenness with which love sometimes pounces.

Before the dancing got under way in earnest, the jazz band took a break and Stanley and Vera's song was played over the loudspeakers. The lights went down and Vera stood across from him in the center of the dance floor, took his hands, and looked into his eyes with entirely genuine feeling, not a drop of fakery about it. She tried to read his emotions, but he was so bent on his "mission" that all she saw was determination, perhaps a hint of gratitude. And then the song began, and they swayed to the gentle rhythm with their bodies pressed against each other.

...I love how your heart beats whenever I hold you
I love how you think of me without being told to

The guests applauded as the dance ended, and then it was time to mingle. On Vera's side of the equation were just Vivian and a compact and antique grandmother who had to be carefully transported like a porcelain tea service. Vera's mother was an only child, her father and his family had been excommunicated from her life, and the few friends she had were too distant in a number of ways. On Stanley's side was his mother's sister, more severe than Martha, wedged into a stiff, black dress more suitable for a funeral than a wedding. Other than this aunt, he had no living relatives as far as he knew. Martha, who sat bravely at her table after her dance with Stanley, had managed to estrange herself from Nick's family, whom she blamed for his eagerness to go off to war in the first place. But Stanley had the family of the entire Hawthorne Hotel, and over the course of the evening he spoke to every last one of them and thanked them for coming—from the downcast, fascinating men who washed dishes, each with his own private reason and means for carrying on in life and his own inimitable style of survival, up the ranks through the maids, the maintenance crew, to the courtly desk and concierge staff, and the lively young porters who were all, to a man, drunk.

The gifts table lurked in the corner of the room, bearing its growing burden. It flourished quietly and humbly until its boards could almost be heard creaking and cracking under the weight, much like Stanley's conscience.

Only the day before the ceremony did Stanley get the courage to confess to Vera that he hadn't quite been able to figure out what to do about the marriage certificate. He asked around and learned that it was something you filed at the courthouse and provided a copy of to your officiant. At first he tried to think of ways to provide false names but then alter the documents before giving them to the officiant, until he realized the courthouse was irrelevant. It was simply a matter of getting a form, filling it in, and giving it to General Bremer. But what if the man filed his own copy with the courthouse or something? To Stanley's knowledge, these military types tended to be awfully by the book. This was just one of many details of his scheme that Stanley had put off until the day before the wedding.

As the two of them settled into the taxi to see Bremer, Stanley said, "I have to confess..." So far, even though she'd offered to help, he hadn't asked anything of her; he hated to trouble her at the eleventh hour. "I'm not quite sure what to do about this marriage certificate business," he said and waved the empty form in front of her.

She sat unmoved. She wanted to make him squirm. The whole time he excluded her from the planning and *now* he wanted her help?

"I thought, maybe... You're smart—any ideas?"

Vera looked out the window. "Nope."

Not until they were outside Bremer's office, waiting to be admitted, and Stanley's forehead was beading with sweat, did she finally produce the pen with the skull on it.

The hardest part of the entire wedding day was the moment when those closest to the couple got up to say a few heartfelt words. It was difficult for Stanley to listen to his mother and Sonny celebrate him in the midst of his treachery, but it was harder still to look over and see Vera as her mother spoke about giving away the one person she loved most in all the world. Vera hugged her mother after Vivian finished demolishing what was left of Stanley's conscience, and the band mercifully broke into an upbeat number that brought everyone onto the dance floor.

Greaper appeared in the current, gripped Stanley's arm, and slipped an envelope into his inside breast pocket. The round little man beamed with joy and looked upon the celebration in a satisfied way.

"You're going to do just fine, son," Greaper said. "Provided you keep your shoulder to the grindstone. Mind your p's and q's..." He seemed hell-bent on dispensing wisdom but had none to give. "Listen to your professors. Call your mother." He let go of Stanley, gave him a mechanical roughing up resembling a sort of hug, and disappeared into the crowd.

After the food was thoroughly enjoyed, and the dancing was done and done some more, and the guests shambled off two by two into the middle of the night, Stanley found Sonny directing the cleanup and said, "Sonny, we need to talk to you." Stanley had told Vera that he would talk to Sonny on his own, but Vera insisted on coming along. "We're a team now," she said. In a cold little storage locker off the loading dock, in the guts of the hotel, where a single lightbulb clung to life on its noose, Stanley asked Sonny if he could do them a huge favor and sell the gifts they'd received. "We want to be discreet about it, because we don't want to offend anyone. But the fact is, we need money for setting up our life together more than we need silver chafing dishes and crystal glasses."

"I see," Sonny said, as Stanley watched him for signs of skepticism. He was a smart and shrewd man. "If that's what you want, then I'd be very pleased to be of assistance," he said, smiling at Vera and still taken with her in her white dress.

"I don't know anyone who's better at taking care of things like this than you, Sonny," Stanley said.

Sonny took a theatrical bow, and for a moment no one said anything.

"Well," Sonny said at last, "let's get on with it." He left momentarily to give a command to his porters to bring the gifts. When that was done, he picked up a pad and a pen and began his inventory, reciting as he wrote.

Waffle iron—Mr. and Mrs. Arthur Matthews
Stereo hi-fi console—Dr. James Crick

Gesturing at the notepad, Stanley said, "Is it really necessary to—"

Sonny interrupted. "How are you going to know who to send the thank-you cards to?" Then he continued.

Cuckoo clock, Swiss—Ambassador and Mrs. Gerhard Hocking
Fondue set—Mr. and Mrs. Robert Shields
Sterling silver flatware, dinner set—The Williams Family
Napkin rings, gold—Congressman Jay Nelson

When Sonny got through the pile of gifts, he opened the cards and added the checks to the list. Vera quickly added the monetary amounts together in her head, but Sonny insisted on checking her work with the enormous adding machine in the shipping and receiving department.

"You're right, Professor," he said with a look of disbelief, after pulling the handle one last time.

"You know, my mom could get you a much better one of those. You should talk to her," Vera said, indicating the abacus-like Zenith adding machine that made loud ratcheting noises.

"That's a marvelous idea. It would be a pleasure to speak to her again. She's a lovely woman," he said. "It wouldn't be appropriate for you to give me her telephone number, but perhaps you could persuade her to call the hotel and ask for me? I'm always around."

"I'll do that."

Stanley shuffled over to them and took the envelope from Greaper out of his breast pocket. The three of them looked at the check. It was made out to Stanley for $1,000. As Sonny added it to the total, Stanley stared at it, sensing little sparks of bad karma snapping from it. Even the lightbulb over their heads seemed to crackle with indignation.

Sonny estimated the value of each gift on the list, catching numbers out of the air, then calculated the worth of the whole lot. He told Stanley to come find him in a week for the proceeds. Stanley had arranged with Vera that he would send a cashier's check to her post office box in New York for her half of the gift money, which came to a grand total of $4,800.

Stanley had a sense of relief that he was inexorably on his way to a freer life, but he regretted putting Vera in the position he had coaxed her into, even though she seemed to be in a strangely elevated mood. Most of all, he just wanted to disappear. Do me one more favor, Vera, he thought. Sketch me with that pen of yours, so I can just vanish.

Vera looked at Stanley and smiled, using all her willpower to act carefree, as if they had just finished the premiere of a new play. The tempo of the situation indicated that it was time to leave, but she didn't know what to do. She wished Stanley would take her to the honeymoon suite, or if not there, anywhere—a supply closet, a laundry hamper, anyplace where they could consummate their marriage in the pyrotechnic fashion that played in her imagination. While Sonny busied himself with the gifts, Stanley took her hand and they left.

They made their way to the elevator and, once inside, stood uncomfortably next to each other. She turned to look at him, but Stanley found it very difficult to look her in the eye. They got out on the fifth floor and faced each other in the empty hallway.

"Well...that's that," she said.

"Yeah, that's that."

She paused and pivoted back to face him. "See you in Cambridge," she said, and ran off.

CHAPTER SIX

It was only a few weeks into the semester, and Vera was already cutting a full day of classes. She sat with her roommate, Abby Giamora, in the Riffraff Café on Mass Ave, a place she and Abby had begun to make their own. The café was decorated like the apartment of an old, Russian grandmother, tiny and cluttered with simple, obsolete things, afghans and doilies, and Soviet-issue household goods that wore the uniform of a generic sadness. It seemed distantly ruled by a communist neglect. But the aroma of the place couldn't have been richer. Small candles glowed close and warm here and there like dishes of melted butter.

The bell on the door jingled and Stanley Owens strolled in. It was the first time she'd seen him since DC. Because it was a Friday and her classes were done for the week, Abby was already a bit tipsy on red wine, and Vera was overcaffeinated. Her heart kicked around inside her like a rabbit in a sack. She didn't dare move.

Lean as he was, Stanley could barely get to the counter without brushing against Vera or knocking a teacup off a shelf, yet he acted as if he didn't recognize her. A copy of that day's *Harvard Crimson* was folded under his arm.

"Is anyone sitting here?" he asked, putting his hand on the back of the empty chair at their table.

Vera just stared at the earthy strata lining her cappuccino cup and didn't move. She imagined she'd been turned to stone.

"Take it," Abby said, scrutinizing him with her arms crossed.

Stanley paid for a coffee and then carefully expanded into the chair, stretching out his limbs as far as he could without knocking into anything. Then Vera heard him say, "I'll bet you twenty dollars I can guess your name in three tries." She looked up. He was smiling at her in that irresistibly playful way that she found in no one else. Abby had a glint in her eye that was enhanced by her inebriated state.

Vera looked up as if she hadn't noticed him. "Are you speaking to me?" she asked.

"Yes," he said.

"You want to guess my name? Why?"

"Oh, I suppose it just occurred to me that it might be fun," he said.

"I don't think so," Vera said.

"You don't think I can guess it?"

"No, I don't think I want to bet," Vera said, and turned her gaze toward the window.

"Oh, come on," Abby said. "Where's your sense of adventure? I'll cover it if he gets it." Then she said to Stanley, "Let's see the cash."

Stanley tossed a twenty-dollar bill onto the table and said, "Andrew Jackson, seventh president..." There was an awkward silence. Stanley couldn't help himself: "...who once killed a man in a duel."

Abby raised an eyebrow, looking like she was teetering on the brink of disliking him.

Vera was trying to think of a way to make him squirm, but her brain had gone haywire at the sight of him. She looked him in the eyes, snapped a match to light, ignited a Chesterfield, and blew smoke in his face. He coughed gently.

She went on staring at him, and as she ashed her cigarette with a snap of her thumb on the filter, she said, "You think you're smart, don't you?"

"Not particularly," he said.

"Okay, wise guy, you're on," Vera said, waving her hand in the air. "Guess away."

Stanley looked at her appraisingly. "Susan," he said.

Abby laughed. She was enjoying herself immensely.

"My God, I can't believe it! You got it on the first try," Vera said. Stanley was stuck in her head, she loved him, she loathed him, and she couldn't drink enough wine to abolish him. Now here he was, hers to tell off, to lecture and lay into, and yet she found herself playing along with him again.

"Did I? Really?" he said.

"I'm a little light, and thanks for the offer, Abby, but I can't let you cover it for me," she said, before turning to Stanley. "Let's say I pay you another time. Bye-bye now," she said, and turned away.

Stanley remained at the table. "Susan," he said. "Remarkable."

Vera looked back at him and made a face. "You actually think I look like a Susan? Come on."

"No, you're right, you don't. Something more exotic. Something with a little shadow and depth. Let me think for a second. Let's see. You are...Lenore."

Abby screeched and covered her face with her hands.

"One more try, mister," Vera said, and did her best to look bored. But she had to admit she loved improvising with him.

Stanley rubbed his hands together and concentrated on the center of the table, putting on a show for Abby. "This is it. I got it. Your name is...Ve...Ve...Venus!"

Abby laughed so hard she fell out of her chair. Stanley helped her up while Vera reached out for the money.

"So...what is it?" he asked.

Vera tilted back her head and blew smoke into the air. The right answer might have been no answer. The right answer might have been to snatch up her things, put a hand on her hip, give him a snappy brush-off, and walk away. But then Vera crushed out her cigarette, looked him in the eyes, and said her name aloud. And as if it were a spell that gave him control over her, she felt herself already giving in again to anything he could ever ask of her. She made a move to get up.

"Wait," Stanley said, and grabbed her wrist. Vera felt a flash of anger. She didn't want this, but then she did. She wanted him to pull her toward him and take her in, but her hand stiffened up in resistance. She found herself wondering if Radcliffe offered any martial arts classes. "Double or nothing if you can guess *my* name," he said.

Vera looked at Abby, who shook her head.

"I have to get to the library," Vera said, reaching for her book bag.

"Please," he said.

"Give me a hint," Vera said.

"It starts with an S."

"Steven."

"No."

"Sven."

He laughed. "No."

"Stanley."

"What?"

"Stanley." She said it so simply, as if it meant nothing. Table. Coffee. Teaspoon.

"Wow, I'm impressed," he said. He took another twenty out of his pocket and handed it to her. "Now we're square."

Vera took the money and Abby followed her out of the café.

Abby Giamora hated everything. She hated the racism that led to the Birmingham riots. She hated the Ku Klux Klan. She protested against both in Harvard Square. She hated the Kennedy Administration's Cuban nonsense. She hated the Seven Sisters' prudish resistance to the movement for coeducation. She hated virtue. She hated vice. She hated the arrogant male students striving soullessly toward their perfect Harvard degrees, struggling under the weight of their books and their unrelenting one-upmanship. One got the impression that the things Abby didn't hate were merely waiting in the wings for her to discover them, so she could hate them too. But she was fond of Vera Baxter. She was Vera's first and only college roommate.

Weekdays, Abby tended a surprising 4.0 average, working at it mechanically like a nine-to-five job. Weekends, she drank red wine, Italian vintages from the land of her ancestors. The first time she and Vera shared a couple bottles together and filled their dorm room in Briggs Hall with cigarette smoke, Vera felt Stanley sweep through and inhabit her like the smoke itself, and she had to go stand in the shower to rinse him off.

Four weeks went by between the wedding and moving-in day at school, during which time she received a cashier's check at her PO box, as promised, along with a businesslike letter about the additional money that Stanley would get to her somehow from the sale of the gifts, which turned out to be more than expected. It was agreed among the couple and their mothers that they would wait to honeymoon until they got their degrees; for the time being, Vera finished out the month with her mother and Stanley with his. It was also agreed that the two of them would live in the dorms, separately, so as to "absorb the full Ivy League experience," as Vera's mother put it.

On moving-in day, Vera waited for Stanley to stop by her dorm and ask for her. She knew he wouldn't be allowed in on his own, so she glanced out the window and down to the entrance below at every opportunity, but he never did materialize.

The week before classes, Vera waited for Stanley in her dorm room, afraid to go out in case he might stop by. When she could stay in her dorm no longer, she looked for him in the Radcliffe Quad, in Harvard Yard, at the bookstore and the little student gathering spots around campus. She had been privately thinking of him as her husband, but told no one about the wedding.

He never did show himself during those early days in Cambridge. "What's going on with him?" she asked herself. "What am I supposed to do?" And so she settled gloomily into a semblance of a student life. She spent a lot of time in the dorm room with Abby, drinking red wine from her Radcliffe coffee mug while Abby blew smoke rings across the room. Every time she drank a bit too much, Stanley made a phantasmagorical appearance amid the furnishings of her every thought, and she went into a mood.

Vera found herself doing quite a lot of doodling in the notebooks that were meant to be repositories of expensive collegiate knowledge. One evening she was in her room with Abby, flipping through the *Harvard Crimson*, when she came upon the crossword puzzle and dispatched it quickly in a burst of nervous energy.

From across the room, Abby scrutinized Vera with one critical eye, pointed her cigarette at her like a professor's stick of chalk, and said, "I figured out what it is I like about you. You have moxie."

Vera, too absorbed in the puzzle to acknowledge Abby's odd declaration, noticed a clue she recalled seeing before, because it contained her name: "_____ vera." Funny, she thought, how aloe is such a common crossword answer. A word with a three-to-one vowel-to-consonant ratio must be a valuable commodity for constructors, she supposed. Then she abruptly tossed the paper aside, grabbed a notebook, and flipped to a fresh page. She drew a grid. She tapped her pencil eraser rapidly on the page, following a skein of thought in a faraway portion of her mind, and scribbled down a list of theme words.

Abby blew a smoke ring at her that opened up and passed around her like a Hula-Hoop and said, "What are you doing?"

Vera didn't quite know how to answer. It was as if a more headstrong part of her had divided off from the rest and gone on an adventure of its own. So she didn't say anything.

Abby got up and looked over Vera's shoulder. "Are you making a crossword puzzle?"

"Apparently so," she said with a half smile, taken with her own moxie.

In her head was a running commentary. *Arrange the theme words symmetrically around the grid, he said.*

B-O-N-N-I-E, she penciled into a space on the upper left. On the side, she scribbled the clue: Clyde and _____. J-U-L-I-U-S, she wrote in the six diagonally symmetrical boxes on the lower right. And in the margin the clue: Ethel and _____. Her theme idea was famous crime duos. After all, weren't she and Stanley a crime duo themselves? Call it what you like, but they had committed fraud. She spiced up the theme by putting the names in reverse order from that by which they were commonly known. She penciled in four other clue-and-answer combos: Sundance Kid and BUTCH, Jesse James and FRANK, Loeb and LEOPOLD, William Hare and WILLIAM Burke. The two five-letter answers and the two seven-letter answers mirrored each other in the grid.

Her commentary continued: *Look for interesting clues for common words, he said.*

She wrote down the clue, "A room that's not savory," and filled in the answer: SUITE. For "City where loads of laundry are done?" she entered WASHINGTON in a row of boxes. "Home for a holiday" was her clue for HOTEL. She filled the grid with these and many other words that were meant to resonate with Stanley and send a signal to him that was unmistakable. And just to make dead sure he got it: "Ninth president," she wrote, penciling HARRISON into the grid. She was certain that if he was in Cambridge, he would do the puzzle. She knew he did every puzzle he could get his hands on, every day, rain or shine, in sickness and in health. And the *Crimson* was free in those steel boxes all around Cambridge.

At the very center she filled in RIFFRAFF, the name of the café where she would be waiting for him. Her clue was "Hoi polloi." VERA crossed the "R" that began the word, and CAFÉ crossed the "F" that finished it. At the top, she wrote the title,

"Partners in Crime." By the time the puzzle was done, Abby was long asleep and the little clock on the nightstand beside her read 3:20. Vera stretched and went to the bathroom down the hall to wash out her mug. As she looked at her tired eyes in the mirror, she reassured herself: He'll figure it out. He may be a fool, but he's not dumb.

The next day, punch-drunk from lack of sleep, she handed the puzzle to the student receptionist at the office of the *Crimson* in an envelope with a polite letter, and walked off with all the confidence in the world. Just a few days later, an acceptance note appeared very cooperatively in her student mailbox. If only everything were this easy, she thought.

And she waited. The very next day, she reached for the *Crimson* at the nearest paper box and riffled through it to the end, as if her puzzle might have somehow skipped through time and into the paper mere hours after being accepted. But of course some other, infinitely lesser puzzle filled the space instead, a limp thing, a puzzle with no purpose. The day Vera's creation finally did appear, she cut her classes and went to the Riffraff Café instead. First she stopped back at the dorm to get a couple books. Abby was blown away by Vera's casual revelation that she had published her crossword in the *Crimson*, and when she met her midday at the Riffraff, she was mystified by Vera's all-day encampment in the café. The more this inscrutable girl baffled Abby, the more she liked her.

"I just want to watch people solve my puzzle," Vera explained.

They spied one solitary woman with the unkempt and forgotten look of a longtime graduate student, engrossed in the puzzle, wiggling a pencil beside her head like a slugger's bat before a pitch.

That's when Stanley walked in, and although Vera had

planned the whole thing, she never really expected her far-fetched scheme to work and was startled to see him. When Stanley finished his name-guessing game and she had his forty dollars in her pocket, she supposed this was his way of giving her the rest of what he owed her for the sale of the gifts.

From that day on, Abby always referred to Stanley as Whatever-His-Name-Is, because she refused to believe that Vera plucked the correct name out of the air. She told everybody they ran into about it, everybody she didn't hate, that is. Abby felt electricity between the two of them, the likes of which she never knew between two people before, and that night in their dorm room she told Vera. Vera disagreed. "Are you joking? Absolutely not." She tossed back her head and laughed with her Chesterfield poised in the air beside her. She thought about telling Abby they were married, or pretend married, or whatever it was, but for a reason she couldn't quite explain preferred to keep it secret. It somehow felt bigger that way.

"No," Abby said. "You and Whatever-His-Name-Is, you've got something boss. I think he's your guy. The phone's going to ring. Watch. Three, two, one." They looked at the phone as if it were about to jump up in the air.

Abby had a guy of her own. His name was Roger, and she didn't like him much. It didn't start out that way, of course. "He was handsome," she told Vera. "Well, *is* handsome. He's not dead. I fell for him from across the room, without the benefit of spoken evidence to clue me in to his stupidity."

Vera gave her a skeptical look and she continued, "Oh yes, there are stupid people everywhere, even at Harvard. His dad's an alumnus." She rubbed her fingers together. "A little donation to the school, and bingo, Roger's in. Anyway, he's easy on the eyes. I imagined what the children might look like. But now I'm thinking of getting rid of him."

Vera was tickled by how bold and unconventional Abby was. Although she hadn't had a lot of friends in the past, she'd never heard a girl talk that way about a boy. As if he was hers to do with as she pleased, instead of the other way around, instead of waiting politely for him to make every move, establish the tenor of their courtship, perhaps make her his wife, or perhaps not.

"He's in danger of flunking out," Abby said. "He tried the peer tutors here—you know, they have this peer tutor program you're supposed to use—but he gave up on them. Or they gave up on him. You don't happen to know of any private tutors, do you?" she asked halfheartedly.

Vera tried to read that night while Abby drank wine and listened over and over again to "Green Onions" with her headphones on, the song coming across miniaturized and squawky. Reading was impossible. More wine was out of the question. *I think he's your guy.* She hardly slept, then the next day she went out walking with Abby and her friend Suzanne from across the hall, and they ran into Stanley again outside Widener Library. It couldn't have been chance, could it? He suggested they sit down on the steps to chat. Vera looked at Abby, who was making a face, and laughed, telling Stanley that Abby hated the Harvard libraries for complicated reasons no one could understand, and Abby said, "Oh, shush."

"Did you know," Abby said softly to Stanley, "that this exceptional young lady published a crossword puzzle in the *Crimson?*"

"Really?" He turned quickly to Vera. "Which one? I bet I've done it," he said, putting on an act. Of course he'd seen it; her puzzle brought him to the café in the first place.

"It was called 'Partners in Crime,'" Vera said.

"That was yours? I thought it was an excellent puzzle," he said. His excitement seemed genuine.

Abby said, "Where did you learn how to do that?"

At first, Vera thought the question was meant for Stanley, because it echoed a question that was in her own mind: Where did he learn to lie about things so casually? Then she realized Abby was looking at her. "Someone I knew in DC taught me."

"You're a clever chick," Abby said. "Maybe you should tutor Roger. For extra cash."

At that, Stanley perked up, which didn't escape Vera's notice. "I'm pretty busy with my own work," she said. Then turning to Stanley, "You don't happen to know any good tutors, do you?"

Roger always arrived about twenty minutes late, every Tuesday and Thursday afternoon, at the little diner far enough from campus that they wouldn't see anyone. Private tutors were either forbidden or frowned upon, Roger didn't really know which. It was immediately apparent at their first session that this was a kid who was deeply committed to a complete lack of commitment. He leaned back in his chair, hooked his thumbs in the pockets of his jacket, and looked at Stanley as if he were waiting for a performance to begin. A feat of telepathy, in which answers to essay questions were transmitted from one brain to another without effort on the recipient's part.

Roger was a history major, a history major without a memory, which was either an oxymoron or a paradox or merely a contradiction—there was a numbing force field surrounding Roger that muddled Stanley's own thoughts. He was helping him understand the Roman Empire in preparation for a term paper he would have to write at the end of the semester. Every time they got together, the kid's memory was a blank slate all over again, and they had to start with the period of transition from republic to empire, and rehash the whole merry-go-round of Octavian and Mark Antony and Cleopatra and Julius Caesar. Tutoring Roger was hard. Stanley, being a natural learner, couldn't understand it. Learning was something that just happened, like swallowing. It made Stanley wonder if he was cut out for the job, but then he thought that perhaps it was just Roger, and he made a mental note to ask Vera if she knew any other students who could use help.

Vera skipped classes some afternoons and followed Stanley to Newton, where he'd found a low-paying job working with the boys' tennis team at a private school for a couple hours a day. From the bleachers, she watched him coach and heckled his technique. Whenever he muffed a lob or a feed to one of his players, she booed him. The kids liked her immensely. Just like Stanley had done before her, instead of reading and writing papers for her classes in multivariable calculus and number theory and physics and French literature, she pored over the crossword puzzles that she was making as she sat in the bleachers, or wrote in her journal with Socrates.

One day Vera borrowed a camera from Suzanne across the hall and managed to fairly casually snap a shot of Stanley looking quite the gentleman under the honey-colored leaves of a maple half on fire with red. It was a beautiful picture, and she stored it inside her physics textbook at the beginning of the chapter about gravity.

She spent so much time lost in a faraway world of her own imagining that her studies weren't going well at all. In fact, Vera

Baxter, child prodigy, was falling behind in every one of her first-semester classes. In half a year's time she had plummeted from perennial A+ scholastic supernova to D for disappointing, an embarrassment to her professors and her institution. The speed of her plummet took her breath away. The desk in her dorm room faced a window, and she sat and stared out of it at the darkness, and puzzled over the reflection in the glass of the specimen she had become.

Stanley was living in a furnished studio at the top of a rooming house on Richdale Avenue, and Vera often found herself walking past it in the autumn night, even though it was as out of the way as a trip to the moon. If a light was glowing in the little dormer window, she would ring the buzzer and go up to see him. They didn't talk about the wedding, not even when they were alone together in his warm, empty garret, with a radiator that growled and snarled from the corner like a chained dog. He talked to her about how much he loved his newfound freedom. He went on and on to a disgusting degree about his plans to travel the world, sending crossword puzzles stateside from places like Helsinki, Taipei, Bora Bora.

"I love travel," she said, hinting that she would be happy to include herself in his plans. But she didn't go further than that. She didn't want to be the clingy hanger-on. She was Vera Baxter, damn it, proud and smart and desirable and independent. And she had moxie! He didn't wear his ring, of course. Her own rings were in her dresser beneath her undies and bras, in a candy tin that had "Candy is dandy!" printed across the lid. Sometimes she slipped her band into her pocket and walked around with it, her hand going to it again and again the way the tongue goes to a cut in the mouth.

In the room on Richdale Avenue, Stanley and Vera made two puzzles together that he sent off to the *Boston Globe* in both of their names. Stanley had become friends with some of the graduate students living in the rooms below him, and they often came up and settled into the deep, enormous sofa that enveloped them like quicksand, drinking tea and listening to records on the little portable record player that they brought up with them. They were gaunt, bearded, and impoverished, receiving the bulk of their nourishment, it seemed, from tea. It was difficult to discern where the tufts of hair on their bony chests ended and the frowsy wool of their loose sweaters began. Stanley gave them copies of the puzzles he and Vera made, to test them out, and they went off chewing their pencils and wrinkling up their heavy graduate foreheads.

"By the way," he said one afternoon, gesturing at her with his teacup, "you don't happen to know anyone else who needs tutoring, do you?"

Stanley was so damn independent, rarely asking for help with anything, that she seized this opportunity to make herself useful. It felt good to say, "Let me see what I can do," and put him in a position of reliance for a change. Over the following days, she set about rounding up clients for her husband, as she still privately called him.

She brought him a Henry, a Mark, and two Roberts. She found them through the grapevine, through friends of the few friends she had made so far. They were the kinds of kids who sat in the back rows of lecture halls with the gloom of hangovers settling around them. Even at Harvard, everyone knew someone who was treating college like a fast track to a twelve-step program, a dress rehearsal for skid row. The officially sanctioned tutoring program hadn't proven fruitful for everyone, the least motivated students in particular, the ones whose parents twisted their arms into attending college and who were prevented from abandoning school altogether only by the threat of disinheritance. He set to work on these Henrys and Marks and Roberts, and found them to be easier boulders to push, but frustrating all the same. If only he could write their papers for them.

Autumn passed in this unsatisfying way for Vera. She was with Stanley, but also not with him, not the way she wanted, and soon it was November. She became ornery and opinionated. One day she was high on herself, and the next, she felt as though she resembled a vampire when she looked in the mirror. Too pale, bags under her eyes, too cunning a brain in her head. She was disgusted by the need she had for love, for sex. She was shiftless and riding the swells of her ferocious mood swings. He secretly loves me, she told herself. Then this thought, too, disgusted her. Nevertheless, she scavenged for clues.

In November, Vera made an effort to reacquaint herself with the library and catch up with her curriculum. But the words on the pages formed a sort of broken netting through which entirely different thoughts would pass unfettered and venture forth into the long study hours. Stanley. Stan Lee. Stan the Man. Stanislavsky.

In the library, trying in vain to study, she slipped the picture of Stanley from her textbook and devoured the image with her junkie's eyes. She looked at it so often those days that after a time it became an abstract thing with all the sweetness sucked from it, like the eye-worn *Mona Lisa*, which she had waited in a long line to see the previous winter in New York when it made a much-hyped visit to the Met. Abruptly the announcement crackled over the loudspeaker that the library was closing, and she packed up her heavy burden and shouldered it back to the dorm, where she struggled once again with sleep.

One day, after walking her to her dorm, Stanley reached into his bag and took out a paper. "Here," he said, handing it to her. "Would you do me a favor and read this?"

"What is it?" she asked, all too happy to take the paper and read what he'd written.

"As you know, I've been tutoring Roger," he said.

"Yes. Oh, by the way, Abby finally broke up with him."

"I heard. About time, right? He seems to be handling it just fine. Unlike his schoolwork, which is abysmal. I've tried, I really have, but I just can't get anything to sink in. So..." Stanley reached out and tapped the paper in Vera's hands. "So I wrote this."

Vera raised an eyebrow.

"For him," Stanley said. "For twenty-five dollars."

Vera turned to the paper in her lap. "Absent Empire: Envisioning a Europe Without the Conquest."

"It's a speculation about how Europe might have developed without the Romans taking over. I hope you can read my scrawl. Let me know what you think, then I'll revise it and type it up."

Vera smiled and clutched the paper. "I can't wait to read it," she said, so heartened by the intimacy of the gesture that the fact of it being cheating escaped her attention.

"I had an epiphany," he said. "I thought, The hell with it, I'll just write his paper for him. It's expedient, and more lucrative."

As soon as he left, she devoured the paper. It struck her that, despite how much he didn't want to go to college, he must have been starved of the academic life that was all he ever really knew.

Here was his chance to show Harvard what he, a civilian with only his own wits and guidance, could do, and he seized it.

"It's good," she said to him the next day, when she met him in the café. "Too good. That's my only worry. It's so good, could Roger have written it?"

Stanley took a deep breath. "Right. I thought of that, but I guess I got carried away."

"Can you muck it up a little? Mangle a few sentences, throw in some bad terminology, a wrong date or place name here and there?"

"I'll muck it up a little," he said with a conspiratorial grin.

So maybe he wasn't her husband, but he was her guy. She was the only one he trusted with this.

The paper was a success. Roger got an A minus, and no question surfaced about the paper's authenticity. Stanley mucked it up ingeniously, going through it and making small inconsequential mistakes, striving to inhabit the mind of Roger and executing the small errors of diction or logic that Roger might make. And the best thing was, it was just so much fun, infinitely more gratifying than coaxing his student toward something he seemed utterly incapable of and uninterested in doing.

After months of listless knocking around, Stanley had a purpose. He wasn't just a tutor; he was a creator. He could knock out a paper in one all-nighter that could stand with the best of them. He approached his Henrys and Marks and Roberts and found them all too eager to conspire with him and bid farewell to the tutoring sessions that ate into their precious drinking time. Stanley walked the paths of Harvard with a breeziness that he hadn't felt in ages. He greeted passersby with a friendly hello and when he bounced up the stairs of his house as briskly as a squirrel going up a tree, he rapped on the graduate students' door to the rhythm of "Shave and a Haircut."

Stanley, Vera, and Abby sat in the café one Friday, the aroma of baba in the oven comforting them as snugly as a sweater, while Stanley finished a puzzle with a winter solstice theme he hoped to land in the *Globe* for December 21. He had begun a Christmas-themed puzzle, but when he mentioned it, Abby stood up and raged against the culture's appropriation of Christmas for commercial means, and so he suggested the solstice, which appeased her. Stanley had sent off the puzzles he and Vera made and was awaiting responses. Vera, now that she had made herself comfortably essential to Stanley as something of a sales agent, was hard at work studying so that she might salvage her semester with a good showing in her own final exams and term papers, come January. There was a small radio on the counter. A hand darted over to turn up the volume. A teacup crashed to the floor. Abby screamed.

JFK had been shot to death in Dallas. Harvard was turned on its head. Out the café window they could see people running by as if enemy aircraft were strafing Mass Ave. Abby and Vera held on to each other, and Stanley began whispering about whether or not his mother might have heard the news. Vera knew about her fragility in the face of even the smallest misfortune, so she stayed by Stanley's side while he made a call at a pay phone out front. Her own mother, on the other hand, would set aside the news as if it were a paperweight on her inbox. The first person Stanley spoke with told him she was at George Washington University Hospital. Sonny was with her. She was okay. Stanley caught the next train.

He didn't return until after the holidays. Stanley invented a story for his mother about making up his schoolwork when he got back to Harvard, and stayed in his old room in the William Henry Harrison Suite. One day he received a thick envelope in the mail from Vera. Inside was a copy of the *Boston Globe*, and there on page C31, between the wedding announcements and the obituaries, was his solstice puzzle, which he'd entirely forgotten about, with a cheerful note paper-clipped to it containing her congratulations decorated with exclamation points. Eventually, Stanley told his mother he had to get back up to his wife, and left her in the capable hands of Sonny. It was the first time they'd seen each other since the wedding, and Sonny had been acting coolly professional toward him, leading Stanley to wonder if he had suspicions about the authenticity of the marriage.

Vera reacquainted herself with her books. She was brilliantly salvaging the semester with a flourish at the end, and a touch of grace from her professors, eventually pulling B's in everything. She couldn't resist her physics textbook and flipped it open to the buried treasure of Stanley's picture and studied it as she reread the chapter about gravity, a love poem about the cosmic inevitability of attraction. Long, wineless days went by, but she didn't feel herself slipping because she knew where he was and what he was doing. And she knew that he would soon return, her Stanislavsky, and they would conspire on his paper-writing endeavor, and be together almost as if they really were husband and wife. Almost. She cracked her neck and tried to turn her attention back to the mathematics journal in front of her.

When Stanley returned to Cambridge in mid-January, he was happy to hear about her holidays (an uneventful week in New York with her mother, who was understanding about Stanley's absence) and how well her exams were going. And in February, after the new semester had begun, he was happy to hear about the classes she was taking and the variety of professors she had, some downright inspired and thrilling to listen to, others in over their heads, apprehensive and watchful as barn cats. They spent some time in a bar that Abby didn't hate, called The Hat, a Somerville cocktail lounge with red banquettes, and a neon Pickwick Ale sign buzzing in the window. Vera was happier then than ever before, and the way Stanley was behaving toward her allowed the hope to keep surfacing that deep down he loved her intensely.

One sunny midwinter day, Vera, Abby, Suzanne, and a whole crowd of young women from their dorm rented ice skates and rode the city bus over to Fresh Pond. Stanley went along too. While Vera was still lacing up her skates, Stanley glided off into a corner of the pond, away from the others.

"Wait for me, Mr. Speedy," she shouted in his direction, laughing as she stood and tried to balance.

Stanley watched her totter side to side on her skates, barely keeping herself upright. She moved along in a straight line on her momentum, absolutely unable to steer herself. She held out her arms for Stanley to catch her, but she was moving at the wrong trajectory, and as she sailed past him he said, "I love your mittens."

She held out her hands in front of her as best she could while trying to keep her balance, looked admiringly at the blue mittens with snowflakes knitted on the backs, and said, "Aren't they cute?" right before she broke through the ice.

Later, Vera told Stanley that, looking back, it felt supremely melodramatic to her, like an opera. She cried out—a soprano— Stanley got on his knees and crawled to her, she remembered a full moon positioned above his shoulder in the cautionary manner of an asterisk, and the whole pondful of skaters watched like a rapt audience until it dawned on them to try to help him. But he had her out before they could get there. He knew that instead of kneeling at the edge and possibly cracking the ice with his concentrated weight, it would be smarter to lie down, distributing his body mass evenly, and crawl to the edge, where he reached in and hoisted her to safety. Fortunately, someone had a car. Vera later recalled feeling not cold at all but richly aglow as if the embers of a dying fire were stewing within her, huddled in Stanley's arms under a blanket as the driver sped toward the dorm. She was as sick as she'd ever been that next week, but she luxuriated in the golden heat of her influenza, propped in her bed feeling victorious as Abby fussed over her, and Stanley—whom Abby smuggled in by way of a side door—paid visits, bringing a flower, a fancy imported chocolate bar, and a thermos of tea with honey and ginger he made on the hot plate in his room. Clues of his love, every last one of them, she told herself as the two of them chattered over her, her stinging nostrils gone scarlet on a face that was otherwise as soft and pale as the belly of a fish.

When she was fully recovered, they watched the Beatles perform on *The Ed Sullivan Show* with Abby and several other students crammed into the Riffraff Café, where a small black-and-white TV was perched on the counter just for that event. When the band played "I Want to Hold Your Hand," Vera reached under the table and felt for his fingers. Two weeks later they were there again, in front of the same precariously propped-up television, and again she held his hand under the table for no one to see.

There at the table, she turned to him and said, "Rumblings

are starting about midterms. Would you like me to, you know, round up a few students..."

"I'd like that, yes," he said. "As many as you can."

"Cheers," she said, clinking her glass against his.

By that point, Stanley's reputation had spread in whispers around campus, among the sorts of students who didn't care if anyone knew they paid for papers. "He's an artist," they said. "He'll ace it for you," they said, "but first he'll go over your old stuff, to get to know your style." Stanley was aware of his reputation, and he aimed to satisfy expectations by playing the eccentric, wearing a trench coat and a cocked fedora that made him look more attaché than student, and cutting to the chase like a lawyer with billable hours.

That semester, Vera did a lot of her studying in his studio room while he alternated between writing papers and making puzzles as the whim took him. She was looking for any opportunity for them to take off each other's clothes, but the graduate students were almost always there with their damn record player, blinking at her from their bearded faces like owls. She fantasized about ripping the needle off their overplayed Doc Watson record, putting on her 45 of "I Love How You Love Me," and pouncing on Stanley right there in front of them. Sometimes he took her in his arms and kissed her softly when she left for the night, but it never went any further, leaving her buzzing and fading away alone in the dark and bitter intellectual Cambridge cold after they parted. On those long walks back to the Radcliffe Quad, the city was a lonely place for the lonesome work of the lone brain. Even its streetlamps shining on empty walkways seemed to be preoccupied with their own light.

"I'm worried about you," she said one evening when the graduate students were at a departmental event and she and Stanley were alone together at last.

"Worried? Why?" he said, hovering buoyantly above a paper he was writing called "Obsessive Tendencies in the Work of Edgar Allen Poe," a title that caused her to wonder about her own obsessive tendencies. And his.

"I worry that you're going too far. How many people know about this now? What if one of them, I don't know, slips. Says something to the wrong person?"

"What if I'm walking beside an apartment building and a potted plant falls on my head? What if I step into a sinkhole? We can't worry about things beyond our control."

"But this isn't beyond your control. You don't have to do this."

"That is true," he said, and looked at her as if seeing something new. "Why are you so concerned?"

"I worry about you," she said, and added, "You're important to me."

"As are you to me." He scratched his head and said, "Vera, I have to confess... I realized in the last couple months that I was depressed for quite a long time. Years. But now I feel so free, and I'm actually happy. I'm living in uncertainty and risk, but I'm happy for once."

"I'm glad," she said. "Just be careful, will you?"

There was a knock at the door and Stanley got up and opened it. It was two of the grad students, carrying a rubber tree plant in a clay pot. "For you," one of them said. Stanley and Vera gave each other a look, acknowledging the weirdness of a random item from their conversation entering the room in physical form. "It was on the curb and we thought, hey..." the grad student said, shrugging his shoulders.

Stanley tried to carry it into the apartment and Vera rushed over to help. "Where shall we put it?" he asked her.

"Anywhere but on the windowsill."

When they set it down, she went over to the door, gave the grad students a wave as if to say "Good-bye now," and bumped it closed with her hip. She felt Stanley's eyes on her, and turned to see him staring. He took her in his arms, finally, and kissed her for real, and as they kissed it felt as if the normal chatter of inanimate objects, the room tone, went dead silent and the apartment held its breath. He let go of her and stepped back. Then he noticed the door. It hadn't shut all the way after all, so he walked to it and slammed it closed.

The slamming of the door touched off something deep in the exhaustion of her, a raw and wild feeling that there was nothing left to lose, an urge to throw away all caution and grab for something at long last that she very much needed. She let her dress drop to the floor and climbed naked into the bed that stood so impatiently in the corner all the time they had spent there. She was still a virgin; she was sure he was too. He devoted himself entirely to pleasing her. He was a bit clumsy with the business about the condom but finally she got to feel what she wanted to feel for so long, his strong naked body up against hers and the heat of him pushing into her. He was gentle and attentive and adoring and it was all extremely good, as if he really did love her. She was certain of it then: He did. There would be no more question of it in her mind. With his actions he praised her slender body and made her feel the weighty, overpowering thing she longed to feel.

She woke the next morning with the sun piercing so blazingly through the window it felt like pinpricks. Stanley was at his table in boxers and a T-shirt, already at work again on the paper, or a crossword puzzle, it didn't matter to her which. She sat on the edge of the bed and wrapped herself in the sheet. He looked up and acknowledged her with a smile, then went back to his work. As he had with the first paper he showed her, he wrote his first drafts longhand, then typed them up on a heavy machine he borrowed from the grad students that snapped hotly as if he were firing a Tommy gun.

She took a shower and dressed in the bathroom, newly shy in his presence. When she came out, she roused him out of his oblivion by clearing her throat and saying, "Well, I'll let you get on with your work."

He looked up, his mind a hundred and thirty years away, with Poe and his obsessions. "Um..."

"I have my own work to do. Places to go, people to see."

"Okay."

She opened the door and, before she left, said, "Let's do that again sometime."

"Yes, let's."

As winter abdicated its brutal regime and the semester moved toward its conclusion, they did do that again sometimes, but not as often as Vera would have liked. Stanley had become a freak for paper writing, lost to his research or obscured behind the attack of typewriter keys, a sonic bead curtain. He was pretending to be a student, for the use of the library, and had crafted his own fake ID by altering one he bought from a dropout. He wrote "The Art of Chartres: A Cathedral More Form than Function." He whipped out "Flemish Politics in the Time of Breughel" for a political science major with an artistic bent. He received an order at dinnertime one evening and at breakfast the next morning put the last period on "Hemingway vs. Fitzgerald: A Literary Prizefight."

Stacks of books were piled on one side of the typewriter, which he had taken total possession of, and on the other was a stack of cash with an apple as paperweight. Behind it all sat Stanley in undershirt and fedora, a term paper pusher man.

Vera was happy for her Stanley, her Outlaw of Harvard Yard, but she was also weary of being ignored. She spent more time out and about with Abby and her friends, meeting new people and providing Stanley with a steady stream of customers. One of them was a freshman named Kenneth from a famous Boston family, the Thornhills, with a great-grandfather who had been chief justice of Massachusetts and another ancestor who had been a Harvard dean back in the eighteen hundreds. He seemed to consider himself appropriately entitled, despite exhibiting none of the intelligence or diligence, or any other ———igence, of his ancestors. His only notable quality was indigence. He was so busy enjoying everything about Harvard except its core function that he didn't have the time or desire to put in the hours of study that survival there required. He flirted with Vera while Stanley wrote his papers for him, and insisted that Vera deliver the papers from Stanley's hands to his. He had no more interest in meeting Stanley than he had in talking policy with Khrushchev. Vera was happy to have the attention, but wasn't the least bit attracted to this kid, who applied the charm as delicately as a bricklayer applied mortar.

"So, Stanley, husband of mine..." Vera said one day just a week before final exams.

"Yes, my dear?" he said facetiously, taking her use of the word *husband* as more of a joke than intended.

"This Kenneth character...I think he likes me."

Stanley looked up. "Does he? Too bad for him."

"He wants you to take his American History exam for him."

Stanley laughed. "Considering the significant role his own family has played, I find that...I was going to say funny, but it's really just sad."

"Isn't it though?" she said. "Anyway, I told him we all know you can't take an exam for him."

Stanley sat up from his work and nibbled on his pencil eraser. "I hate that word."

"What word?"

"Can't." His opinion of himself as an academic maestro and a superman of the deadbeat class had gotten the better of him lately.

"Well, it's true. There will only be twenty students in the room. What could you do, dress up as him?"

"Let me talk to him, at least, before I say no. Maybe there's a way."

One week before the exam, Professor Lamb of American History 101 gave his students five possible essay questions for which to prepare. The final exam would be a one-hour session in which they were allowed as much space as they required in a single blue book to answer whichever one of the five questions the professor handed them. Kenneth gave Stanley the five questions, along with a sample of his handwriting, and Stanley bought five blue books at the student bookstore. Then he and Kenneth sat down and made their plan for the day of the test. Stanley would write answers for all five possible questions and give the blue books to Kenneth that morning before the test. Kenneth would tuck the blue books into the waistband of his trousers and keep his jacket buttoned. After receiving his essay question and blank blue book from the professor, Kenneth would drop the blue book on the floor and, in picking it up, swap the blank book for the one Stanley had provided that matched the question.

The week before the test, while Stanley was hard at work answering the five questions in Kenneth's handwriting, Kenneth was hard at work trying to seduce Vera. He stopped by her dorm and asked to see Abby, hoping she might bring Vera down with her, which she didn't. In their conversation, he teased out the fact that the two of them liked red wine, so the next day he stopped by again and dropped off a bottle of 1953 Château Latour. When they called to thank him, he hounded Vera until she promised to take a walk with him on Thursday, the day before the test. Vera enjoyed flirting, although she found Kenneth dull, and was wondering how far to let this go. She decided to give in and take a short walk, only within the confines of the two campuses, and then that would be the end of it.

Thursday evening found Stanley walking down Quincy Street on his way home from a research session at Lamont. Down the block, he caught the movement of two figures backlit along the side of the Carpenter Center. He thought he recognized Vera's familiar contours and elegant way of lifting her hand, and turned in that direction. No, couldn't be. But then he saw the other silhouette pull the shape he thought was Vera toward him and press his face against hers. Stanley stopped, and his heart climbed up into his throat. He was moving, running a few steps toward them as he watched the woman—yes, it was Vera—watched Vera struggle, a flash of arms and twisting shapes, then saw them stumble into the light and saw her slap Kenneth hard and take off in the other direction, and as he watched her go, Kenneth vanished in the dark. Stanley started to walk toward her dorm, but then thought, No, leave her alone, she probably wouldn't have wanted me to see that, and anyway, I have a better idea.

When he thought it through, his better idea required that he still go to her dorm. He called from a pay phone and asked Abby to come down and smuggle him in. Vera was on her back on her bed, reading a book, her chest rising and falling rather quickly. Stanley hadn't said a word to Abby about why he was there, and Abby stood blinking presumptuously at them both as if inviting them to welcome her into whatever the hell was going on. Vera mentioned none of it. Stanley made benign chitchat as Abby grew increasingly irritated at being ignored. Stanley covered Vera lovingly with a blanket and said, "Hey, next week let's go see that *Dr. Strangelove* movie you've been wanting to see," then asked Abby to work her magic again and help him sneak out. On his way out of the room, while Vera reached for another volume on the shelf beside her bed, he soundlessly lifted Socrates from the pen cup on her desk.

When the bookstore opened at eight o'clock the next morning, Stanley was the first one through the door, popping out moments later with five more blue books. Working briskly as a bomb defuser, he put himself through the grinding tedium of copying all five essays from the old blue books to the new, while the skull on the passive end of Socrates bobbed in the periphery of his vision. The test was at noon. With his eyes flicking occasionally to the church clock outside the window and back to the essays, he finished the last one, messy and ragged, just at 11:30, his wrist a rusted joint, the pinkie side of his hand long gone numb, the last few pages of letters woozy on their spider legs. He had just enough time to get to the rendezvous point outside Robinson Hall by 11:55, if he hurried. But he didn't. Stanley let the bastard sweat it out, and met the frantically pacing Kenneth at precisely 11:59.

Stanley approached Professor Lamb's office a half hour after the test was over, fully prepared to present himself as a reporter from the *Crimson* with questions about the historical context of the recent political turmoil, prepared even to take the professor to a nearby restaurant for a free meal and further questioning if necessary to prevent him from grading the not-yet-disappeared essay. But Stanley was relieved to find the back of the man diminishing down the hall with nothing but jacket in hand, and a sign on the door that read, "History 101 exams will be graded after the weekend and results posted forthwith."

If Stanley had actually been a reporter for the *Crimson*, he might have seen it coming. He might have at least gotten some advance notice, not for himself, but for Vera, and been able to warn her, though that would have done little good. He and Vera spent part of the weekend working—she studying for her last exam and he putting together a new puzzle—and part of it sharing the bed in the depth of night with the open window carrying in the narcotic scent of spring in full bedazzlement. So it was with relaxed body and mind that the two of them eased their way into the last week of the term. Vera knocked the stuffing out of any semblance of a challenge that her exams presented, and returned to her dorm to find her resident advisor waiting for her, fanning herself with a piece of paper. "Baxter, I've been looking for you. The dean would like to see you," she said.

Vera felt herself going weak, and had to take a deep breath and steady herself. "The dean? What dean?" she asked.

"Dean Martin," the advisor said. "What dean do you think? Walsey, the Dean of the College."

"Oh." Vera had a feeling, but no, it couldn't be. "About what?"

"I don't know. Go find out."

The dean was perched on the edge of his desk when she came in, his pant leg rucked up and a comical length of sock on full display. She quickly sensed that she wasn't the only other person in the room. As she turned her head, she knew what she'd find. Sitting in a chair with his elbows on his knees and a wounded look on his face was the descendant of a man who had occupied this office back when it was lit by flame, the troublesome Kenneth Thornhill.

"Did you know..." the kid began to say in a high-pitched whine, but was quickly interrupted by a sharp "Please" from Dean Walsey.

He held up a blue book and turned the pages, blank, every one of them. "This is Mr. Thornhill's essay for the American History final exam. It's a pity that this is all he knows about the subject." Kenneth squirmed in his chair. "Apparently a fully filled blue book was provided to him by a young man named Stanley Owens, in exchange for money. Yet somehow this is what Professor Lamb found, with only Mr. Thornhill's name on the cover. In his discomfort at being swindled, our young man here told us quite a story, involving purchased papers and many unwise undergraduates. It's a story I sorely regret happening on my watch."

Vera sat down. She had a sensation then that it was *she* who was becoming invisible, and within twenty-four hours she would exist only if she alone wanted to believe she existed. She knew what was coming. She wished she could just return to her room and pack her things and go already.

"Apparently you were good friends with this Mr. Owens? Dating, perhaps?"

Vera nodded.

"Would you be good enough to tell me where we might find him?"

Vera shook her head.

"No, you wouldn't care to, or no, you don't know where he is?"

"With all due respect, no, I don't care to."

The man stood up and did a lap around his desk. Then he sat in his chair and picked up a pen. "Most of my responsibilities here are an absolute pleasure. I go through the day singing to myself, I really do. But then there are times when I have to do things that make me hate my job. Vera, today I hate my job. I hate having to turn away hardworking, gifted young people whose only crime is aiding those of others. But I'm going to have to ask you to leave, and never come back."

Vera told herself she wouldn't cry. She pressed her hands together and fed all her emotions into those pressed hands, and did not cry.

"Let's do this my way. You leave of your own accord. You're free to transfer your solid academic record to another institution. You don't talk about it, and I don't talk about it." Then, as if he'd forgotten that Kenneth was in the room, he looked up at him and said in an entirely less gentle tone, "And you don't talk about it. About Ms. Baxter, I mean. Or any of it. We'll do our best to stop this here," he said, pressing his finger onto the desk, "if it's not already too late."

He looked over again at Vera. "That's all."

She got slowly to her feet. But part of her never left that heavy wooden chair in the dean's office in Massachusetts Hall. It had happened so fast. She had wanted it to be over and now that it was over she wanted to stay with this nice man in this room, minus Kenneth. But then she knew she needed to do as the dean said as quickly and with as little fuss as possible. Thankfully, Abby was not at the dorm when Vera returned, senseless to any of the end-of-term hoopla going on around her. She packed up the things she needed and left a small pile of things she could do without on her desk for Abby to use as she pleased. Vera was too mortified by what had happened to write a note, telling herself that the less Abby had to do with her anymore the better for Abby. She called a taxi and asked that it meet her on Shepard Street, and carried down her suitcase and box one by one. Inside the cab, she leaned her head on the window, watching Radcliffe slip away.

"Good-bye, Stanley," she whispered, drawing his name in the condensation from her breath on the window, then rubbing it out. She had the driver take her into Boston, to "any inexpensive hotel," she said, and the driver looked over his shoulder at her with a judgmental smirk, and dropped her at the Hotel Paramount. She put her suitcase and box in the corner of the room she rented for the night, and sat down on the edge of the bed. Small steps, she told herself. She wanted to go back to her mother but her mother thought she was married, and she didn't want to confess two crimes at once. She didn't even want to confess one crime. Small steps. Tomorrow, I'll find a cheap place to live, she told herself. The thunder booming in her head became sheets of rain, soporific sheets of rain, and she fell asleep.

CHAPTER SEVEN

Stanley had been in love once. There was a maid, a perfectly different kind of girl of sixteen from Bolivia whom Stanley fell breathtakingly and hazardously in love with at first sight when he was fourteen. Her face was a startling arrangement of wonders that delivered a thump to the chest whenever he saw it. There was no explaining it because he never once spoke to her, and the only things he knew about her were the things he could observe: She was a lefty, she carried a parchment-colored satchel, she did all sorts of fabulous things with her hair when she wasn't wearing her cap with the frayed brim, and the only shoes he ever saw her wear were black Mary Janes. She had big brown eyes, and an infinite world lay hidden in the whites of those eyes every time he caught a glimpse of them. It was impossible for him to speak to this girl, not because her English wasn't very good but because the internal control systems that operated Stanley wouldn't allow him to approach her. The closer he got, the more his entire body shuddered and began to break apart. Then one day she was gone, and he fell into a suffering that was a frightening emptiness like a terror, and it was intolerable, but he suffered through it for over a year until time healed him. Stanley had a fondness for Vera, but he didn't think he loved her. Catching a glimpse of his reflection in the window of a women's clothing shop on Brattle Street, he was convinced that it was his destiny to only ever have the women that he was warm to, not the ones that burned him up from inside.

That was what he told himself, at least, in the depth of his intelligence and the shallowness of his wisdom. Until he realized Vera had vanished.

On the Wednesday morning two days after Vera's final, Stanley left his room, jogged down the stairs, and headed for the diner on the corner for the dollar pancakes-and-coffee combo. And as he sat and rotated playfully right and left on the toadstool at the counter, it passed through his mind as gently as the sweet scent of butter and syrup that Vera was done with school for the year, and that he ought to stop by and congratulate her.

To the left of him occurred a rustle of activity and the sudden absence of a person Stanley hadn't noticed, leaving behind the artifacts of his presence there: greasy plate, bent cigarette butt sending up a last choked complaint of smoke, folded *Boston Globe* bearing the headline "Cheating Scandal Exposed."

Stanley snatched up the paper and took in the article in one swallow. He left instantly and was probably halfway to Vera's dorm before the counter stool stopped spinning.

Abby met him in front of Briggs Hall, more glum than ever, pulled him around to the side of the building and into the shadows, and told him that Vera's things were gone—the small number of clothes she owned, her hairbrush and its relatives from the bathroom, a few books and a suitcase. Gone. She left behind her Harvard coffee mug and a lamp she'd bought and a macramé sweater that Abby liked to borrow.

"She got expelled," Abby said, with a blank look of loss on her face as if Vera had passed away. "No, not expelled," she corrected herself. "She was asked to leave." Abby handed him a copy of the *Globe*, folded to the article he had already seen. "I won't state the obvious and say who's to blame here," she said, forming her mouth into a straight line of resigned dissatisfaction with the whole sorry state of affairs. "I don't wish you any ill will," she said as if trying to convince herself. "If I were you I'd make myself scarce as well. I don't know what they have the legal power to do to you, but I'm sure they can cook up something."

Stanley didn't know what to say. He was thinking only about Vera and where she might have gone. "I guess you're right," he said, and turned to leave.

As he left, the thing that was bothering Abby the most finally forced its way into expression. "She didn't even say good-bye."

Looking over his shoulder at every phantom sound behind him, Stanley made his careful way back to his studio apartment and packed up the few things he owned. He knew of a cheap rooming house even farther from campus for vagrants, addicts, professional gamblers, and others just on this side of hobo-hood. He returned the typewriter, still hot and smoking in his mind's eye, back to the graduate students and bid them a brisk and mysterious farewell. He took his suitcase and his library books and teapot and closed the door on the little garret where he and Vera incinerated their virginity together. In the dark of night, he walked to the rooming house where no one knew who he was or that he was possibly wanted by the Cambridge police for fraud or some such thing.

He lived there like a squatter. He signed the register as Owen Baxter. He had no bills, no way to be tracked, aside from the post office box he rented under his real name so he could receive the rejection notices and the occasional acceptance of his puzzles. He showed his face outside the rented room as little as possible, inhabiting it like a hideout. He unscrewed the one lightbulb. To the casual observer, the only difference between Stanley and a gangster drawing back the shade was that in his free hand there was a pencil and not a pistol.

In late June, as his paranoia subsided, Stanley put on sunglasses and his fedora, turned up his collar, and looked cautiously for Vera around Briggs Hall, in the café, the student union, the empty lecture halls. He was certain she had left Cambridge, but he poked around the campus anyway, wherever there were no security guards or campus officials to be seen, sifting the crowds for one face. He waited in front of the library, hiding behind a newspaper and staying until the very last monkish form shambled out and the perimeter was deserted. He went to the places she liked to eat. When he ran out of places to look, he even checked for her in places he knew she would never be: pool halls, the Harvard boathouse, travel agencies, phone booths—as if they were playing a game of hide-and-seek. He might catch the flash of a familiar shape passing through a door and he would go after it whatever the consequences: not her.

He checked with Abby, who, because of the earnestness of his search for Vera, had forgiven him just enough to allow him to speak to her. She was preparing to go abroad to the Mediterranean with her mother and sister for the summer, but she hadn't received any communication from Vera. She claimed to hate the Mediterranean. "Bourgeois getaway for the rich," she said, as if she wasn't a member of that group herself. She talked about how she hated to leave the country with Vera still unaccounted for, while Stanley helped her carry her bathtub-sized suitcase to a taxi. When they finished wedging the suitcase into the trunk, she put her hands on his shoulders and said, "You find our girl." Stanley nodded, and she went off grumbling and snapping at the cabbie.

Stanley didn't know where else to look, so he stayed in Cambridge, hoping she might turn up there. He still had his part-time job teaching tennis, but other than that he had nothing to distract him from his loss. Everywhere he went he was in a mode of preoccupation, searching faces for that one brilliant spark. For the first time in months his crossword notebook lay untouched on the floor of his room.

His conscience was poking him sharply, reminding him that no matter how he rationalized it to himself, he had done wrong. And rationalize it he did: The privileged kids he took money from were responsible for their own decisions, and had he not written their papers for them they would have flunked out anyway. They didn't need the money they paid him as much as he did. No arms were twisted. There wasn't any real harm in it. But inevitably he was forced to face the truth by his conscience, an extremely rude and unpleasant little character with a Napoleon complex that always seemed to know better, forced to confront the fact that he had indeed done harm, to Vera. Real, irreparable harm that he would desperately like to undo, or to make up for in some way. Stanley made his way around Harvard incognito, downcast and desperately worried about Vera, and about the money that was slowly running out. In a way, skimping felt like an art form, but eventually he would have to do something, and he was worried about lingering around the scene of the crime. Though he didn't want to leave the place where he and Vera had shared so much, he figured he ought to move out of Cambridge.

Vera was gone. Abby was gone. The students were gone. Stanley's future was a wispy, diminishing thing. His half-baked moneymaking scheme had ruined everything. He became particularly observant of loss. Places where there had been buildings became vacant lots. Folded-up old widows sat alone on bungalow porches. Harvard itself seemed to be crumbling away, and Stanley took refuge in the public library, a building so sturdy it looked as if it could never be gone. Stanley spent most of the summer there. The enthusiasm he had for crosswords no longer felt sharp and original and forbidden but was starting to take on the flabby, hulking feeling of an obligation. He still did all the puzzles in all the papers he could get his hands on every day, in the library, so as not to have to buy them. As a token of peace to his ever-more-impertinent conscience, he copied the grids with tracing paper and solved them there so as not to ruin the challenge for the next reader. He was becoming conscientious like that in small ways, trying to change into a person who was better than that fool who had done so much harm. As much as he enjoyed wearing the shoes of a rebel, he couldn't forgive himself for what had happened. Midday he could be found staring into space with his pencil lolling in a limp hand. How could he have put her at risk like that? He had never thought so carefully about Vera until she was gone. By August, he was no longer bothered so much by the fact that he lost her, like a set of keys, but rather by the obvious implication that she didn't care to come and find him.

"Dear Dad," he wrote. "Now I've lost two people. You're gone. Vera's gone. If you've seen her in that otherwhere that you inhabit, send her back to me. I think I need her. I live in the hope that her vanishing is temporary. Your son, Stanley." He put the letter into an envelope and reached for a stamp, then stopped. "It's about time you grew up," he said disgustedly to himself, crumpled the letter and envelope and threw them into the trash.

Stanley read newspaper articles about the Civil Rights Act and the Congo Crisis and the bombing of Vietnam, scanned library books, and watched whatever was on TV in an East Somerville cafeteria where he always went for the dollar meals. It was the kind of place that had gunk around the baseboards so dark and everlasting, you couldn't help but picture roaches scampering free there at night. Every day he also spent an hour in the Riffraff Café, lingering over the cheapest thing in the place—cup of coffee, twenty-five cents—because if Vera returned to Cambridge, that was where she would most likely surface. He stopped actively hunting for her, having tried everything he could think of, but as he wandered the sidewalks he scanned every face he could see with a feeling of panic that if he missed just one it might be the very one he sought.

He economized. He had three or four changes of clothes that he wore in succession, washing them in the disgusting sink of the shared bathroom with hand soap and laying them out on the bare floor to dry. He nibbled on day-old bread from the wholesale bakery down the street. The last bit of money from the paper-writing business was nearly gone. He had published seven more puzzles since the New Year, which brought him the great fortune of thirty-five dollars. He could survive a whole week on ten dollars. It was a welcome challenge, in his barren summer, to encounter so many dazzling things in his day and not buy a single one of them. It gave him a kind of power, when he was feeling his most powerless.

Already, the students were beginning to reassemble for the fall semester, but they seemed like a different species entirely, insubstantial and less authentic than the crowd that left in the spring. Imposters. Stanley searched the campus with renewed hope, wondering if she would be back for the new semester. He dared a visit to the registrar's office and asked the uninterested clerk if Vera Baxter was registered for classes. Despite her poorly concealed contempt for her job, the clerk proved to be stubbornly conscientious about the privacy of student information and refused to tell him.

He was intensely lonely, a condition that manifested itself as a physical ache, a shivering when he took a deep breath. He tried to strike up conversations with the people he encountered but he found he wasn't his old self. He wasn't a part of any community like he had been at the Hawthorne. He used to be able to burn away great fistfuls of time playing the young gentleman and chatting with friends and doing the crossword puzzles in the hotel lobby that he missed so much now. Up in Cambridge on his own he continued to time himself doing the *Globe*, the *Post*, the *Times*, and recorded the results in a pocket notebook. But he was slipping. He rarely managed to do a puzzle in under four minutes anymore. And he really tried—or at least he tried to try. He sat in uncomfortable chairs, breathing, thinking, feeling his powers slip away, seep from under his collar, evaporate from the ends of his hairs. His brain cells dizzy and idle.

Vera.

In those days it seemed he would find her name in almost every puzzle, since it was part of a common clue: "_____ vera." Blank Vera. Blank Vera. One day he even saw a play on that clue in a puzzle in the *Globe*, just like in the crossword Vera planted for him a year ago. "Aloe ____." It caused the faintest of smiles. He filled in VERA with pleasure and turned his attention to the theme of the puzzle. He identified the key clues and solutions.

Municipal legume: BOSTONBAKEDBEAN
Baseball team accessory: BOSTONREDSOCK
A Henry James title: THEBOSTONIANS
Keep a stiff upper lip: NOTSOB (He liked that one.)
The world in your hands: BOSTONGLOBE

Clever. The clue that stopped everything though was this: "Erle _____ Gardner." Now that's odd, he thought. Vera and Stanley were both answers in the same puzzle. And a puzzle themed for the city just across the Charles River, no less. In his mind he took a step back and then everything became clear. Clues were everywhere. A hankering: JONES. Writer Nathaniel: HAWTHORNE. City planned by L'Enfant: WASHINGTON. Small cut: NICK. Word war: SPELLINGBEE. Chills traveled along him as if some virtuoso were thrumming him with the cottony drumsticks of a xylophone. He jumped up from the floor and dashed out of the rooming house and was lucky enough to find a taxi right away. He got in.

In the pandemonium of his thoughts the scenario got flip-flopped and he said to the cabbie, "Where to?"

The driver looked at him as if he suspected he was drunk. Then Stanley realized he had no money in his pocket and no idea where to go once he crossed the river.

"I'm sorry," he said, and climbed out.

He knocked around Cambridge in a state of shock. Inside his rib cage was a rattling heart and a bottomless sensation as if he were falling forever. She really wrote another puzzle for him? She did: There it was, still in the crook of his arm, touchable and real. He found himself walking Brattle Street, passing her old dorm, staring into space on a bench along the Charles River. So she was in Boston. Suddenly he realized it was night. He was surprised that he had first discovered her secret message many hours ago, around midmorning. It felt like only a matter of moments. He went to the Riffraff Café, her place, and sat down to pore over the puzzle and decode where exactly in Boston she might be expecting him.

CHAPTER EIGHT

Chuck Reese came into the bends of Highway One so quickly that Vera's fingers ached from gripping the passenger seat handles of his Corvette Sting Ray, the rattle and shake of the car itself causing her to imagine the worst, picturing its seemingly flimsy exoskeleton flying apart entirely and leaving her skidding across the road surface on her bottom alongside the transmission shaft.

"Slow it down? A little?" Vera said.

"What?" he shouted over the sonic terror of the car, delightedly tuned in only to the road and the car and the play of his feet on the pedals. "Can't hear ya!"

"Slow down!"

He let out a full-throated laugh. "S'alright, exit's just here!" he said, and swung them off the highway in a meteoric gather and sweep of vectors. The downshifting engine growled in disagreement with the reduction in velocity.

Vera loosened her grip and counted her blessings. It's good to be alive, she thought as she emerged from the crypt of her fear and let out a hard sigh of trapped breath. She had started working for Chuck, as he preferred she call him, shortly after escaping to Boston. She'd needed a job, and fast, so the first thing she did after snapping up the one and only inexpensive apartment she looked at was to leaf through the *Globe*, quickly bypassing the puzzles-and-games page, to the classifieds. "Wanted: Exec. Assistant, p.t.," read the first ad to grab her attention. Part-time was what she was looking for. "Get your foot in the door in the exciting television industry! Must be personable, professional, good with numbers." The numbers part sealed the deal. She couldn't have cared less about sticking her foot in the door of the television industry, which seemed as dull to her as the exciting mathematics industry did to most of her peers.

Chuck was the GM of WNAC-TV, the Boston affiliate of ABC. "The abecedarian network," Vera said when he mentioned its initials in the interview, and Chuck slapped his thigh and let out his wrecking ball of a laugh even though (or perhaps because) he had no clue what she meant. She started as a part-time assistant to a junior account executive, about as thinly sliced and marginalized a job title as she figured it was possible to have. The station had plenty of extra work with the glut of new shows premiering that September, including *Bewitched*, whose star, Elizabeth Montgomery, Chuck had met in LA and was in love with, or so he said; claustrophobia-inducing *Voyage to the Bottom of the Sea*; the evening soap *Peyton Place*, with the bookish Allison MacKenzie played by Mia Farrow, an actress Chuck told Vera she reminded him of; the *Hootenanny* replacement, *Shindig!*; Chuck's favorite, *The Addams Family*, which always lagged disappointingly in the ratings behind the "copycat" *Munsters*; and *Jonny Quest*, the Hanna-Barbera production for kids. These new properties generated a lot of work in the accounting department, and as Vera quickly found out, the staff on hand wrestled with simple computation the way Ahab wrestled with his fish, giving the task an almost metaphysical worthiness. But Chuck liked her, and in short order she was appropriated to replace his own assistant, who had disappointed him by getting a job elsewhere.

Toward the end of her first day working for him, his bulky form shadowed her desk as she sat hunched over a spreadsheet and she looked up, and in an awkward businesslike moment full of propriety, he said to her, "Do you have a boyfriend?" She replied, "I'm married," hiding her ringless left hand under the desk. "Oh, of course," he said, and that was that. Lying to him in that way was simply the first defense that came to mind, but she knew the idea of being married to Stanley had been buried alive in the dark graveyard of her temporal lobe and was only waiting for the right moment to rise up out of the dirt. From then on she kept her wedding ring in her pocket and put it on when she got to the station.

Chuck liked to play hooky, and often went on death-defying tears in his car, laying scratch on Boylston Street, to escape the constant pressures of his job. There were impossible sales goals to meet, forever just out of reach to a scientifically exact degree, like the proverbial carrot on a stick. There were advertisers to please, who were always just less than satisfied with the excellent fare his station offered—*Bewitched*! *The Addams Family*!—their drooping faces resembling that of the sea bass. And then there was the FCC, peering over his shoulder at the most inopportune moments, like when he was trying to coax an ad buy out of a vendor. They considered that a violation of the rules. Reciprocal trade, they called it, while to Chuck it seemed only fair. The compression of these competing forces would pop him from his office high in the brand-new Prudential Tower and into his Corvette, keen of shape like the fletching on an arrow, with Vera beside him to write down ideas and to-dos as he released his tension onto the roadways of eastern Massachusetts. Vera had enrolled in Boston University for the fall semester, and the plan was for her to work for him only through the summer, but then summer waned and the school year started up again with the heavy unslumbering of its august gears, and she stayed on without either of them mentioning it.

That fall, Vera was taking classes in mathematics and waiting for Stanley to come and find her. When she wasn't busy crunching numbers for Chuck or taking his machine to the Esso on Columbus for an oil change, she spent time studying on a bench in the Museum of Fine Arts, whose name she placed at the exact center of her published crossword puzzle. Clue: Where you'll find Water Lilies. Answer: MFABOSTON. The bench she studied on was situated directly across from one of those famous paintings by Monet, and she would look up at it and recall Stanley rescuing her from Fresh Pond.

She was not lonely. She made several friends at the station and at BU, and in the apartment building she moved into, and she often met them for coffee or drinks or a walk through Boston Common on a Sunday. One of her classmates, Lisa, had a border collie that was addicted to flinging itself into the air after a tennis ball. Her colleague Dawn had a gigantic Irish family that was horrified by Vera's aloneness and treated her like an adopted sister. But in fact none of these friends really meant a lot to her; her relationships, if you could call them that, were simply a way of taking her mind off things. She deliberately found chores to do when she wasn't studying or working, because she believed that it kept her from losing her mind. She would go very slowly about the business of doing her laundry and washing up her dishes and cleaning the apartment, working carelessly so she had to crisscross the apartment to retrieve things.

Among Vera's acquaintances were a few interesting young men, but for the time being, all other men were ruined for her—slack and shapeless. For the time being, their gender was dominated by one man only. Whatever black magic he had worked upon her she was dead set on undoing. She had given up trying to remove him from the epicenter of her thoughts and now accepted that there he would remain, imperfect and impossible and never to be trusted. She was not lonely but sometimes she almost wished she were, the better to wander the Back Bay in the bottomless throes of a heavily romantic desperation, welcoming remembrances of him and the doubts they brought.

Vera introduced a BU friend, Farid, to the practice of studying on the bench in the art museum. They were there one afternoon, deeply mining their thoughts silently and independently, when Vera felt a kind of summons in the air. She looked up. In that instant when her eyes settled on him, she saw him slip from fantasy to reality, going realm to realm smoothly and omnipotently. She looked at him coolly. A smile threatened to form itself, trembling at one corner of her mouth.

"May I?" he asked.

She nodded. He sat. After a moment of silence he said, "I finally found what I was looking for."

"Excuse me?" she said, looking up from her book.

"I can't get enough of Monet. I've seen that image so many

times but it's much more impressive in person." He nodded his head toward the painting directly in front of them.

"I agree," she said. "It reminds me of something."

"Sorry to pry, but I have to ask: Is that group theory you're studying?"

"Yes, it is."

"That's a branch of abstract algebra, isn't it?"

"Mm-hm."

"I'm fascinated by math, but I'm no good at it. I'm Stanley, by the way."

"Vera," she said, and shook his warm hand.

At this point, Farid peeked his head out from behind Vera and she introduced him. "We're in a seminar together at BU. He's from Iran."

"Really? Mesopotamia, where the sexagesimal system came from—the sixty-second minute, the sixty-minute hour..." As soon as Stanley spoke he looked as if he regretted it. Then he said, "I have some friends from Iran. Members of the consulate." Vera realized how pompous he must have sounded to himself as he tried to explain. "I grew up in DC. A lot of embassy business happened right under my nose."

Farid asked, "Are your parents in that line of work?"

"Not at all. My mother's a copy editor. My father died in World War Two. Normandy."

"Oh, I'm sorry to hear that," Farid said.

Looking back to Vera, Stanley asked, "Where are you from?"

"New York. Although, as I grew up, my mom started traveling more and more all over the East Coast, first as a secretary to a salesman and then as a sales assistant, so I kind of lived in hotels a bit."

"Me too! I lived in a hotel all my life until I came up here," Stanley said.

"How did that come about?" Farid asked.

"My dad was the concierge at a hotel in DC, and after he died in the war, they gave my mom and me a suite to live in. So we just stayed there."

Farid was about to say something in response but Vera spoke up. She wanted Stanley all to herself. She coveted him and wanted to lay herself over him like a blanket and protect him, and simultaneously to strangle him. "I bet we'd have a lot to talk about," she said. "My hotels were only the most lavish affairs, a personal attendant outside every room, foot massages, food service under sterling silver domes, that sort of thing."

"That must have been wonderful," Stanley said, happy to go with whatever she was saying.

"Fabulous establishments, but alas...only in my imagination." She laughed at herself. "Honestly, my hotels were mostly cheap country wrecks—walls, a roof, a door, and one window that hadn't been cleaned since it was put there." She laughed again and so did Stanley.

"Who's your favorite artist?" he asked her.

"Picasso," she said, as he already knew. "I'd love to meet him. Who's yours?"

"Van Gogh," he said, as she also knew. "Is Boston your favorite city?"

"No, DC," she answered.

"Mine too," he said. "It's where I met all my favorite people."

They chatted this way for a short while, Stanley and Vera trading information that they already knew about each other, with Farid looking on. Stanley asked if they'd like to get something to eat.

"Sorry, but I have to get to a class, actually," Vera said.

They agreed to meet for dinner Saturday, Vera and Farid and Stanley and maybe more of her friends. He asked for her phone number and then she asked for his.

"At the moment I don't have a phone number."

"How about your address? I'll send you a letter," she said, and laughed.

"Listen, I'll call you. How about that? I'll call you Saturday at noon and we can decide where to meet. Will you be home then?" She had the suspicion he was living on the streets—days in the library and nights in South Station. But maybe he had a room somewhere and a part-time job, she reassured herself.

By the time Vera had adjusted to the cold weather and the wearing of jackets, the leaves had left the trees and mornings came formally attired in frost. At dawn, when the sun was just at the height where she could reach up and touch it, she took brisk walks to clear her head, over to and along the Charles River. It dragged itself, cold and steel, continuously downward without ever a change of pace. She quit smoking her beloved Chesterfields, cold turkey. The FTC recently ruled that health warnings would have to appear on cigarette packages, and that spooked her. Quitting was a personal passage of torture that she had known all along she would someday have to go through, and it was everything she feared. Quitting was a Hieronymus Bosch painting, a diabolical tincture of infinite longing and irritability and the bone-deep application of blacksmith tongs. But she declared that she was the master of herself and she did it. She felt as if she was only just regaining control of her heart, and by God she would not lose command of her lungs. Stanley occasionally stayed the night. He told her about his euphoria the moment he found her secret communication hidden in the puzzle, about how he'd been doing the puzzles in all the major papers every single day, no matter what, desperately hoping she might send out another secret call to him but never really expecting to find one concealed there with its back up against the comic strips.

They were living as a couple, but guardedly, laying low, living on the straight and narrow, happy to be out of trouble and just doing what life required of them. Vera was busy with school, studying and doing exceedingly well. Stanley was wizarding up his crossword puzzles. Every week or two he burst in on Vera with the pride of a boy, announcing the great news of another accepted puzzle. Vera listened but didn't reveal that she too had sent off several of her own. She managed to find time for a puzzle now and then while she was on the T or had downtime at work, and she was quick.

She studied the wedding ring that played a part-time role on her finger. It was a sad statement. A stand-in for something real. This gave her an idea for a puzzle. The theme would be phrases containing the word "ring"—three-ring circus, ring in the New Year, ring true—but in place of the word "ring," there would be the letter "O." LORDOFTHEOS, then, would be one answer. That will really trip people up, she thought. She titled it "Ring-a-Ding-Ding." When this puzzle was accepted, the editor sent along a handwritten note praising the idea. Never before had he seen the substitution of a symbol for a word in a puzzle. Maybe it had been done before and he hadn't seen it. Or maybe she originated the idea. He ended his note with, "Please send more!"

Vera and Stanley spent time together almost every day like lovers are supposed to do. But it always felt to her as if he was holding something back. She didn't allow herself to believe the things he said. He called her Beautiful. He said he was crazy about her. "Well, I know you're crazy," she said to herself, "so that doesn't particularly help." He confused her by saying he enjoyed being married to her. She corrected him: "We didn't really marry, silly."

"Didn't we?" he said. "It sure was a convincing performance. I wonder if actors ever believe they are the roles they play."

"Do you believe we really are married?" she asked, posing the question that she herself once considered.

"Maybe," he whispered, kissing her ear.

Deep in the hollow of one of those hushed nights in her apartment, when he thought she was asleep, he said he loved her. She didn't let herself accept it; it was too late and he had proven himself untrustworthy. By this time her heart was hardened to him, or at least she hoped it was. She wouldn't put herself in mortal danger again, so she let his mumbled confession of love lie there in the bed between them.

Stanley had recently landed a part-time job at a library. Even though he had no experience aside from having read half the books in it, he impressed the head librarian with the knowledge that he rattled off the top of his head, from the life of Melvil Dewey to the history of the company that produced the banana lying on her desk, and she gave him a chance. He also had a part-time job at the 7-Eleven, where he often worked a night shift. Sometimes Vera drifted off and woke in the dark as he was leaving, and she watched him go, his bony legs wriggling into his jeans, his loaded smile as he looked back at her, the door slowly closing behind him. "Please don't disappear again," he said on one of those occasions. Then she turned away and made a sound as if she was glad to be rid of the fool and went back to sleep.

When he wasn't with her, Stanley was staying in a room in a town house near the Fenway, on St. Stephen Street, sharing a bathroom and kitchen with eight other impoverished individuals, each of them parceled away into his own box, three tiny lodgings to a floor with a damaged old stairway running like a crooked spine down the middle to the kitchen in the basement, which they also shared with a notorious rat that scuttled about as boldly as if it were paying rent.

Vera brought Stanley to the station one day and introduced him to Chuck as her husband. Stanley wore his wedding ring. "Ah, so here's the lucky fellow," Chuck said, clapping Stanley on the back and setting loose his wild laugh. He asked all sorts of impertinent questions, only half-seriously, offered to take Stanley for a ride in his Corvette, and then hurried off to meet a client for martinis, much to Stanley's relief. Vera was making herself indispensable to Chuck, and at the same time attracting attention and causing beards to be scratched in the patriarchal mathematics department. Her professors—intense people but in extremely distant and private ways, as if carrying the charge of their knowledge were to possess some horrible secret—came out with bold statements about her natural gift for math that stood out awkwardly from their modest personalities. She aced her finals, her pencil scratching briskly across the paper in the light-filled hall, and then it was time for winter break.

Stanley took a bus home to DC for a week, while Vera went to New York City to spend Christmas Day with her mother in the little-used Upper West Side apartment. As soon as Stanley arrived and was seated across from his mother, he began to try to unfold the truth of his origami lies by telling her as gently as possible that Harvard turned out to be less spectacular than he had imagined. He planned to confess the whole thing then and there, working backward: the Harvard lie, then the wedding lie. But even at this modest beginning, the warm-up before the dive, her eyes opened wide and she gripped the arms of her chair as the word "No" popped out of her mouth like a small dark bird.

"Mom, it's fine," he said, giving her a reassuring hug. "I'm making the best of it." She smiled at her little soldier of academia and nodded.

Vera's mother, on the other hand, was perpetually sharpening her perception and went through life in skepticism of everything. Vera treated her to dinner at her favorite Italian restaurant, Barbetta, as a Christmas gift. She toyed with the idea of confessing everything right there over pasta, but in the end decided she didn't want to risk throwing a wrench into the works because, she admitted, she was having fun with her Stanley. Ever since Vera switched to BU, the move had been a cause for argument between them, and she spent much of dinner trying to convince her mother that Boston University was a better place for her than Harvard. There were some excellent mathematicians doing exciting work there, she said, which was true. She tried to be as honest with her mother as possible, with the exception of the business with Stanley, which was a big exception. Vivian was under the impression that Stanley also transferred to BU, and that he and her daughter were living together in marital bliss.

When they left the restaurant, Vera's and Vivian's steps aligned as they walked down the street. They looked at the scenes around them with the same sort of detached understanding. For the first time, Vera felt that she could appreciate her mom's assured poise. Vivian was a survivor with style. Vivian dropped her off at Grand Central Station on the morning of

December 27 and looked back once to smile and wave before cutting into traffic.

Chuck had been to LA for Christmas—"Gosh darn sham of a Christmas holiday, I tell you," he said sadly, a true northeasterner. "But! But," he said, Santa Claus full of good cheer, "I have something for you. We had a meeting with a producer, Jack Lansdon— funny guy, smart guy—and..." He made her wait for it. "We bought his show! A great new show. It's called, get this: *The Just Marrieds*," he said, spreading his hands around the words in the air.

Vera stood there feeling it coming, the ice cracking beneath her, not sure what to do with her hands. She flexed an elbow, rubbed an eye.

"It's a game show. Newlywed couples come on, and the host, this guy Johnny Rocks, he asks questions to see how well they really know each other, and then...Anyway, look at me, an old news guy and here I am, burying the lead. You, young lady, are going to be in the premiere! You and Stan. You're *perfect* for it. Absolutely perfect."

He ticked off the facts, switchblading out a finger for each one.

"You're a lovely young couple. You've been in front of an audience before. You're both smart. Basically, you fit the qualifications, you're good. I got you all signed up, got to get your plane tickets..." he said, trailing off, his thoughts outrunning his speech. "Got to call a sales meeting too, they're going to love this..."

Stanley and Vera spent the rest of winter and the early spring in dread-filled anticipation of another lie in the distance, their fragile lives gimping across the perilous surface of falsehood, the

DC scam living on to torment them, a creature under the ice. Vera tried to get out of it by telling him they weren't exactly newly-weds anymore, but Chuck waved that away and said if it was a problem he'd deal with it. Then she tried every excuse that came to mind: I'm afraid of flying, Stanley can't get away from work, my mother forbids me to be on TV, I think I might be pregnant. Chuck wouldn't hear any of it, waving it all away with closed eyes and a smile. "I saw the fear in your eyes the moment I first mentioned it. Sweetheart, this will be the best thing for you, don't worry. They'll hold your hand, it's a piece of cake, they shoot it in little pieces, it'll be fun!"

Neither Vera nor Stanley had a television, but as they sat without talking in the diner on the ground floor of Vera's apartment building, the voice of Vic Perrin declared from the blue-gray tablet of glowing glass above the cash register that they should not adjust their screen, that they were not in control, there was no recourse but to sit passively as they were taken on a great adventure into the awe and mystery which reaches from the inner mind to—*The Outer Limits*. There was no escaping. So they might as well not try. They were the perfect couple, the test victims to be sent in an airship to the otherworldly land of Los Angeles and inserted into the sterile laboratory atmosphere of the United Artists television studio and recorded answering questions from an alien life form terrifying them with his probing inquiries and humanoid smile.

With mechanical precision Vera put her sword through her final exams and executed her long and challenging papers. Stanley took a brief leave from his shifts at the library and they allowed themselves to be airlifted out of Boston and into LA. The production assistant assigned to them was a woman named Mary-from-Wisconsin, whose regular-folks demeanor dulled some of the sensation of being mildly electrocuted. Johnny Rocks took a moment out of his collection of valuable moments and gave it to them in the form of a personal coaching session, generously spreading the schmear of his charisma over the proceedings and then again leaving them to the comfort of Mary-from-Wisconsin. As Vera nibbled from a box of raisins, they were informed that there was a certain value to the unpreparedness of the couples on the show, ensuring that the whole thing had an authentic feel, and with the suddenness with which a visit to the doctor becomes an injection, they were taping.

Lights. Applause. Horns, drums, and piano forming something resembling music. The studio audience in the watchful dark. Vera shuffled out into the light alongside Stanley and they took their place behind a polyurethane lectern. Johnny Rocks spoke about his enthusiasm in hosting the first-ever episode, then introduced the first two couples and quickly moved on to "Stanley Owens and Vera Baxter! Stanley and Vera met at the National Spelling Bee, where they won in a tie, how wonderful is that?"

The APPLAUSE sign blinked on and the audience obeyed.

"Vera," Johnny said, gliding over to her as if on roller skates. "You kept your last name. That's very unusual. How did your hubby feel about that?"

"When I asked him why it was that I should be expected to take his name and not him mine, he was very understanding."

"A couple of Bolsheviks, you two," Johnny said.

Obedient laughter from the audience.

Vera played along, smiling shyly. The husbands were dismissed to the seclusion of a soundproof room offstage, and the game was explained. The "girls" would be asked three questions and would give their answers. Then the husbands would return and provide their own answers to the same three questions.

Vera felt as if her head were stuffed with cotton balls, and the sound of the host's voice came to her as if from under a blanket. She cracked her neck and tried to stave off her hypoglycemia by force of will.

For each matching answer, Johnny Rocks continued, the couple would get ten points. Then the process would be reversed, the wives removing themselves and the husbands providing the first answers to three questions. The game would end with a bonus question. The couple with the most points would win the prize lurking behind a heavy red curtain at stage left. For all Vera knew or cared, it might as well be a furry monster drooling heavily and waiting for its opportunity to lunge. There was no chance of anything good coming from this.

"Ladies," Johnny began. "What will your husband say was the first thing that caught his attention about you?"

The first woman—Vera missed her name—answered in a breathy voice that was an outright heist from Marilyn Monroe, "My hair."

"And what wonderful hair it is," Johnny said.

The second woman, Margaret, answered with a giggle, "My laugh."

"Your laugh," he said, a master of repetition. "And Vera?"

What caught Stanley's attention? She had no idea, but she looked the host in the eyes and said matter-of-factly, "My spelling."

Johnny's carefully jacked-up smile started to fade before he regained his composure and said, "Ah, yes, you met at the spelling bee. Fair enough."

He moved right along, apparently determined not to trip up on his very first show. "Our next question: Where did you go on your first date?"

Wife number one, in her imitation voice, said, "To the movies."

Wife number two said, "He took me dancing."

As they took their turns, Vera searched for an answer. Had they ever even had a proper date? The only encounter from the regrettable events of their time in DC that might resemble a date was their Washington tourist day. She forgot the name of the museum they visited, but she happily remembered one stop they'd made.

"Vera?" Johnny Rocks said, standing uncomfortably close to her.

"The Mathematical Society of America," she said resolutely, not minding at all how incredibly uncool she sounded.

Rather than giving the answer its due as a naturally humorous bit of spontaneity, Johnny dropped his hand to his side and said, "The Mathematical..." Realizing he was not holding his microphone to his lips, he quickly returned it there and said, "The Mathematical Society of America?"

"Yes."

"Alrighty. Strange place for a date, but okay."

From the quiet of the audience came the sound of someone chewing gum.

Johnny took a few steps back and tried to rekindle the dying show with the tinder of showmanship. "Last question," he said with a flourish. "What is your husband's favorite sport to watch on TV?"

Vera was feeling the dry, hot lights, the alien-abduction sensation of being examined by the probing pupils of the television cameras, trying to do as she was expected but also trying to play the game to win, a competitor to the last. Stanley loved tennis, but she couldn't recall him ever watching it. Then she remembered sitting in the Riffraff Café with him back in Cambridge and watching twenty-year-old Bobby Fischer in silent combat at the US Chess Championship, and remembered Stanley insisting they stay until the very end to see the outcome, which was spectacular: a predatory win by Fischer and the first perfect score ever in the history of the tournament. Johnny, already finished with the other two contestants, stood in front of her with the microphone to his lips. He raised his eyebrows and looked to Vera with the trace of a wince in his expression, knowing he needed a response from her but recoiling from whatever was coming.

"Chess," she said boldly.

He stood there a moment and blinked. "Chess." Wearily he walked back to his place of safety on the stage and turned a fresh page by saying, "Let's bring out the gentlemen!"

It was a relief to Vera to see good old Stanley loping out onto the stage with his eyes on her and an authentic smile on his face. He stood by her side. Johnny commenced the questioning. Husband number one said that the first thing that caught his attention about his wife was not her hair but her chest. A whirl of laughter, embarrassment, and recrimination ensued. Husband number two went the lemming route and stole from the first couple, saying, "Her hair," eliciting groans from the audience.

Then came Stanley. He thought about the question, rolled it around for a moment, and said, "Her spelling."

Johnny kept his cool admirably. "That is correct. Ten points for couple number three."

When it came to the second question, couples one and two both scored, and by Stanley's turn, he was ready. "The Mathematical Society of America," he said, adding, "of course."

For the third question, after the first two, husbands both matched their wives' answers, Vera watched Stanley thinking it over, puzzling out what he thought she thought he would say. Johnny looked uneasy. "Stanley?"

"Chess?"

A smile as real as the Easter Bunny spread across the host's face and he said, with a slight crack in his voice betraying him, "A perfect thirty points for couple three, and that brings an end to round one."

Vera was relieved to be off the stage, away from the lights and the people. For the first time since she quit, she craved a cigarette. In the awkward silence of the waiting room, wife number one, Charisse, soaked up Vera with her eyes and tucked a hand alongside her neck and said, as if she'd just remembered something, "You're interesting."

Back on stage, Vera was grateful that the host whipped the show along, probably as eager to be done with it as she was, and she fantasized about being free on the sidewalk outside the studio.

"The question we asked your husband is: What one thing is your spouse best at?"

"Group theory," Vera answered without thinking.

Johnny, failing to capitalize on improvisational gold when it fell in his lap, raised the microphone to his lips and said, his voice descending the stairs of pitch as he spoke, "Yes. Group theory, whatever that is." He looked to the audience and laughed nervously. "Ten points."

Around they came again to Vera with the next question. "How many pairs of shoes, to within three, do you own?"

"How many pairs, or how many shoes?" she asked, barely tethered to the present moment now.

"Pairs."

"One. One pair. Two shoes."

The other wives craned their necks to get a closer look at her, observers at a crash site.

Johnny looked offstage to the producer. Then he said, "Ten points! For the couple with a wife who owns one pair of shoes.

"Last question," he said, looking thankful. "What is one word that could describe your mother-in-law and could also apply to you?"

Running through her head was *What would Stanley say? What would Stanley say?*

"Itinerant," she said, smiling the way she did when she knew she'd won the spelling bee, in a tie, with him.

Johnny shook his head, and a genuine laugh escaped. "*Itinerant.* Where's my dictionary?" He laughed again. "Correct. Our very first show, and we already have a perfect score. And now, our bonus question. For this one, we'll have the men do the honors and remove themselves."

As fortified as Vera was by the prospect of a win, she was still suffering from the feeling of being pinned to a specimen board, and hurried the host along. "What's the question?" she said, twirling a finger in her hair.

"What is the worst thing that happened on your wedding day? The worst thing that happened," he repeated, "on your wedding day."

As Vera waited for her turn, the answer crept in shame from the triple-locked, dank labyrinth where regrettable memories go to hide. There was no question what her honest answer was, and since they were assured of a win, she gave it. "Signing the marriage license."

A gasp escaped from the darkness of the studio audience. Mr. Rocks short-circuited, a bundle of competing impulses, lurching on tangled legs and then stopping and laughing a laugh made in China. He wiped sweat from his forehead and, taking refuge in the comfort of repetition, said, "Signing the marriage license." It sounded like a call for help. Vera caught sight of the producer stretching out from the wings on a jackknifed knee desperately whispering, "The guys, bring in the guys!"

"Bring in the guys!" Johnny repeated. "Bring in, I mean to say, let's bring back the husbands."

When Stanley came bouncing back in, Vera took it upon herself to ask him the question.

Stanley's cheerful expression went dark. "The worst thing. There weren't many. It was a wonderful day. But if there's one thing I wish had happened differently, there's no question it was the way we signed the marriage license."

With great efficiency of movement and clarity of purpose, Stanley and Vera run-walked through the backstage warren toward the dressing room. As they hustled along they witnessed a chamber-of-horrors kind of set piece featuring Johnny Rocks stripped to his underwear and splayed out in a chair with a drink in one hand and a producer applying a compress to his forehead as he said, "...that couple belongs on that other ABC show, *The Addams Family*." Mary jogged after them. "Wait! Wait!" There were details to be worked out, papers to sign. "Your motorcycle," she said, imploringly. The prize that Johnny Rocks managed to tear the curtain from before stumbling into the wings and collapsing into a chair was a shiny new Harley-Davidson Duo-Glide, custom painted the ebony and cream of an eight ball and fitted with chrome everything and a deluxe passenger saddle, about as likely to be ridden by Stanley and Vera as a fire-breathing dragon.

They sat illuminated by the showbiz razzle-dazzle of the dressing room mirror and talked details. Papers had to be signed, first the sheets that had to do with permission to use their likenesses in any which way, shape, or substance, sideways or upside down as the producers saw fit. Then of course there were the papers attesting to the fact that they were married and had been so for no more than one (1) calendar year.

"Got a pen?" Stanley asked, directing the question at Vera. Mary-from-Wisconsin had already retrieved one in a move that was apparently too brisk to be captured by the human eye, and held it out between them, but Stanley said, "No, thank you. I prefer to use my wife's."

With Socrates, they both laid down their perishable signatures, "here, here, here, here, and here," as Mary guided them through the pages.

As for the prize, "We would rather not take it," Vera said, to Mary's seeming befuddlement. Mary glanced over in the general direction of the Harley, still on the stage, with a look of longing. Stanley imagined her slinging a leg over that proud stallion and spurring it out the studio bay doors and across the country, its engine saying "potato, potato, potato," all the way home to Wisconsin.

"Really? You'd rather not take it?" That gorgeous, gorgeous

machine, she seemed to append to the question with her eyes. "You're saying you would prefer the cash equivalent?"

Stanley and Vera looked at each other. No, that was not what they were saying, their looks agreed. Vera thought it might be fraudulent to take any sort of prize, and after all, they'd caused enough trouble for themselves as it was. She could tell Stanley felt the same way. "We hate to decline," Vera began.

Mary took this to be in reference to the motorcycle, and said with rare irritation, "Very well. I'll have a check cut and mailed to your current address."

They settled the logistics of their return to Boston, and then Stanley and Vera made themselves as gone as a rabbit vanished from a magician's hat.

Vera dropped her small duffel bag on her apartment floor, the events of the past couple days swirling in an unsettled arrangement in her head, when it dawned on her: *It won't be long now.* She knew then exactly what would happen, laying down the sequence of events in her imagination. Here we go again, she thought, as she stepped into the bathroom to check her reflection, touching her face to verify its substantiality.

"Someone will see them," she said out loud to herself. The papers will come in front of an assistant of some sort, she told herself. A filing clerk. She'll lick her thumb and flip through them, not expecting anything out of order. Then she'll stop and make a face. *These aren't signed*, she'll say to herself. *Idiots*, she'll say. *Do I have to do everything myself?* She'll take them to someone, maybe Mary, maybe the producer, or a lawyer at the studio. They'll question Mary. Mary will swear we signed them. She'll probably be smart enough to hit on a suspicion about the pen. *They were strangely insistent upon using their own,* Mary will say, smart girl. They'll call Chuck. Chuck already has the FCC breathing down his neck. Any hint of impropriety will bring the house down. He's a nice guy and he likes me but he's not going to let the station take the fall. He'll throw me under the bus.

Vera chewed her nails as she paced her short hallway. She held her hand out in front of her. Already she saw herself beginning to slip away. Her diaphanous skin was paler and more translucent than it had ever been, blue veins visible beneath it. She asked herself why on earth they signed the damn papers with Socrates anyway. It was a stupid knee-jerk reaction from a couple of novice con artists. They ought to have used Mary's pen. Maybe if they had done that, the whole business would have blown by without further trouble. But then, of course, there was the possibility that one or more of their recent friends or acquaintances might tune in for the show.

Her pacing picked up speed and she missed her turn in the living room and kept walking out the door and down the stairs and out onto the sidewalk and down three blocks to the filling station and rented herself a one-way van just before closing time and parked it in front of her building.

Back inside, she couldn't sit still and resumed her pacing. She asked herself, "Why not just tell Chuck the truth and see what happens? Because then he'll be obliged to tell me directly that he can't help me. That the production company is a separate entity that won't sweep this under the rug for him, especially now with all the heightened sensitivity because of the quiz show scandals from several years back, so damaging to businesses and careers that Congress even passed amendments preventing the fixing of these shows. I won't put him through the pain of having to watch me take the blame. Besides, if I stick around, I could be expelled. Again."

She knew this wasn't really Stanley's fault, but it all led back to the fake marriage that ruined everything for them, and she was just plain tired of all that smoldering wreckage behind her. Maybe she was tired of trying to make things work with him too.

She woke up in the middle of the night on her bed with her clothes on. She got up and walked out, this time making her way toward his building near Fenway. Half a mile out, she stopped and turned back. "Forget it," she said to herself, and made her ghostly way home in the thick indigo night. "Home." What an absurd concept, she thought. She had gotten only a couple hours of sleep. The thought occurred to her that maybe it was better to make important decisions in the misty neverland of a tired mind, when she might be closer to her real desires, than using all the well-rested but suspect might of logic.

She wasn't worried about what harm might come to her at this time of night. She had nothing to lose. In fact, she wished that chance might step in and force a new direction for her. "But the universe doesn't come to our rescue, now, does it," she said to herself. "Fate will never intervene on your behalf. You are yours and yours alone to save."

She was tired.

Her keys in the door made an especially loud, jarring sound, like sleigh bells. Morning was peeking around the corner, revealing the shapes of objects with a deft touch. Vera had a month-to-month lease. She wrote a note to her landlord telling him she was leaving, slipped it in an envelope and stamped it. The rented van waited on the street below. She took a deep breath. There were very few things but still . . . She had a mattress, which she dragged to the door and then pushed down the stairs. It was a twin so it wasn't too hard to carry to the van and shove in through the back. The chairs she had picked up at a rummage sale were not a problem. The legs of her table had already been unscrewed and were lying by the door. Smaller things she tossed into boxes very quickly, and she carried the boxes down one by one without stopping to rest. Soon the apartment was empty. She caught a glance in the hallway mirrors on her way out the building and was fairly certain that nothing was reflected there but a bobbing duffel bag and box. She walked to the corner for some milk and fruit, got into the van, started it up, and she was gone.

CHAPTER NINE

Stanley sat on the edge of the bed in his shoebox room with its table and chair, its drafty window slightly crooked in the frame and its single exposed bulb, on top of which a cake of dust was gently cooking, in the center of the ceiling. He sat blinking and staring through the wall at the future that he was just now seeing come into focus. He hadn't slept well, and was roused by the half-waking train of thought that paralleled Vera's and ended with the two of them in trouble once more.

"Oh God, not again," he mumbled. He rose up off the bed and grabbed his keys and walked out to the street. He headed in the direction of Vera's apartment, quickening his pace to a brisk walk, and by the time he arrived at the spot where her rented van had pulled away several hours earlier, he was panting from running. His forefinger pressed the buzzer once, a second time, then jabbed it six times in a row. He stepped out to the curb and looked up at the window. He resisted the urge to yell out her name.

The walk back to his little cell was one of those preoccupied insensate teleportations, and by the time he got there it felt as if

Vera had been gone for months. Yesterday's kiss good-bye as they parted at the airport seemed so distant as to be only another concoction from the laboratory of dreams. But there was something in that moment that told him things were different now, that another wall had arisen between them. On a hunch he went to the door, opened it, peered down the hallway, and saw nothing but a haunted emptiness and peeling paint.

He was hungry. There was no food of any kind in his room. With exceptional agitation he rumbled down the stairs and over to the corner store and grabbed a goddamn sandwich and some juice and slapped down his money on the counter and stormed back to the apartment with a bolus of dark cloud gathering in a nasty way directly above his head. Where the hell was Vera? Where was she speeding away to at this very moment? She could be anywhere. Unable to accept that she was no longer at her apartment, he went to the pay phone in the hall and dialed her number. He let it ring twenty-nine times and then he slammed down the handset so hard it cracked. She could be headed for Los Angeles for all he knew. She could be hitchhiking and having herself abducted. She could be humming brightly to herself in a rented car, happily renouncing crossword puzzles and lies forever. She could be meeting another guy, at a rest stop, a dashing young man stooping to pick up the keys she dropped and falling in love with her at first sight. Anything was possible. That was the problem with the world.

He ripped open the paper around the sandwich and flung it across the room and force-fed the sandwich into his mouth. He drank down the juice in one go and threw the container against the wall, off of which it bounced unsatisfyingly. He didn't expect to be living there much longer, if living was indeed what you could call the thing he was doing, but nothing was out of the question. In fact, everything was *in* question. Everything was up in the air, shifting and in flux. Wasn't that what he wanted? He washed up in the rusty communal shower and dressed, then walked to the Charles River and sat down on a bench, where it seemed he remained for six months.

Spring was cooked away by the increasingly oppressive afternoons of the impending summer, and then summer itself ripened and rotted and was gently laid to rest. From his place on the bench, to which he returned again and again, he observed these changes while the better part of his mind tried to tell itself that he was living an extraordinary life.

Stanley got to know his boss at the library. She lived in Brookline in an old white house with green shutters and a husband, two daughters, and a tumbledown dog whose jowls were attached to the floor of the foyer. She would sometimes invite Stanley over for a barbecue and a romp in the backyard with the kids and the sleepy old dog whose windy woof seemed to erupt from the deepest hollow of its canine soul.

Stanley would have liked to talk crosswords with other constructors, but those he knew of and admired lived in New York, Chicago, Fort Lauderdale, Baltimore, and parts of Connecticut, and Stanley didn't have a telephone. The pay phone in the hall was uninviting, and besides, long distance was expensive. So he wrote them letters and they wrote back, but that was the extent of it. At the library there were a few people who came in regularly that he got to know, including a talkative old lady named Lucille whose shockingly progressive viewpoints and colorful way of speaking always tickled him. She was much shorter than he was and he would look down upon her coarse gray hair and her chalky pink scalp revealed through a part as wide as a finger. Then there was Sasha, a young woman who had just graduated from Smith and moved to the city to work as a photographer's assistant. She didn't have many friends and liked to read but didn't have money for new books, so there she was. The woman who read to the children every morning at Story Hour, Elaine, was just about the kindest person on the planet. She could talk about anything, just like Stanley, and had an infectious laugh, and it made him feel warm and fulfilled to sit and chat with her in the miniature but sturdy children's chairs.

What did he tell them about himself? His story was a mixture of truth and lies. He let them know about Vera—not about the marriage or the Harvard trouble or the TV show, but that he had a very close friend named Vera who had moved away. He told them he won the National Spelling Bee in a tie—with Vera—and used to study constantly but that he lost interest in academics and that all he wanted to do with his time now was create and solve crossword puzzles, which was as true as it gets.

Throughout the rest of that lonely summer there was only one imperative: that he continue to solve every crossword puzzle in every major newspaper every single day. He picked up a roll of tracing paper at an art store and rolled it out across the puzzles in the library so as not to mark up the originals, like he'd done at the library in Cambridge. It was a peace offering to his conscience, which still nibbled at him frequently. He wanted to believe he was not a bad person, and providing this courtesy helped him believe that.

The joy of solving crosswords was sometimes edged out by desperation as, day after day, puzzle after puzzle, his search for a signal from Vera yielded nothing. At the start of every fresh puzzle he would wonder, with the futile hope of a lottery ticket holder, Could this be the one? But then the clues and solutions would turn foreign or strange or complicated and he would see that she was not recognizable there, and the once-momentous puzzle would become small, like a train that passed without stopping and disappeared into the horizon. It was unlikely she would even communicate with him in this way. But it was his only chance to locate her. The honorable thing would have been to drop the whole foolish game and begin down the long twisting path of forgetting her, but he couldn't help himself. He kept his hopes alive in the empty grids in the back pages of the major newspapers.

One November evening, the single light went out in his room as he was reading, and he stood up and looked out the window and saw nothing but darkness. A whisper of some presence, a coldness, passed him and he said, "Vera?" Then he heard voices on the street, saw people moving under candlelight, and spent the night of the Great Blackout of 1965 huddled under the blanket on his bed, deep within the vacuum of his life, blinking his wet eyes at the darkness while along the Eastern Seaboard other men started families.

At the library, he started to notice Sasha more and more and began to wonder if maybe she didn't really come there just because she liked to read. He tested out his conjecture one afternoon, approaching her at the round table in the center of the library and asking her what she was reading. She looked up with a quick smile and flipped over the cover of the book so he could see it. *Herzog* by Saul Bellow. "It's new, just came out," she said. "Haven't read it," he said. "You should," she replied with a smile. "You really should." The conversation drifted to how she was settling in to Boston. "How's the apartment?" he asked. "Oh, the apartment," she said. The apartment was okay but the landlord was a bully. He kept coming by and pestering her about this and that. He came by to fix things that weren't broken. She was a little worried about her safety. The man was a big Russian and the way he spoke to her in broken English was forceful and a little scary. Stanley said he'd like to meet this man and she brightened up. "Come over," she said. "When?" "Come over right now," she said. He looked up at the clock and back at her and said, "How about in an hour when my shift's done?"

They walked to her building, chatting all the way. She had a bright personality if not Vera's bright mind, and she was curious and talkative, a tiny little thing unable to contain the energy within. When they got to her apartment it was a revelation to Stanley: very nicely set up, with striking photographs pinned all over the walls. She had made resourceful use of common things to decorate the small space. It never before occurred to him that the apartment of a young single person could be like that. He was so used to living in a starkly functional way, going from page to page of his life with as little friction and as little shopping and decorating as possible.

She made them coffee in a rustic way, heating water in a pot, dumping in grounds, popping a filter into a funnel and pouring it through that into two cups. He sat on the sofa and she hopped up next to him, curling her legs under her and diving right in. "So, tell me everything!"

He told her everything except the most important thing: how he felt about Vera. Sasha was fascinated by his passion for crossword puzzles. She was fascinated by his upbringing in a hotel. She was fascinated by and very sympathetic about his father's death at

Normandy. He felt exotic and very, very interesting with her. She looked him in the eyes as if he were some kind of incredible zoo creature. Then she looked at the coffee table as she reached forward to set down her cup and said in an offhand way, "Tell me about this friend of yours, Vera."

There was a single loud knock at the door. Full of excitement, she mouthed the words "It's him" and crept dramatically toward the threshold. She opened the door a crack and peeked out.

"Yes?"

"I come to fix shower head."

"There's nothing wrong with my shower head."

"Please. I tell you last week I come with new one."

"You never told me that."

"Permit me to come in. I will demonstrate how this works."

She opened the door to let him in and Stanley stood up.

Sasha said, "This is my friend Stanley."

The landlord studied him as if he were a particularly challenging plumbing problem or invading pest.

Stanley walked over and shook his hand. "Stanley Owens. Of Owens and Baxter."

"Owens and Bax...?"

"Attorney-at-law," Stanley said.

"Attorney," the landlord said.

"Yes. We specialize in tenants' rights."

The man blinked dumbly at Stanley and puffed out his chest. Then he let out a sigh and turned to leave.

"Well, I leave this. You look at it. Tell me if you want it put in."

Stanley said, "I've told Sasha to keep a record of every time you come here without her asking you to. If I have to, I'll prepare the necessary documents to have this matter investigated by the district attorney's office."

After the landlord crept away, Sasha closed the door, clapped her hands together, and said, "Well, well, Mr. Owens."

They both laughed.

"I had no idea what I was talking about," Stanley said.

"It sounded legit to me, but what do I know?" As she walked off to put the coffee cups in the sink she sang out, "You're a bad boy, Stanley."

She led him downstairs to the Chinese restaurant on the corner and when they returned with a bag of food she poured wine and lit candles, although they felt redundant considering the way she brightened up the room with her laughter. Stanley was elated by the attention, and before he knew it he was finding her extremely attractive. Her face in the candlelight drew him in and he kissed her. An hour passed this way. Sleepily, as if he had dosed her into a narcotic pleasure dream, she kissed him good-bye at the door and he tiptoed backward into the hallway.

Now what? It felt wrong to see Sasha. But then, there she was as the centerpiece of his days, and she was lovely and he was lonely. In the end he decided she was a healthy distraction, and he went with her to movies, to restaurants, to the park even though it was cold, to her apartment where it was warm. He couldn't help wishing she was Vera and he hated himself for that.

Every day his search through all the major crossword puzzles became more and more hopeless. He worried that he was over-looking a paper in a smaller market that happened to be just the one where she sought him. If she even sought him at all. After the way he messed up her life, why would she? So he took Sasha to matinees with two-for-one admission, to Chinese joints and diners and pizza places where they could get a meal for two for a buck and a half. She would say, "Let's go Dutch." He never heard anyone use that phrase before Sasha did, and he liked it.

He tried to play the gentleman, but more often than not she invited him in and they wound up on her couch. He felt that it would be dishonest somehow to stay the night with Sasha, considering that his heart was elsewhere, but he very much wanted to and it seemed the feeling was mutual. One night on their way back to her place, she led him by the hand into a drugstore and marched him up to the counter, braced herself for what she was about to say by straightening her posture and lifting her chin up, and said to the pharmacist, "One package of condoms, please." Stanley, who knew full well the pharmacist was doing them a favor by overlooking their ringless fingers, as contraceptives were banned for the unmarried, happily paid as she smiled at her boldness, at her pride in the man she was with, at her immediate future. Stanley's immediate future was fantastic even though it was suffused with guilt. Candles burned down to their bases, clothes on the floor, music until the record came to an end and the needle reported and reported and reported that fact with a cottony sound. When he woke up she was there within the semi-circle of his body and it felt as if every part of her was touching every part of him. Yet all he could think that morning was Vera, Vera, Vera. And even though Sasha fashioned their morning into an extremely pleasant, fluid, beautiful thing, he managed to get himself out of there without showing his guilt and without leaving the shell of his gentlemanliness.

Soon after, Sasha told him her uncle was coming to town. He wanted to take the two of them to dinner wherever Sasha wanted to go. She picked an Italian place that always attracted them every time they passed with its busy self-preoccupation and its steamed-up windows and its enticing aromas. When the uncle walked in, a barrel-chested man in a pinstriped suit with a drift of white hair, skin as pink as a picture book pig, Stanley recognized him immediately. He had been a frequent guest at the Hawthorne, a lobbyist of some sort. Stanley vaguely recalled talking to him about crossword puzzles and the launch of Sputnik 5. And he remembered seeing the man at his and Vera's wedding, as a guest of someone he'd invited. But, for the time being, the man didn't seem to recognize him.

"Well," the man said. "Isn't it fortunate that business brings me to Boston," he said to Sasha, gripping Stanley's hand. Sasha beamed. She wanted to know all about his trip so far.

Stanley was terrified that the uncle was going to remember who he was and reveal the truth. His mind searched frantically for excuses: We got divorced; she left me; she came down with a fatal illness right after the wedding—what luck, huh? As the uncle spoke about his trip, his eyes lingered on Stanley, and it seemed he was trying to place him. Stanley knew he met so many people in his business that there was a chance he'd simply be lost in the shuffle. The dinner was awkward. They could not break through the barrier of small talk. Sasha seemed disappointed. The uncle paid for the meal and said he had to get back to his hotel to prepare for the next day's meetings.

The two of them walked back to her place. She was quiet. He was lost in images of the past that the man's appearance called to mind: Sonny in motion, Greaper bobbing absentmindedly around the hotel, the revolving door spinning and Vera's face presenting itself. He heard the rhythm of her name running through his head, noticing it rhymed with Hera, who was coincidentally a goddess of marriage, among other things. Where was she? What city was she in right then? What were her quick and graceful fingers doing at that very moment? It had been so long. Without fanfare the holidays had come and gone, a distant shaking of bells, and soon it would be a year since she left. Back at Sasha's apartment they nestled into the sofa briefly, but they were both so moody that soon Stanley found himself wandering back to his frigid little room nearby.

He took off his clothes and went to bed as usual. He got up in the morning to the excitable windup alarm clock with its clapper dashing between twin bells as usual. He waited his turn for the dingy old shower as usual and, as usual, arrived at the library to continue the pursuit of his perhaps not so extraordinary life. The old woman, Lucille, engaged him in a conversation about the Jimmy Hoffa conviction. The woman who read to the children, Elaine, was out sick and there was no Story Hour that day. Stanley's boss scurried around shushing the scattered children, and finally tried to replace Elaine herself, with mixed success. Amid all this, Sasha appeared and came straight for him. She whipped off her hat and mittens and tossed them on the counter and said, "You're married!"

"I..." He stood with his fingertips tented together.

"I can't believe this. It turns out you're ... you're a *scoundrel*." She said the word as if it was a fact as plain and indisputable as a job title.

"No, no. Sasha ... I'm not married. I'm not. I was. But it didn't work out." It didn't work out. As soon as he said these words a surge of emotion came through him that blocked out Sasha and her whole furious storm of grief. It didn't work out. Failure. Loss. He had an intense urge to make it right. But he didn't know where she was, and all he could do was grow old waiting and searching for a signal that may never come. Sasha was speaking.

"...understand why you didn't tell me that to begin with, then. You're divorced, then. I don't know if I should believe you. Are you telling the truth now, or are you lying again?"

Was he? Was he married? Stanley was momentarily frozen in a strangely calm state of self-ignorance. It felt pleasant, ironically enough, to be stopped there in a place of nothingness, not recognizing the Stanley he had become. Thoughts in his head were desperately trying to form but were not gathering enough force to declare themselves. There was this woman standing in front of him whom he liked and wanted to respond to, and he felt awful and misunderstood, but he could express nothing to her. Over it all was Vera's absence, a fact so potent as to make Sasha utterly irrelevant. An absence as vast and boundless as the sky.

She slapped him, then turned in all her smarting anger and hurried out, forgetting her hat and gloves.

The rest of the day forced itself by with such agonizing tediousness that it seemed at certain moments as if he could feel the friction of time itself grinding past. Stanley retreated to the cover of the library stacks and buried himself in the dusty oblivion of stacking and sorting and arranging. It was routine physical work that allowed his mind to unravel and examine its most recent errors. What if word somehow got back from the uncle to the people in DC who gave him monetary gifts that there was no marriage? Would someone's offended dignity lead to his being tracked down? Surely what he'd done had to be illegal in some way? It was fraud, that was what it was, fraud. He knew there was a degree of paranoia in these thoughts; nevertheless, that night he wrote a grateful and apologetic note to his boss and friend stating that he wouldn't be returning to the job, without citing a reason. Under the darkness of a March night—a darkness that seemed to be the true condition of things, daylight being only an illusory reprieve—he walked all the way back to the library and dropped the envelope into the book-return slot.

He moved out of the grim little room near the Fenway and into a grimmer, littler room in the North End. He found himself a new library in which to spend time and do the crosswords, but it was a branch with a limited newspaper selection. He tried to catch the rest of the puzzles by buying papers at newsstands, but he knew that he missed a few and he felt certain that in one of those missed puzzles was the coded message from Vera that would have changed his life.

Stanley left off the electric heater in his little room so as not to incur the expense, and then as quickly as the turning over of a hand of cards the weather became warm and he kept open his single window. He ate like a homeless man, stuffing in chunks of bread, fruit, food straight from cans. One silent evening he sighed and whispered to himself, "Good-bye, Vera, wherever you are. I wish you the best possible life." And then, on a day soon after, as if fate or time or God or the universe or whatever it is that makes these perverse decisions about our lives was simply waiting for him to surrender in order to pardon him, there it was.

Aloe ____.

"*Vera*," he whispered.

The rest of the clues smoked on the page.

Stinger: BEE.

Where you may hang your hat: HOTEL.

1936 quadruple gold medalist: OWENS.

The paper was the *Globe*. Did that mean she was still in Boston? Not necessarily. He knew she wanted to finish her degree but it was very possible for a young woman with Vera's grades and recommendations—and intelligence—to transfer at will. But then again, it was possible she was hiding in another corner of Boston, a small city but one with many corners. He hoped the puzzle would answer his question.

It was titled "Just Friends." The theme words popped into place.

Videotape format: PAL.

A type of Holly: BUDDY.

NATO nation: ALLY.

Motorcycle starter?: SIDEKICK.

The whole time of course he was scanning for a clue that might render the answer of her present location, and he stood up as he filled in:

Fate: PROVIDENCE.

University color: BROWN.

The women's college at Brown was called Pembroke. Eventually he found it in the center of the puzzle, with this clue:
_____ Pines, FL.

He dropped the puzzle and pencil on the floor and slid his

suitcase out from under the bedsprings. He placed it on the bed and with a quick move of the thumbs flipped open the latches. In went the sweater, the turtleneck, the boxer shorts, the jeans, the corduroys, the jacket, the socks. He threw in a small bag with the simple toiletries that he carried into the communal bathroom every morning. There were half a dozen library books, which he loaded into a shopping bag. He snatched up his notebooks and pens and pencils and tossed them into his satchel along with the crossword puzzle and glanced around the room. He slung the shoulder bag over his head, picked up the suitcase and the bag of books, turned out the light, and closed the door. He left his keys in the mailbox and scribbled a note for the landlord, which he left on the radiator cover in the front hall. He walked to the library, where he fed the books into the depository slot one by one, then he turned and started walking to the bus station, while tickling the back of his mind was that title: Just Friends.

CHAPTER TEN

One year earlier

Theodore Leviticus Wellington IV was a man who was imprisoned by money. He had so very much of it that over the years he took up a defensive position behind the great bulwark of his desk in the center of his office, which itself was in the central rotunda of his house in Newport, a structure that bore a stronger resemblance to the United States penitentiary at Leavenworth than any sort of residence to which the human eye is accustomed. There he sat from dark of morning to dark of night with only the shortest of breaks. It was essential that he hold his ground there in order to watch over and protect his worldwide holdings. It was important that he remain vigilant against the invading forces of the world, which might breach his defenses and carry away the immense treasure that had been passed down from his father, and his father's father, and the fathers before them, and which he'd so painstakingly tended and grown.

His son and daughter too were imprisoned by the responsibility implicit in the great sum that they were so fortunate to have been born into and that would one day embrace them as snugly as a boa constrictor. From the shelter of their bedrooms, which were under the protection of a seeing-eye security system, the only evidence that they resided on the seashore was the occasional startling flap of a gull's wing passing too close by their double-insulated, bulletproof glass windows.

Unless he was away on a business trip, on any given day, be it a Monday, a Sunday, Christmas Eve, or tax day, Mr. Wellington could be found behind the stronghold of his desk, as broad as the deck of a merchant ship. He wore an expression of importance on his face at all times. He had his important suits custom sewn by an important tailor. He flew in his important helicopter to important meetings in important buildings with important men. He brushed his important teeth with an important toothbrush, which was in fact the most expensive toothbrush money could buy, made with the bristles of an albino piglet and tracked down in a men's grooming shop in London by one of his important assistants.

On one of these countless days in his home office, his chubby hand made its way across the desk toward the telephone when a very unimportant young boy ran into the room, tripped on the deep nap of the carpet, and sprawled across it. The man's personal secretary rushed in right behind him, followed by Vera, who said, "Sorry, sir." He raised his eyebrows in confusion at the lad on the rug as if to say, "Why, who the devil are you?" The boy responded in equal measure, standing up and backing away with a terrified look as if he had discovered himself in a place as strange and frightening as a courtroom.

Vera thought that perhaps the father really didn't recognize his son, and who can say? They were strangers occupying the same building. These parents had as much to do with their children as President Johnson had to do with Bozo the Clown. A nanny woke them. A chef fed them breakfast. Tutors taught them. When it was playtime, a physical education instructor escorted them to the yard for jumping jacks. More often than not, another nanny read them their stories and tucked them into bed, while the woman who Vera could only suppose gave birth to them in some impossible past, Edie Wellington, spent the night at the Waldorf=Astoria in New York City with a security detachment in the adjoining suite, or simply let her tennis engagement run too late, and by the time she poked her head into their bedrooms, the offspring had escaped through the walls of daily life and into the open fields of their dreams.

Vera's role was to teach them mathematics, and simply to be their friend. Theo and Thea took to her right away. In fact, they picked her out, as they were fond of telling Vera. It so happened that one day they were waiting in their limousine on Westminster Street in Providence, outside of the building where their mother's charitable foundation had its offices. Edie had made an excursion into town that day to meet with officials from the government of Taiwan. She wanted to show them that she understood children, having two of them herself, and so she brought them down with her and trotted them out in the conference room in front of the perplexed team from the Far East and then sent them back downstairs to wait in the car while she finished her meeting. Theo nudged his sister with his elbow and tapped on the tinted glass of the car window. In the next building was a remnant of the ancient species of soda shop that was already in those days approaching extinction.

"Let's run for it," Theo said.

Thea glanced up at the fat neck and bald head of the chauffeur, who was engrossed in the sports page behind the glass partition.

"Shhh!" She put a finger to her lips as Theo reached for the door handle.

They crept out soundlessly and made for the door of the shop. They hopped up onto stools at the counter and politely placed their orders.

"One double fudge chocolate sundae, please," Theo said.

"One ice cream cone, please," Thea said.

"What flavor, princess?" the counterman asked. "We have 'em all."

"Chocolate, and vanilla, and strawberry, and peach!" she answered.

"Sorry, no peach. And here I thought we had them all. I'll get you the other three though, how's that?"

Vera sat at the counter on the stool next to the children, having a grilled cheese sandwich and arranging a stock of mathematical symbols down a page as if diagramming an escalator.

Vera turned to Thea and said, "You must really love ice cream."

"I think so."

Theo, two years older than his sister, said, "She's never had ice cream before. But I have. Ingrid gave me some."

"Ingrid's my friend. She reads us stories," Thea added.

When the counterman brought the ice cream, the kids gripped their treats and stared at them in awe. "That'll be one dollar and twenty-five cents, please."

A state of confusion slowly came over the two of them. It became clear that not only did these expensively dressed children have no money, they didn't even know what money was, and the counterman stood across from them awkwardly trying to think of what to say.

Vera reached for her wallet. "Let's see now. I think I just might have that exact number in here somewhere," she said. The children watched her pay the man as if she were performing a feat of prestidigitation. When she thought back on it later, it occurred to Vera that people with lots of money hardly know it, whereas those without two coins to rub together are intimately familiar with currency, constantly wrestling with money and their lack of it, forever reckoning with the cost of things.

Vera gave each of the children a quarter to leave for a tip. "Do you know what a tip is?" she asked.

They shook their heads in unison.

"It's a little something extra you give to someone to thank them for serving you. Usually it's a percentage of your bill."

"Per-cen..." Thea started to say.

"Would you like to know what *percentage* means?" Vera asked.

The children nodded.

Vera was completing as meaningful an explanation as she could muster when the chauffeur came flying through the door, hat in hand, brushing sweat from his bald head. "There you are!" he said. Close behind came the *rat-tat-tat* of Edie Wellington's heels. Like her husband, she was short and plump. She wore a pink jacket and matching skirt with a string of pearls, and had a habit of looking upward. In fact, every element of her face seemed to be striving for altitude, her nose up, her lower lip thrusting against the upper, her eyebrows painted on quite a bit higher than nature originally decided, everything below her chin difficult for her to observe, as if it were underwater. Theo held his spoon in the air, poised over the sundae, and Thea gripped her ice cream cone with both hands.

"Theodore the Fifth. Put. That. Down." She wasn't kidding.

"Mother . . . we . . ." Theo began, but the force of that personage was much too powerful to attempt a debate.

Edie turned to the chauffeur. "Pay the man and put the children in the car."

"It's paid for, ma'am," said the counterman.

"Paid for? By whom?"

The kids excitedly pointed out Vera. "That lady," Thea whispered.

"She told us what *per-cen-tage* means!" Theo said enthusiastically.

Edie glanced beyond her chin to where Vera sat. "Did she really?"

"Yes, ma'am. It means part of something. Like if you have a hundred apples and you give someone ten. That's percentage. Ten . . . I mean one hun . . . one hun . . ." He completely lost his train of thought under his mother's stare.

Vera introduced herself and explained that she was a student at Pembroke, majoring in mathematics, with the goal of getting a PhD. Seeing the instant connection the young woman had with the children, Edie asked Vera if she might be interested in tutoring them. The next week, Vera was established as a part-time tutor in the Wellington household, one of the fifty wealthiest households in the country—if not one of the top twenty-five—as Edie did not fail to point out to her in their more formal interview on the grounds of the estate.

When Vera had first arrived in Providence in her rented van, the summer before Stanley discovered her puzzle in the *Globe*, she'd quickly found herself a cheap but pleasant off-campus apartment and a part-time job in an accountant's office. The accountant, a bony, outdoorsy man whose aim in life was to make enough money to spend every free moment in his canoe, was happy to have a whip-smart math major to assist him, but she found the rituals of office work intensely dull. When she started tutoring the Wellingtons in mid-July, she worked with the children for only an hour a day. But as the summer wore on, Mrs. Wellington noticed a significant change in the children's attitude toward learning. During a little chat she had with Vera on a bench under the wisteria, she told Vera that her arrival in the children's lives was doing wonders for their education, and asked Vera to spend as much time as she could with little Theo and Thea. Vera's junior year was about to start up at Pembroke, so they worked it out that Vera would quit the job with the accountant (most likely delaying his canoeing plans) and come to the house every weekday afternoon. Whenever she could, she would also take dinner with the children in the gymnasium-sized dining room with its breakfast nook–sized fireplace. It was at this point that Edie seemed to accept Vera as a part of the family, giving her a full tour of the residence and pointing out all the little touches she'd implemented in a rustic French style, which was so convincingly done that in fact to Vera the place very much called to mind the Bastille.

Vera was done with Stanley. Done. That's what she told herself, and that's what she believed. She made light of it. "C'est la vie," she sang out to herself one day in her little studio apartment, shrugging her shoulders while she washed her dishes. Without Stanley, the air was fresh and clear again and she no longer had to occupy herself with therapeutic chores or medicate herself with a bottle of bottom-shelf wine to treat the symptoms of her frustrated love for him. She made peace with her own mind and finally found a way to tuck him into one of the pockets where all of the incidental characters we encounter throughout our lives eventually take their places, waiting for the archivist of memory to come poking around again, coming across one here and another one there and saying, "Ah, there's Arnold Grant, the funny red-faced boy from first grade who used to get scolded for ripping off his shirt at recess and beating his chest like Tarzan." Stanley's pocket was a very prominent one, but Vera convinced herself that one day it would become as inconsequential and as seldom touched upon as poor Arnold Grant's.

School went well. During her disastrous year at Radcliffe and her much more productive year at BU, she completed many of the foundation classes that colleges required, and now at Pembroke she could zero in on math. It was a wonderful experience for Vera to spend mornings and early afternoons doing the quiet, rigorous work of serious study among the crisp minds of her professors and fellow students, and then to plunge into the wildly arbitrary imaginative lives of the children. Her professors praised her. She was said to have a natural mind for math and she was a disciplined student. Edie complimented her on her success with the children every time she ran into her, although those occasions were very few.

As she explained to Vera, her husband, Teddy, was permanently busy with his international snack-food business—"Whatever that's all about!"—which she waved away and seemed to take pride in not knowing a thing about. So she had to manage the estate entirely on her own. It was just her and a staff of twenty-six. "And then," she said, "and then, I'm off on my trips to the poorer countries of the world so much of the time, doing all I can for the children. That is to say, to help provide food and shelter to the starving children of the world." She shook her head and looked frightfully distraught. "It's a crisis. Don't you agree?"

Vera agreed wholeheartedly. She said she was behind Edie completely and asked if there was anything she could do to help.

"Be with the children, my dear. Be their friend." She popped her glasses into her purse with an exasperated sigh and encircled Vera in a hug. "Life can be so awful for children. We must do what we can do." And then she proceeded to leave on a weeklong trip to Mexico, in such a rush to get to her departure gate that she had to ask Vera to kiss little Theo and Thea good-bye for her.

It was a long and solitary year for Vera. She worked at her studies rigorously, forgoing all other pleasures. The only joys in her life were the simple thrill of fitting together the interlocking teeth of a logical truth after long effort, and immersing herself in the delightful spontaneity of the children. The New England autumn and winter rolled by heavily and sullenly. The melancholy of the days seemed to be at one with the massive stone walls of the Wellington fortress, built of sleepy blocks each as big as an Easter Island head, each one exhaling a gloomy fog.

Vera rang in the New Year of 1966 alone in her apartment with a book. Her mother, who was trying very hard to prove herself as a sales assistant in a masculine world, was on business in the state of Maryland, from where Vera received hastily scribbled postcards detailing little tidbits of business intricacy that, without context, meant nothing to her. Winter gave way to the relentless rains of spring, which the sky pitched down in ferocious overhand strokes. While waiting one day in the grand foyer for the children to be delivered home from their sailing lesson, Vera found the *New York Times* sitting on the divan next to her like an old friend. The headline read, "'Sound of Music' Wins Oscar as the Best Film of 1965." She hadn't seen it. She picked up the paper and leafed through it page by page, all the way to the back, where the crossword puzzle popped out at the end of the gray woolen text like a jaunty checkered hat. She had stopped doing puzzles, stopped making them, and it amazed her that she had gone without them for so long. She took a pen from her bag and quickly dispatched it. It was immensely satisfying, like tasting after a long absence what was once your very favorite dish. That day, Vera began doing crossword puzzles again. She figured there was no harm in it.

She started with the *New York Times*. It didn't take long before she was doing the puzzle every day. Then she added the *Boston Globe* to her ritual. Then the *Washington Post*. The *Wall Street Journal*. The *Philadelphia Inquirer*. She even took on the *New Hampshire Gazette* and the *Newport Daily News*. Mr. Wellington received all these papers, more as a matter of course than as things to be routinely read, and Vera would politely ask his secretary if she could have the games pages after he was finished with the papers. Suddenly she was doing seven crossword puzzles a day, sometimes more. Her renewed love for them overcame her totally and helplessly as if she were a drunk who fell off the wagon. Occasionally she came across one that contained words or phrases that struck a familiar chord, and she wondered if it might be Stanley's handiwork. For a moment she would pause, but then push him out of her mind and carry on with the puzzle as she hummed a tune, working on it with a critical eye and saying to herself, "I could do better."

While Theo and Thea climbed all over the marble hooves and togas of the statuary in their seaside yard, Vera would sit on a bench absolutely lost in one of her puzzles. Like Stanley, she began to record her times and found that she was getting progressively faster. She could knock out a challenging *Times* puzzle in six minutes, and the *Newport Daily News* sometimes went down in four, the only limit being the speed at which her nimble fingers could move. She once treated herself to a movie on a Saturday night and, not even fifteen minutes in, pulled out her stack of puzzles and began flying through them in the dim red light of the EXIT sign while the soundtrack droned on in the distant present. On the bus, in diners, standing in line at a shop, in the park, under a bridge, at the seashore, she couldn't tear her eyes away from a crossword puzzle, and she thought to herself, This is the strangest thing.

Another day, a quiet Sunday when the sun filled the lemon-yellow rooms of her cheerful little apartment, her schoolwork advanced as far as possible and the semester's topics virtually picked clean, she looked down on her open notebook with its blue horizontal lines, and began crossing them vertically. She made a grid. A theme came to her, the theme of nautical knots, and she spent the afternoon knitting together what turned out in the end to be a fine puzzle. With that, Vera began constructing crosswords again. She figured there was no harm in it.

Her priority was her schoolwork, and as she understood her studies of matrix groups and abstract groups and algebraic topology better, she also got faster in her work and still more focused. When she was certain that she had covered everything that she set out to cover, and had progressed through all the math journals, she let herself set aside the schoolwork and make puzzles late into the night with a cup of mint tea and a bedside lamp that looked over her shoulder curiously. During her second semester at Pembroke, she published almost a dozen crossword puzzles, although no one would know unless she chose to share the information—the important thing was that she was aware the puzzles she published were hers, and she took great pride in them. When the two or three weeks surrounding finals came, she focused the totality of her intellect on her papers and exams with such force that it was as if the whole lot was blitzed by the kind of electrical storm that is talked of with reverence long after the season has gone.

Then in June, with the smoldering wreckage of the semester's final challenge behind her, she returned to crossword constructing, but no theme came to mind. She was on a bench at the seashore when a seagull dangled for a moment on the wind above her, trained its black buckshot eye on her, and mocked her loneliness with a singularly sarcastic squawk. That set her off on the thought of friends, wondering why she didn't have any in Rhode Island—after all, she was a sociable person, friendly, agreeable, an attentive listener and polite. Above her grid she wrote the title, "Just Friends," and began thinking of synonyms for "friend" as her theme words. PAL, BUDDY, AMIGO, COMPANION, CHUM . . . She made a list and fitted them all in. Later she would clue them but already ideas such as "videotape format" for PAL were teasing her imagination, and she scribbled two or three of them in the margin. OWING filled a space on the right side, crossing several words very luckily, and it touched off something in the back of her mind. WILMINGTON took its place cooperatively in another difficult spot and she was pleased with that. Then it finally dawned on her why OWING—"Writing an I.O.U."—tripped a catch in her mind. Stanley Owens. She looked at the title, "Just Friends." How perfect a message to send him. It's all over now and we can just be compadres. She erased the second, third, and fourth letters of WILMINGTON and changed it to WASHINGTON. She found places to tuck in other code words, like SONNY, MARTHA, NUPTIALS, even her unmistakable twist on the common ____ vera: aloe ____. The "V" in VERA crossed the "V" in PROVIDENCE. She would send it to the *Boston Globe*. Maybe Stanley was still living there. She knew he did all the major puzzles every day and would see it and understand, just like he did before. Maybe he would come visit her. She didn't see any harm in it.

Sometimes Vera thought that she experienced more than her fair share of disappointment and struggle, but her puzzle was accepted and published only two weeks after she sent it. What's more, the *Globe's* puzzle editor sent along a letter saying how thrilled he was to hear from her again. He even took the unprecedented step of offering to let her choose the date of publication, and she wrote back, saying, "As quickly as possible, please." Without letting on much to herself why she was doing so, she began to make a public presence of herself around Pembroke, bringing Theo and Thea with her to the campus green to study "in the inspiring atmosphere of higher learning," as she reasoned to Edie when making the request. They enjoyed picnics on the lawn, with the giants (her name for the children's two bodyguards) gnawing on chicken bones at a remove of ten feet. It was July, so the campus was fairly empty, and Vera stared at their surroundings quite often and paused to stretch and say things like "What a beautiful day!" But the cool figure of Stanley did not present itself on the campus green.

Back in her apartment, she watered her plants, put away the dry dishes, stacked up the books that lay about, and wiped down the bathroom sink. Drumming her fingers on her desk, she pulled open a drawer and took out the puzzle in question. She looked it over as she imagined Stanley might have, searching for some bit of misdirection she may have slipped in unintentionally. Her index finger stopped over the answer HOTEL. It happened to cross with ADDEDON, for which the clue was "Built more."

The next day, Vera again took the children to the campus green, looking around at the beauty of nature and casually slipping in story problems here and there: The number of birds in a tree divided by the number of nests equals how many birds per nest, that sort of thing. After their picnic she and the children went for a lengthy walk, with the giants laboring along ten steps behind and the limousine skulking at the end of the procession. She pointed out the ornate old Biltmore Hotel and Theo was immediately drawn toward the revolving doors, with Thea following on the invisible elastic that connected them. Inside the small lobby, it was cool and dark. Ferns abounded, giving the place the deep hush of a forest glade. Vera scanned the space, but didn't see him there. After wandering around as long as she could without making a nuisance of herself, she led the children out.

The following day, Thea asked to go to the hotel again, and Vera immediately responded, "What an excellent idea!" As soon as they entered the dim lobby, Vera saw that in one of the overstuffed chairs was a pair of crossed legs with the back of a *New York Times* floating above them, held wide open by a pair of hands. When Thea, a bit lost in the darkness after coming in out of the bright world, shouted, "Ve-ra, where are you?" the newspaper lowered itself. Vera introduced Stanley to the children, who had the magical power of nullifying the awkwardness of the situation. The giants stood by warily. She was thrilled to be in the presence of a friend once again, but she too was wary. She would not let herself trip up again. She was beyond that now. Things would never be the way they were. Just friends.

The children saw the comics on an open page of the *Newport*

Daily News lying next to Stanley, and Thea leaned in with a hand on his knee to get a closer look.

"I hope we're not interrupting anything," Vera said.

"Absolutely not. In fact, I was struggling with something there and maybe they can help."

Next to the comics was a word-find puzzle.

"These words are hidden among these letters somewhere and I just can't find them," he said to the children, pointing to the list beside the square of letters. "Do you think you can?"

Theo said, "I can! I can!" while Thea, who was still learning to read, poked her head forward like an eager turtle.

Stanley handed Theo his pen, and the boy found every word on the list with his tongue sticking out of the corner of his mouth. When he finished, Stanley shook his hand and said, "It's a pleasure to make your acquaintance, Theo. I'm always eager to meet smart people."

The giants inched closer. The chauffeur made an appearance and announced that it was time to get the children back for dinner.

"When the weather's nice, we have picnics on the lawn at the university," Vera said. "Maybe you'd like to join us sometime?"

Theo nodded enthusiastically. Vera smiled down at the poor friendless boy and put a hand on his shoulder. Stanley furrowed his brow and said, "Well, let's see, I just might be able to make time for that in my schedule."

As they parted out on the sidewalk, Vera asked Stanley how he liked the Biltmore, even though she knew he couldn't afford it. "Oh, I'm not staying there," he said with a laugh. "I just stop in for the atmosphere." He pointed out the place down the street where he was staying; its overcast façade of faux brick might be best described as no color at all, and its windows were covered with exhausted-looking curtains in shades of stained bed linen.

Always the gentleman with his tweed jacket and his courtly manners, he shook all three of their hands good-bye, and he looked into her eyes as if something could be found in them besides the usual parts of the eyeball. In his hand was her puzzle, and she noticed that he had doodled all around the words at the top. Just Friends.

CHAPTER ELEVEN

Stanley knew that the code word for the Allied invasion of Normandy was Neptune. He knew that the sodium and chloride ions of a table salt molecule bond in a crystal lattice structure, and he could draw you a diagram. He knew the names of the Seven Sisters—Alcyone, Asterope, Celaeno, Electra, Maia, Merope, and Taygete—and what's more, he could spell them. Stanley knew many things, but he still didn't know that he should go to Vera straightaway and tell her how he felt about her using just three little words, and ask her to be with him forever, then take her to Washington and marry her for real in a simple and honest ceremony, and slip a legitimate ring on her finger, and sign the marriage certificate in the unexceptional variety of ink that normal people use in their wonderfully normal lives to write checks and grocery lists and make signs about lost cats.

But those with a richness of talent in one respect tend to suffer a deficit in others. Stanley suspected he had shortcomings in matters of the heart, and theorized that there's a finite space within a person for ability. In most people that ability is evenly apportioned, so that they know how to do all the things a person has to do capably but without distinction, while in others ability is apportioned unevenly, great talent mixed with woeful life skills. Stanley had the book smarts of three PhDs combined, but was blind to the obvious path he should take in his relationship with Vera.

The Wellington children were having a wonderful Christmas Day, right up until the time came for them to be removed from the boisterous staff dinner and escorted to the grand dining hall of the Wellington estate. They heard that it was snowing, but couldn't see for themselves because the windows of the dining hall were covered over with complicated drapery bearing a tasseled cord that looked as though, if pulled, it might bring down the constellations with it. There they were greeted by Mrs. Wellington and formally wished a merry Christmas in front of the fire, which held its tongues of flame at a respectfully sedate level. They stood side by side and watched as two lethargic ponies with giant red bows hanging from their necks were paraded by stable boys quickly in through one door and out through another, and they were told that a small island off the coast of Madagascar was being named Theonia as a gift to them from that country's prime minister.

Stanley had a squeaky bike that was lent to him by the old man who ran his rooming house, and he rode it all the way from Providence to the Wellington estate in the light snow to join them for Christmas dinner. Stanley and Vera tried to make themselves comfortable among a dozen or so other guests, who arrived in black tie and stood around the table in postures more rigid than the supports of the Washington Bridge. When the children were dismissed, Edie invited her guests to sit, and after some routine conversation she invited them to go ahead and eat. "If we wait for Teddy we'll be here all night," she said with a laugh. After the soup course, Theodore Leviticus Wellington IV arrived at last, getting a few gruff "Merry Christmases" off his chest on the way to his chair, into which he delivered himself with a lot of grunting, as if he were a heavy parcel.

Stanley and Vera were seated near the middle of the long table. The hostess was at one end, the host at the other. A string quartet played from a distant corner of the hall. The main nuclei of conversation clustered at the polar ends of the table.

"Nutrition," Mr. Wellington said from his end, in a mocking tone. "It's a free country, and if the children of America want to eat WellCo's snack chips and cakes with whatever we put in them for flavor, what business is it of the government?" Holding up his plate and displaying its contents, he said, "There's plenty of beef and vegetables available. We're not stopping them from eating those." After pausing to set the plate back down, he continued, "If we put monosodium what-have-you in our products, that's our concern."

On her end of the table, a softer-spoken Mrs. Wellington could be heard saying, "Malnutrition is the real problem in these poor countries. Sure, Stamp Out Starvation can try to deliver enough rice or porridge to the poor children of the world, but a child cannot live on that alone. Nourishing foods are what is needed."

Stanley heard crunching sounds and turned his attention back to Mr. Wellington, who was holding a snack chip in his hand. "You simply can't get this wonderful color without a substance called Orange B. But now our supplier is being visited by the FDA. Even though—how many complaints have there been from our customers about it? Zero!" He banged his fist on the table, causing his finger bowl to jump in the air.

Startled by the noise, Mrs. Wellington looked down the table and, appearing to recall that a notable acquaintance of hers was seated there, said from her end, "Darling, Teddy, please!"

"It's these *people*. These infernal, busybody..."

"I know, dear," she said with a pacifying smile. "I know. Now settle down and eat your roast beef."

The husband smiled back at the wife he hardly knew, and the two halves of the table were united in a beautiful moment of joy and light. The candles flickered, the quartet played on, and soon the forks and knives joined in with their soothing cricket-like dissonance.

After dinner, they adjourned to a more intimate room cluttered with untouchable objets d'art and the sort of elaborate furnishings that require a person to perch on the edge of his seat. While not making a point of it, Stanley managed to engage them all with his ability to be interesting on any topic. Mr. Wellington produced one of his rare smiles—a kind of squinting-into-the-horizon expression—and patted Stanley on the back. "If I had a son... What I mean to say is, I hope that my son turns out to have half the brains you do. And now I have to leave you all," he said, standing up to go back to the bunker of his office. "It's morning for our new suppliers in the Orient, and I have calls to make."

Ever since he was welcomed into the Wellingtons' circle, Stanley had frequently sat and talked with Mr. Wellington in his private library, filled with books that were touched only by a feather duster. They talked about general things—politics, business, current events. They didn't share the same views at all, but Stanley was as diplomatic as ever. The elder man worried a lot and was soothed by his chats with Stanley, who tried to be a reassuring presence. Mr. Wellington perceived his world as a fragile one in which everything was poised to perish at any moment. Despite his enormous wealth, a wealth so cunningly tucked away in myriad vaults at the far corners of the world and invested so very carefully by the most inscrutable accountants one could hire, he felt that it was nothing but a nomad's tent. It may contain emerald-encrusted samovars and chests brimming over with gold and myrrh and dancing girls with rubies in their navels, but it was his everlasting worry that a piece of misfortune would come along and wipe it all away.

Stanley had found a part-time job at the Providence Central Library. He kept his cheap lodging at the Squire, the decrepit rooming house down the street from the Biltmore, but on Christmas night he stayed with Vera. Although she normally held herself at a careful distance, she took down the barrier this one night and the two of them came together like powerful magnets, bruising body parts, knocking each other's teeth. They spent so much of their time without sex that when they were together it was two starving souls arriving at a sumptuous banquet. Yet Stanley had received firm clarification from Vera that although they slept together that night, they were just friends who had simply been through a lot of things together, just friends who were so much alike and so different from everyone else that they might as well enjoy each other. He accepted her mandate, unaware that in her well-fortified heart Vera abhorred the idea of friendship between them and was holding out hope that he might leap marvelously across the gap of distrust with all the swashbuckling gusto of a Zorro, liberator, or waxed-mustachioed mutineer and make a grand gesture, something that would smash the shackles of friendship and at the same time repair what was broken in the past.

Lying in Vera's bed that night as she breathed earnestly next to him in her sleep, possibly dreaming of the aforementioned grand gesture, Stanley remained unaware of the absurdity of this so-called friendship. Now that he had found her, the urgency and crippling emptiness of his time alone in Boston had eased away unnoticeably, a pickpocketed emotion. And so although he had a vague idea of what the right move might be, he was carried along by inertia, doped up with the sedative effect of happiness. So he let the months slip by, the grand gesture not coming in the winter, not coming in the spring, comfortably living a non-life with her, a life without substance, written in ink that fades away.

Vera was on the phone with her mother, talking graduation, while Stanley stood next to her in the Wellingtons' kitchen, an industrial kitchen that reminded him of the one at the Hawthorne, his nose buried in the *Times*. "My husband is fine," Vera said softly, dangling the black coil of cord in his direction and looking around to make sure no family members or staff were nearby. Stanley lowered the paper, smiled at her, raised it again. She had long ago told her mother about her transfer to Pembroke. Her mother wasn't thrilled that she left BU and was on to her third college, but she accepted it, and Pembroke was an excellent school too, she admitted. Anyway, Vera had just completed her last undergraduate exam and would be graduating cum laude. She excelled in her math classes, writing papers that were of genuine interest to her professors, who assured her that any coed graduate school would be thrilled to have her.

Stanley's communication with his mother was less fact-based.

He was still trying to figure out a way to gently undo the Harvard lie. Occasionally he wrote her a letter, went to the Greyhound station, and asked a trustworthy-looking person who was waiting for the express bus to Boston to mail it for him when he got there in exchange for five dollars. It was a high price to pay for a Boston postmark, but cheaper than traveling there and back himself, and easier than hitchhiking, as he did occasionally to check his Cambridge post office box. He was keeping it solely for his mother's sake, so he could receive her letters there and she could go on believing he was still at Harvard. As the ostensible end of his senior year approached, his mood sank at the prospect of forging a diploma. Martha had already asked to see it after the graduation ceremony, which, he knew, she would attend only if it were to take place in the Hawthorne Hotel. Of course, she would want to see a photo too, and his mind spun out solutions involving either a staged portrait in a borrowed gown or the doctoring-up, somehow, of another graduate's picture with his own face. He had grown very tired of lying, and sometimes he fantasized what it might be like to tell the truth about everything, no matter the consequences.

When Vera got off the phone, Stanley put down the paper, stood up, and said, "Speaking of your husband, he's been thinking," the grand gesture bubbling up at long last. Maybe it was time to say to her, Let's do this: Let's confess everything to everyone. Let's have it out in the open. With all the momentary agony and fireworks it might entail, let's undo and then do. Let's tell everyone it was a horrible thing that happened and we're going to fix it. *I'm* going to fix it. I'm going to get that genuine ring and get down on my knees and beg you . . .

"My dear Stanislavsky," Vera said. "You've been thinking? Tell me about this thinking you've been doing."

Just then, Mrs. Wellington flew in through the swinging door as briskly as a sparrow. She didn't normally enter the kitchen, and never in her life had she even so much as boiled water or made toast. But there she was, a newspaper in her hand and her facial features stretched to their capacity with astonishment.

She stopped in front of Stanley and Vera while the swinging kitchen door sliced the air.

"You're married!" Edie blurted out, as if telling them they were on fire.

She hoisted the paper up as evidence, gripping it with her stubby fingers. "I...I was reading this article. Right here in the lifestyle section. About marriages, unusual marriages. And there you are!" Reading the article now with the paper held at arm's length to accommodate her aging vision, laying out each word as if dismantling a complicated piece of machinery, she said, "Stanley Owens and Vera Baxter, who were joint winners of the National Spelling Bee in a very rare tie, were married in grand style three years later in the very same ballroom..." She blinked ferociously at the couple in question, screwing her mind around to the impossibility of their being married and hiding it all this time. "Here's a photograph. It's you!" She shoved the paper forward and sure enough, there they were, in another dimension, a wrong turn into the Twilight Zone or a dip into the Outer Limits, another position in the space-time continuum, an unshakeable scrap from the fabric of the past that still clung to them wherever they went.

"Well look at that," Stanley said. He eyed Vera. She eyed him.

"That's us all right," she said.

"It certainly is," Edie said. They all looked at each other.

Stanley said, "Well, anyone for a game of croquet?"

Edie let the paper fall to her side. "Why didn't you tell us? I could understand why you'd pretend to be married if you weren't, but I can't figure why you'd pretend you aren't married when you are. It doesn't add up," she said, a twist of befuddlement dragging down her normally elevated features.

All eyes turned to Stanley. It was his moment to spring forward and be Vera's hero. It was his time to shine, to bring all the deception creaking to a halt and sit Edie down and confess the whole sordid truth, diagram it out, from beginning to end. It was a thing he did not do in this moment. What he did do, as Vera's hand ever so slowly moved to her hair and felt for a strand and began to wind it around a finger, was pause. She could see him thinking, could imagine him thinking how he might spin another lie to their advantage. Thinking how he could drag that chain of falsehood a little further along into the uncharted reaches of improvisational bullshit just one more time. It was a pause that became a chasm through which his future fell. Vera dropped her hair and sprang to her feet and brushed herself off.

"We're not married," she said bluntly, coming to her own rescue.

"Of course you are, my dear," Edie said in protest. With the patience of a schoolteacher, she added, "Why, it's right here in the *Boston Globe*."

"Well, we're not," Vera repeated. Among all the emotions churning within her just then, there was one word that expressed how she felt more strongly than any other: alone.

Finally, Stanley pulled himself from the muck of wrong thoughts, agreeing too vehemently, too late. "She's right. We're not married. We faked the whole thing."

Edie laughed. "Nonsense!" she said with great mirth, grasping

Stanley's joke completely. "Hah! Of course you're not. What I don't understand is..."

"We're not married and that's that. Can we please drop this?" Vera said, moving away from them and then clutching the stainless-steel prep table for support.

"My dear, it's all right," Edie said. "Whatever you're hiding, it's all right."

Stanley put up a hand. "Can I ask a favor? Can I have a moment alone with Vera?" Edie nodded, and absented herself from the exotic territory of the kitchen.

"Now you've done it," Vera said sharply. An atmospheric disturbance shadowed her, a dark cloud of anger gathered above, shot through with the occasional needle of lightning.

"Done what? Listen, Vera, let's get married for real. Why not?"

Vera took his hands in hers. She looked at him seriously, her brows knitted. "Stanley. Listen. I'm going to get a PhD in mathematics. I'm going to be a professor and do something with my life. You do as you like. You have talent. I wish you all the success in the world with your games. Your puzzles."

Stanley's head drooped and he said to the floor, "Vera."

"Stanley. Let's stay apart for a while. A long while. Maybe as long as forever."

"Vera."

"*I am not a grifter*," she said.

"And I'm not either."

This was all going so wrong so suddenly, he thought. She couldn't be saying these things. She couldn't be leaving him again. She couldn't be, could she? Not after all this. Then she said the worst thing of all.

"The fact is I'm not sure I love you anymore. I thought I did once. I believe I was in love with you...no, I know it. I think I even loved you way back when you misspelled *exsiccosis*," she said, and he set those words aside, never to be forgotten.

"But that was a long time ago. And now...well, I fear this relationship is too far gone," she said.

In his head, Stanley tore apart that cliché the moment she uttered it.

"The problem I'm having is...I'm not sure you really mean what you say. You're a very kind and gentle young man, and you're awfully handsome, but the fact is I find it hard to trust you. You say you care for me, but I always seem to end up getting hurt."

Stanley ached with the need to protest, but there was too much truth in what she said, and his mouth opened but no words came out.

"My heart is already fractured, I'm afraid. There's at the very least a crack in it. A broken heart doesn't easily fix itself," she continued.

"Vera, I really do love you," he said at last. "You can trust me now, I..."

"Shhh," she whispered, putting a finger to his lips. "Everything you say or do seems to be an act to me. It's too late for 'trust me.'"

These confessions of hers only made him want to set things right even more. And setting things right, to him, meant marrying her for real. He told her so, or at least he tried, but she didn't want to listen, and said she was done with all that, and furthermore she declared she was done with love, and she left the kitchen, going someplace where he couldn't find her.

After stumbling around the estate for a while, he walked down to the stables, where he stored his borrowed bike. Down the long twisting drive he went, the bike saying "creaky, creaky, creaky" every time the crank went around, past the tall fortification of hedges that separated the estate from the road, as tightly knit as pool table felt, past the other cleverly hidden mansions that peeked out shyly from hedgerows. Down he went along Main Road, the landscape disengaging from its fixed relationship with the earth and floating by most gracefully, across the Mount Hope Bridge and down Hope Street. "Hope," he said out loud in disgust. "Hah!" On he went past a gardener clad in gray and wielding the lobster claw of his pruning shears, on through Barrington and East Providence, past the campus and through town, and finally back to his room in the Squire, where he took off his shoes and lay down on the bed.

The next night, Stanley returned through the evening fog to the estate to try again with Vera. He felt strikingly out of place there in the mansion on the finger of land that stretched out into the Atlantic, and utterly confused. The man at the door told him the Wellingtons wanted to speak to him and deposited him in a small room he hadn't been in before, with two high-backed chairs and a round table arranged in front of a fireplace, a room that somehow felt as if it were occupied by ghosts. He looked at the image of the young man reflected in the mirror above the fireplace. In the fog of his bewilderment, an almost physical thickening of the mind that seemed of a piece with the very mist gathered outside the windows of the estate, he said, "Charlatan." Then he tried out another label to see how it fit: "Fraud."

With the crisp sound of a door latch, the Wellingtons entered and Stanley turned. All three of them said at the same moment, "Where's Vera?"

"We thought she was with you," Edie said.

"Oh," Stanley said. "I thought she was here."

"We've been looking for her. For both of you." Edie turned to her husband, who held a white box with a gold bow. "We want to give you this. As a belated wedding present. Congratulations," said Mrs. Wellington, the hint of a question in her voice. "Teddy?"

Mr. Wellington raised up the package and, after what seemed to be a brief moment of nostalgia for its contents, allowed it to pass from his hands to Stanley's. "A little something..."

"Let's not be modest, dear," Mrs. Wellington said. "It's a lot of something, but it's for the two of you to buy yourselves a home and start a life together. Take it to her."

Not quite knowing what to do with the box, Stanley lifted the cover and parted the sheets of rustling tissue paper inside. Lurking within were stacks of hundred-dollar bills, silent as sticks of dynamite.

"There should be twenty thousand there," Mr. Wellington said.

Stanley looked up in surprise. "Thank you, Mr. Wellington. Thank you from the bottom of my heart. But we can't accept this."

The man was at a loss. He was accustomed to two forms of communication: issuing commands and negotiating ruthlessly with the sharp blade of his self-interest. "Edie?" he said. "He won't take the money."

"Of course he will," she said calmly, patting Stanley on the shoulder.

"No, I really can't," he insisted.

"You must," Edie said. "You simply must. It was the children's idea, in a way. They wanted to buy you a house. We thought this way you can choose for yourselves. There are many pretty cottages across the bay in Bonnet Shores."

"It's just..."

"I won't hear any more about it." She touched Stanley's hand, then straightened her clothing and turned to leave.

Stanley stood with the box in his hands. "Cash?" he asked softly.

"Taxes," Mr. Wellington whispered back.

"Take it to her," Edie repeated, and they left him alone in the room. Stanley dropped into a chair. Silence. Even the ghosts in the room, elderly, sophisticated types, held their breath. Through the door was a world existing in his absence, with Stanley apart from life in this silent antechamber.

A chauffeur appeared to drive him back into town, the borrowed bike already placed in the trunk. Stanley was delivered to the door of his flophouse in a stupor, as if he were boozed up or out of his wits. When the car pulled to a stop and he didn't move, a hand reached in to help him out, taking the box on his lap containing twenty thousand dollars and placing it on the ground beside the bike leaning on its kickstand. The car made a dismissive sound as he watched it pull away, and the twin red taillights disappeared around a corner. He went to his room and sat on the edge of the bed in the dark with the box beside him, surrounded by the creaking and digesting sounds of the old hotel, which were hard to distinguish from the wheezing and groaning sounds of the old men who inhabited it.

Then he got to his feet and went out and rolled the bike out of the lobby and rode it all the way back to the Wellington residence in the cracked-open night, the bike saying "guilty, guilty, guilty" with every turn of the crank. Stanley shoved the box under the iron gate at the end of the driveway and scaled the thing, throwing a leg right over its W medallion in the fog-softened moonlight. He walked in the quiet grass along the edge of the drive and set the box down outside the front door, rapped on it three times, then returned down the drive to the gate, climbed it once more, and began the long ride back to town.

By the time he got to Vera's place, it was five a.m. Her lights were out. He entered the building and went up the stairs to her door on the second floor. There he stopped and sat down against the wall and permitted himself to close his eyes for a moment. When he opened them again, everything was shockingly bright. He stood up, brushed himself off, and knocked. No answer. The door was unlocked. The room was filled with emptiness. The wire for the phone lay twisted in the dust. Amid the visual oddity of all that naked wall, the white noise of the bare rooms screamed out at him. She was gone.

Stanley returned to the Squire, packed up his bag and paid his bill, and walked to the train station, where he bought a ticket to Washington. Mulling over the misdeeds of the past few years, he became paranoid and imagined that the police were looking for him. Surely the sum total of all the wrong he'd done added up to some sort of crime. The wedding scam alone was fraud; of that he was certain. As he sat on the train, the moving landscape set a rhythm, dragging along the picture show of his prosecution. He imagined that with no trouble at all he was captured and incarcerated by the gentlemanly police force that he wanted to think existed, handling him with a Sherlock Holmesian courtesy. At a table in a nasty little interrogation room, as comfortable as the inside of a lightbulb, he was shown the blank wedding certificate from '63, which, when the prosecutor held it at a slant toward the light, revealed the indentations of a pen spelling out their names. Stanley pictured a courtroom where a team of lawyers was arranged in the first row behind the prosecutor with their shoulders angled forward like the teeth of a saw.

"Stanley Carl Owens," he imagined the judge saying. "You have been convicted of fraud in the inducement." Looking at his documents, he said, "This is a shame. After having looked over your file, I must say you strike me as the kind of man who could have been anything he wanted to be."

The judge peered at Stanley over his bifocals. "What kind of man *do* you want to be, Mr. Owens?"

Stanley looked out the window of the train. What kind of man did he want to be? He supposed he wanted to be a crossword puzzle wizard. He wanted to be a man who knows all things. He wanted to be a great traveler. But then, maybe he really didn't after all. Maybe all he wanted in the end was something very unextraordinary. Yes, it was nothing special that he wanted, but yet it seemed so very hard to achieve.

"I want to be a happy man."

The judge responded, "You'll get another chance after you serve six months in the Rhode Island State Correctional Institution."

There was the sound of the gavel striking its target, but no, it was the blast from an air brake rousing Stanley back to reality as the train pulled into Union Station.

CHAPTER TWELVE

I'd like to begin again." The words tumbled out of Vera as she sat staring into space on the half-empty train to New York.

She recalled the well-meaning but stern teacher who taught her the rules of spelling bees, way back in third grade at P.S. 199, and pictured the same teacher instructing her now that in life, as in competitive spelling, starting over is permitted, as long as you begin with the decisions you've already made. "What kind of starting over is that?" Vera thought when she first heard the rule, and she felt the same frustration now. She could start a whole new life, she could and would reinvent herself, but whatever life she constructed from the scraps at hand would always be connected to what went before, no matter how different she made it or how hard she tried to forget.

First order of business was leveling with her mother. When she arrived at the apartment in New York, it was a surprise to Vivian, who was packing to come up for Vera's graduation. But Vivian had her own surprise as well. She told Vera that on her business trips to DC, she had begun seeing Sonny, and that they were dating.

"In fact," she said nervously, "he's come up for a visit. He's here now."

With that, he stepped jubilantly out from the kitchen with a wide smile, like a guest on *The Tonight Show* coming out from the wings. He hugged Vera and told her what a joy it was to see her again, and then, awkwardly, told her how grateful he was to be part of Vivian's life and that he hoped the two of them would become good friends.

Vera was amazed that her mother would choose this man of all people. They were so different. Then again, they were similar in some ways, always hustling, always taking charge. Vera liked Sonny and was happy for her mother, and responded warmly, but didn't have a lot to say, as she was preoccupied with an entirely different matter. Hastily, before any further diversion could occur, she sat them both down and confessed everything. Vivian was absolutely floored—and furious, of course—but after all, this was her daughter, her only child. Sonny admitted that he was suspicious about the wedding but decided to say nothing, and never imagined the truth would be something like this. It also explained something else: In Sonny's correspondence with Stanley, Sonny told him that he had heard, through Vivian, that he had transferred to BU, and Stanley had asked him to keep this news from Martha until he told her, which he never did. For her part, Vivian wasn't exactly appalled by the immorality of the whole thing—after all, she prided herself on the fact that she and her daughter were creatures of independent thought living trailblazing lives—but she was upset about the lies. And she was upset that, as it turned out, she hardly knew her daughter. It was her own fault. She was upset with herself for keeping distance between them all those years, focusing too much on her quest for a husband and working too hard in pursuit of a job as a bona fide saleswoman at IBM—which, she confided, might finally be coming to fruition. The three of them spent the next few days reconnecting, venturing out via Checker cab to interesting restaurants around the city, including the legendary Delmonico's, spackling the mother-daughter relationship with the peculiar form of love that existed between them, somewhat formal yet also charged with the intensity that sizzles between a single mother and her only child. They talked about Vera's next move, and then said their good-byes, this time with Vivian promising to visit soon and often.

Second order of business was disappearance. Vera wanted to go somewhere she couldn't be found, so she packed a rented Ford van and motored on to graduate school at Princeton University, a destination she disclosed to no one but her mother. She moved into a unit in graduate student housing. New student occupancy wasn't expected until August, but they made an exception for her. After she settled in, Vera purged herself of all the grim business with the fake wedding and the cheating scandal and the god-awful television appearance by writing it all down, using Socrates, in the hope that its disappearance on paper might hasten its disappearance from her memory. With a hearty welcome from the dean of the School of Mathematics, who admired her academic qualities despite all the hopping around, she began her first day of classes as a graduate student with the shed skin of an old life in the distance behind her.

She lived alone. She lost herself in her work. She cooked for herself and cleaned for herself and went to the park alone. Her graduate school years were as steady and uneventful as her early undergraduate years were reckless. Her intelligence and her determination carried her through. As a woman and a social creature, her self-esteem was in the basement, a crippled and beaten thing. But as a student of mathematics, her confidence soared and guided her. Her friends were all math people: fellow graduate students, professors, the occasional promising undergrad. She didn't let the flash in the eyes of masculine specimens she crossed paths with—one of whom followed her into Fine Hall to tell her she had a beautiful smile—distract her. Men were not to be trusted. She surrounded herself with female friends, and even though she was determined to keep her focus on her studies only, she did attend an occasional feminist meeting on campus. She didn't talk about Stanley. She was a woman without a past. Silent, observant, listening. Her friends came to her with their troubles and she was quietly grateful that hers were over. She could please herself in much the same way that a man could please her, and when she got that urge that felt so slippery and acute, she would go to her bedroom and do so, and then it would quickly be over. Nothing much after all. She was convinced she could spend the rest of her life without a man. Instead, perhaps she would buy one of those nice Japanese teapots.

In the two years that went by with the flap of a sparrow's wings she earned her master's degree. She discovered during that time a fascination with the new discoveries that were being made in group theory, and her work on her PhD focused on that. She was frequently amazed by the hidden symmetry of things. There was a professor at the university—Professor Lehnert. Peter. Imported from Germany. He was known around the world for his work in that field and she absorbed everything she could from him. He had several cats and a spindly vegetable garden that Vera took care of for him when he traveled the world to attend conferences and work with other luminaries in his field, and he was constantly being visited by professors from West Germany, Finland, Italy, England, and even, on those rare occasions when they could get a visa, the Soviet Union. Vera worked on proofs. Professor Lehnert worked on proofs, sometimes in partnership with one of these foreign professors, and every so often, after much quiet preparation, one of their successes would appear in a mathematics journal like a ripe fruit appearing on a tree. Vera had two articles published as she labored on her dissertation. Nothing extraordinary, but getting published was a point of pride nonetheless, and an eventual necessity. After four years of doctoral work, she typed the title of her dissertation at the top of a sheet of paper and began her final draft: *Algorithms in Combinatorial Group Theory.*

By her late twenties, Vera had amassed many acquaintances and good friends, all university people. Most of them were intelligent and serious and witty and silly all at the same time. Being among those people after so many years of struggling through life as a misfit sort of creature, like a kind of Sasquatch or unicorn, she felt that, at last, she had found her lost tribe.

As a teaching assistant, Vera occupied a small bare-bones office in the building that housed the math department. She usually kept a few fresh-picked flowers in a wine bottle to add color to the place, and tore funny headlines from newspapers and taped them to the wall—"Kids Make Nutritious Snacks." There weren't a lot of extraordinary highs, like there had been in her younger years, but there weren't a lot of extraordinary lows either. Just an even sort of satisfaction. And when she got restless, and began to yearn for a life she could not have, she very deliberately made herself a cup of tea, stood in one place, breathed deeply in and out, and enjoyed a silent time of peace.

Her teaching assistant stipend was just $8,000 a year. She owned one plate, one bowl, one set of flatware of four pieces each. She had a casserole dish, a pot with a lid, a frying pan, and a cutting board. She had one spatula, one sharp knife, a wooden spoon, a ladle, a grater, a can opener, and a wide tomato can to keep them all in, with *San Marzano* printed in dancing yellow script across three fat tomatoes. Once or twice a week she drank a glass of wine. She did not own a television. At the close of the day she leafed through the *New York Times* but there was never, ever any question of looking at the crossword puzzle.

There was no avoiding the fact that she missed his body. She was flesh and blood after all. But she wouldn't say his name, or even let it whisper through her mind. If she felt the "S" coming, she would quickly bend it into something else. Sss-tandard. Sss-tarlight. Two times near the end of her graduate years her human need for companionship and the circumstances of her social universe colluded to put her together with someone who was no match for her. The first one was an undergrad she was teaching. He was smart, although not in a mathematical way, and easy-breezy like Sss-paghetti, and she wouldn't have let him kiss her if he hadn't been so damn cute about trying to hide his attraction to her and getting all flustered when they worked on problems together, boyishly ruffling his fingers through his hair. He seemed wonderful at first but in the end the veil lifted and he turned out to be awfully immature, and she wondered what blinders she had on not to see he wasn't very smart at all. They slept together once at his run-down place off campus and then she called him to say he had to switch his section.

The second one was a highly regarded professor she met at a party when she had two glasses of wine too many. In the light of day it turned out that his face looked like a potato, but he couldn't have been more attentive to her. Yet there was something missing. It felt as if there was a layer of something between them. She couldn't put her finger on it. He too she slept with only once. It was like an awakening: There were simply no men in this world who were right for her.

After passing her orals and having her dissertation accepted, Vera received her PhD in the spring of 1973 at the age of twenty-eight. Her mother drove to the graduation in her new Mercedes-Benz, a thing with a chrome grill in front shining like a pawnshop window, with Sonny in the passenger seat. Vivian had finally gotten that sales job she had spent a decade chipping away at the glass ceiling to attain, and she was making the most of the opportunity. She had put extra effort into selling new clients in the DC area, just because Sonny was there, and eventually she secured some contracts with the federal government. IBM was doing well with its IBM System/360, and so was she. For the past four years, she had been dividing her time between his apartment in DC, her apartment in New York, and the road. She described to Vera how, when she returned to DC from one of her trips, it was always a very special time for the two of them. She talked about how Sonny, unable to contain himself, would take the bus all the way out to where I-95 met the Beltway, exit 27, a desolate patch of nowhere scarred by winters, where long lonely weeds grew. She would stop to pick him up there, and they would drive into the city together. Sonny would have a feast cooking, and there would be a bouquet of flowers waiting for her.

Vera learned the details of their relationship, more of them than she in fact wanted to know, from the frequent phone conversations she had with her mother ever since her confession. Now

Vera and her mother talked on the phone nearly every day, and visited each other often. At least something good came out of the awful end with Sss-talagmite.

Sonny, for his part, changed dramatically. With Vivian to occupy his thoughts, he no longer obsessed about every detail of the Hawthorne's management. He no longer needed to be in perpetual motion. He went from addict-thin to Capone-like, which made his filled-out face look friendlier, almost innocent. He behaved like a bloodhound who had been searching rather pathologically all his life for something and had finally found it, and now there was nothing left but to keep it between his paws and protect it. The one and only project that remained to him was to make Vivian feel good about herself. Vera was astonished by the whole thing, and thrilled for her mother, though it served to highlight the lack of romance in her own life.

At Vera's doctoral commencement ceremony, Sonny presented her with a bouquet of flowers so large that it took the two of them to carry it back to her apartment in the graduate housing section, now so cluttered and homey after several years of life there. Vivian and Sonny camped out in the living room for several days while Vera prepared for yet another transition. For their meals, Sonny cooked dishes such as chicken cordon bleu, salmon in a light lemon sauce with asparagus tips, pork tenderloin, and quiche lorraine. In the mornings, Vera and Vivian awoke to the smell of blueberry muffins baking in the oven. There was so much food that, in the evenings when he left them so they could have a little time together, he had a full bag of leftovers to take to the soup kitchen nearby.

Over dinner one night, Vera told them about the job she had lined up. Assistant professorships for mathematicians were scarce

enough, she explained, but jobs for mathematicians who specialize in specific branches of group theory were so hard to find that
there were only a handful of them in the world. She might have
ended up in Zurich or Zagreb, if she ended up anywhere at all, but
with the help of Professor Lehnert and his networks, she found a
job at the University of Nebraska in Lincoln.

After a week spent catching up with her mother and Sonny at
a campus emptied of students, Vera rented a U-Haul, and Sonny
loaded up the thing almost entirely by himself, taking everything but the very lightest of objects out of the hands of the two
women. They were permitted to carry a spider plant in a macramé
hanger, a small framed picture of mother and daughter, a lamp-
shade, and an empty basket. Finally, Vera said good-bye. It felt so
far and unreal, Nebraska, Nebraska, Nebraska, a mission to a fic-
tional place, to do a fantastical kind of job, as if she were going to
see the Wizard of Oz or build a ladder to the moon.

The U-Haul started with a big hollow fuss, Vera moved the
long gearshift into first, and during the four-day drive she had
nothing to do but think. She thought about him. Sss-tatistic. Did
he stay in Providence? Maybe he got a college degree after all and
became a high school teacher. He would have been good at that.
It would have worn him out but he would have been happy doing
it. Maybe he even coached tennis after school. Six years was a long
time. He could be anywhere.

Images came to mind like they do in dreams, liberated from
any relationship to the possible. Vera imagined him bent over his
notebook on a park bench, carefully etching the letters of a puzzle.
What was he wearing? A filthy peacoat over a torn sweater. Un-
shaven, unshowered, his mind a little gone. When she got a closer
look, she saw that his fingers were filthy and were busy filling

the entire page with minuscule characters resembling the letters of no language, like the coils of a fine necklace. His pencil occasionally slipped off the edge of the page, which roused him for a moment, but then he went right back to his mad scrivener's work. She imagined him looking up and staring right at her and saying, "I told you life without you would drive me crazy."

Vera stayed in hotels on the road. In her mind she was that singular, lonely child in the backseat again. Numbers and fanciful symbols and their puzzling relationships swam through her thoughts. On her journey to Nebraska, Vera lay on the marshmallow surfaces of the hotel beds and stared at the ceiling. Did he feel remorse? Of course he did. But she felt remorse too. To be honest with herself, she was complicit; she got a thrill out of playing the outlaw with him and being in on secrets only the two of them shared. And although it was essential for her survival, she felt guilty for leaving him. She thought of him alone, picturing his meager and stretched-out shadow stealing through some unforgiving eastern town. She wondered if he was still making his puzzles. It had been his whole life. She hoped he was happy.

Vera wasn't cut out for driving. The monotony of staring at the road was torture. By force of will she turned her mind away from Sss-tanza and instead to math. She had the most fantastic ideas for problems she was working on. To her frustration, she had the most beautifully lucid ideas at such moments as this, when she was unable to fix them on paper. Several times she tried to pull over to jot them down, but often she was unable to, and although she repeated them over and over so that she might not forget them, in the end the ideas simply flew off, untamable as birds. And in their place those thoughts of him rushed in again.

As she drove, Vera wondered what sort of place was awaiting her in Lincoln. She wondered if her life there would be a success. What sort of people would she find? Would she like the town? Most of all, during that unrelenting drive, what she tried so hard not to let herself wonder was, Does he still think about me?

CHAPTER THIRTEEN

May 1967, six years earlier

The Truth. Stanley stood in front of the Hawthorne Hotel with his satchel in his hand, stuffed with crossword puzzles and a change of clothes and his wedding band. It was all he had in the world. He had just arrived in DC from Providence, and the truth be told, the Hawthorne really wasn't as spectacular as he remembered it. Stripped of the sparkle his youth had given it, it looked a bit long in the tooth, its limestone frosted with the black particulates of vehicle exhaust, its awnings dotted with pigeon shit. It was a breeding ground of persistent old politicos with dollars swarming in their heads and lies flying from their lips. Well, the hotel sure produced a champion liar in him. When he first got off the train, looking in the filthy mirror of the bathroom in Union Station, he made a promise to himself: He would tell no more lies. Even if it proved to be as challenging as bending a spoon with his mind, he would stop the lying. It was time to take up The Truth, and see what damage it might undo.

Stanley didn't recognize anyone in the lobby, and he was glad. He hadn't spoken to Sonny in a long time. Stanley had called his mother a month ago from a pay phone in the lifeless lobby of the Squire and told her he would come visit her after graduation, bringing his yet-to-be-forged diploma and doctored photo to show her. Stanley didn't know that Sonny was in New York for a visit and had already heard the truth from Vera.

Stanley took the stairs to the fifth floor and rapped on the door of the William Henry Harrison Suite. Martha answered, gripping her bathrobe shut under her chin. "Stanley! My baby." She hugged him tightly, pressing her soft cheek wet with tears against his. She wiped her eyes and settled in her chair, which was deeply rounded out and surrounded by all the things she might need—her pencil sharpener, a box of tissues, her teacup, the ivory telephone that had once been white, a tower of manuscripts, the clock radio, her timeworn dictionary, a cup of red pencils, all the tools of her trade at arm's length in the style of a dentist. Stanley pulled up a chair to face her and took her hand.

"So, tell me all about graduation," she said.

"Mom. I have something to say and you're not going to like it. Please listen to me. Hear me out. As bad as it may sound, everything is all right. Okay, Mom? Everything is all right, and everything is going to continue to be all right. Are you with me?"

She blinked at him.

"Everything is all right," he said. "Say it."

"Everything is all right."

"Okay." He patted her hand, gave her a smile, and began. "I've done a lot of lying. Now I'm going to be telling the truth, from here on out, for better or for worse."

She swallowed hard and nodded.

Stanley told her everything, starting with the lies about his college applications.

"I never sent any," he said. "Not one. Not even to Harvard."

She tried to stand, in her confusion, but he rose up and put a hand on her shoulder and helped her lower herself back into her chair.

"I make crossword puzzles. I know it's not lawyering, but it's become my life's work. Like it or not, there's no stopping it now."

She seemed to be looking right through him, but she didn't cry out; she didn't collapse.

"I'm good at it, Mom. I've been published in papers all over the country and I'm proud of that. Now," he said, and took a deep breath. "About Vera."

She looked into his eyes, as if to say, "There's more?"

"Mom, the wedding was faked." He squeezed her hand. "I was very angry, and very confused."

She looked at him with a courage in her eyes that was unfamiliar to him; a realness, as if she had declared to herself at long last, "Enough with the pretense of fragility." Stanley said he was angry that his father was taken from him. Taken with less outrage or retribution than if someone had taken his backpack. He was angry that he was—the way he saw it—pressed into service as an academic slave. All so that his bright light might compensate in some way for the absence of Nick. Stanley told her he wanted to extract money from the wealthy people he knew, to start a life on his own. He told her about the disappearing-ink pen, the selling of the gifts, the new life in Cambridge. He told her about the cheating scandal at Harvard, and about how he jeopardized Vera's future in his blindness and selfishness. Then there was Boston. The fraudulent wedding doggedly following them and leading to more lies on national television. On to Providence. He found her there. He wished he had put an end to it all, but he let himself be complacent, and then more trouble, although to be honest—and that's all that mattered now was being honest—he could have done the right thing by Vera. "But I didn't," he said. "Not properly, anyway.

"After that, she left. I think she's going to graduate school. She's brilliant, Mom. Absolutely brilliant. Anyway, all I can guess is she left Providence. That's where I've just come from. There was no graduation. I am not going to law school. I have never spent so much as one hour enrolled in a college course. I don't know where Vera is." He was shaking. He put his head in his hands.

To Stanley's surprise, his mother held him, stroked his hair. She said, "It's all right, honey." She put her hand on his chin and lifted his face up to meet hers. "Stanley, look at me. Everything is all right, and everything is going to continue to be all right." She stood up from her chair and helped him into it. It struck him that it was the first time he had ever sat in it. Martha unfolded the kitchenette to make him a cup of tea.

He was amazed that she wasn't more undone by his revelation, but then he had a feeling she had her suspicions, kept hidden deep within herself. After Stanley recovered his composure, he took his satchel and said to her as she fumbled in a cabinet, "On the bright side, I have this." He opened the bag and out spilled hundreds of sheets of paper. Crossword puzzles of every stripe, a pixilated swarm of them, his best work ever. During the year in Providence, he completed several beauties every day, his mind freely escaping into an untroubled world of creation. Martha fanned out the puzzles on the kitchen table, took up a few of them as she sipped her tea, looked them over and smiled. He showed her a *New York Times* puzzle page from several months earlier, and told her that although there was no byline, only the name of the editor, it was his work, a Halloween puzzle, by special request.

"Well. I am proud of you. I really am." She looked into her teacup. "I blame myself, Stanley. I pushed you too hard. I didn't allow you to be a kid. I didn't listen. I didn't let you be yourself."

"No, Mom," he said. "No one's to blame but me."

After a long silence, she said, "I'm happy you've decided to tell the truth. I would like to do that too." She sighed and looked into her lap. "Stanley, I have something to tell you. I too have lied."

He looked up at her, his mind racing. What could she have to lie about?

"I lied about your father. It's not clear that he was killed in Normandy. He was missing in action." She stopped to let this soak in.

Stanley just sat there, staring, as everything but Martha and the chair receded into nowhere. "Not killed? MIA? So..."

"So, yes, he might still be alive somewhere," she said. "Stanley, before you get excited, it's doubtful. Very doubtful. They say only a very small number of these cases are actually found alive after they've been declared MIA. And after all this time, the chance is virtually nil. If he was alive, surely he would have found his way back by now."

Stanley stared at his mother with a strange expression forming on his face.

"Why," she said. "That's what you want to know, isn't it? Well, to be honest, I couldn't bear it. I was weak then and I still am, frankly, although I've gotten stronger here on my own. I didn't want you to spend your life wondering, wishing, hoping he might come through that door at any moment, as I had done. For a long time after that terrible day when Sergeant Promise knocked on our door, I held out hope. I think you were five years old when I gave up hoping. I wanted to forget. Telling myself he was gone was the only way to go on. I would've gone mad if I'd... And he never was found. For a few years the Air Force sent me letters—'We're looking. We're looking. We've stopped looking.' Then I started getting checks every month. 'Death benefits,' they call them. Someone ought to rethink that expression. Stanley, don't go thinking he's out there..."

He jumped up, his chair skittering across the floor. "I can't believe this. Mom. My God. That's not something you..." He stopped speaking, with his mouth still open, and dropped back into the chair. Martha reached across the table for his hand. He had to get up again and go. He had to go to Normandy right away. But he didn't have the money for that, nor did his mother. Unable to continue the conversation, he closed himself up in his old room and didn't leave again until that night.

Stanley stayed with Martha in the William Henry Harrison Suite for several days. Things were tense between them. He was angry that she lied. She was angry that she accepted his confession graciously but he didn't accept hers. She found him standing in front of the photograph of Nick in the hallway, studying it, as if a clue might be detected there. He wrote a letter to the United States Air Force asking for his father's files. While he awaited a response, he worked on puzzles, many of them containing words that might mean something to Vera, simply because he couldn't help himself. He also began the project of sending off the puzzles he had been accumulating, and started to think about putting together a book of his own work. He ran into Sonny, who was back from New York, and they began to talk easily, as if Stanley had never left.

"How was graduation?" Sonny said with a laugh.

"Sonny, I have a confession to make. There was no graduation."

"I know." Sonny always seemed to know everything, soaking knowledge up from the atmosphere without ever opening a book.

"You know?"

"I heard from Vera."

Stanley had prepared himself to make an explanation to Sonny, and he didn't let Sonny's unexpected response stop him.

"Imagine having to live a prearranged destiny," Stanley said. "Someone else's idea of how you should live your life. I couldn't stay here anymore, and I couldn't face going to college. I guess I could have asked people for money, but that's not me. I only did it to make a break from this place. It was the best I could come up with."

"The best you could come up with?" Sonny shook his head. "Well, I wish you had come to me first. You know, you're not the first kid who didn't want to go to college."

"Sonny, I want you to know it was all my doing and Vera had no fault in it," Stanley continued. "She only did what I asked her to do. Reluctantly, at that."

Sonny nodded.

"I'm sorry," Stanley said. "Look, here's the thing: I wanted to make crossword puzzles."

"You wanted to make crossword puzzles?" Sonny said, repeating it back to Stanley.

"I'm very good at it. It's the only thing I love doing. Call it stupid, but that wedding was my way to make a clean break and start doing what I love."

"You faked a wedding so you could make crossword puzzles?" Sonny said, scratching his head, looking like he didn't know whether to laugh or cry. "Okay, look. I understand. Let's leave it in the past."

"I promise you, I'll never lie to you again."

"It's okay, my boy. Everyone makes mistakes. Some are bigger than others," he said, and laughed again. Sonny was not one to hold a grudge or be judgmental. He looked healthier than Stanley had ever seen him. He was involved in a momentous project: quitting smoking. He told Stanley that he had been up in New York to see Vivian, Vera's mother. He couldn't help mentioning offhand a few things about her that apparently lived in the forefront of his mind, like the fact that she loved seafood, especially oysters, and that she sang beautifully in the car when no one could hear her but him.

"Did you know she's a history buff?" Sonny asked.

They both stood looking at each other, hesitantly. Sonny knew what Stanley was thinking.

"Do you know where Vera is?" Stanley finally asked.

Sonny nodded. Stanley stood there, waiting, knowing he wouldn't get an answer. "You promised not to tell me, didn't you?"

Sonny nodded again.

"Is she well?"

"Yes. She's fine," Sonny said, and put a hand on Stanley's shoulder.

In the quiet of the suite, with Martha's spirit sucked away into her manuscripts and the occasional snarling of the Point-O-Matic pencil sharpener bringing them both back to reality from time to time, Stanley thought of puzzle themes. Every morning, Stanley visited the lobby and picked up the crosswords from all the

major papers, which Charlie, his old newsstand friend, had set
aside for him. In the time it took him to drink a cup of coffee,
he worked half a dozen puzzles, just in case there might be a
message from her. *Her.* The train he took from Rhode Island to
DC passed through a town called Berlin, and it stuck with him.
He started a puzzle with the theme of small American towns
bearing the names of famous cities: Rome, Wisconsin; London,
Kentucky; Paris, Texas; Athens, Georgia; Moscow, Pennsylvania;
Venice, California. He used the city name as the clue and the state
name as the solution: "Rome, _____," for instance, was one clue,
a piece of misdirection that thrilled him. If only the state names
were the same number of letters as their original country names,
now that would be perfection. Poring over his United States map,
he even discovered a Normandy, Tennessee. He arranged all these
theme clues on the grid and began filling it in, when his mother
knocked on his door with a letter from the Air Force. She waited
for him to open it, wanting to see what it said, but he gave her a
look as if to say, "You've kept this from me for all these years and
now you expect me to share this with you?" She turned and left,
and he opened the letter.

Dear Mr. Owens:

*We have looked into your request for the personnel files of a Private
Nicholas William Owens, enlisted 1944. We regret to inform you
that we have no records for such an individual. Is it possible that
there is a different spelling of the name? Or is it possible that you
meant to contact a different branch of the armed forces? We are
sorry for any confusion in this matter. If you would like to pursue
your inquiry further, please contact Corporal Randall Jacoby at the
Department of Records, who will be happy to assist you.*

That night he slept poorly, flung in and out of nightmares, one of which featured his father in permanent suspension above an icy beach in his parachute like a target in a carnival game, punctuated by a gunshot, wet blood splattering Stanley's face and snapping him to a sitting position in bed. In the morning, while Martha was in the tub, he went to her bedroom. A picture of Nick was tucked into the corner of her mirror. It showed him standing in a T-shirt and khaki pants against a brick wall. The photo could have been taken anywhere. Across the back was scrawled, "Greetings from training camp in jolly old England!" On the dresser was a stack of bills: grocery delivery, newspaper subscription, stationery store. In the stack was a canceled check with "death benefit" printed at the lower left corner. The originator of the check was the law firm of Driver & Jennings, of Memphis, Tennessee.

The purgatorial bus from DC crept along with high regard for every speed limit and stopped far too often. The first thing Stanley did when he finally arrived in Memphis, of course, was find the law firm. But the polite receptionist made it clear to him that all client business was confidential, even if he did claim to be related, and in any event, Mr. Driver and Mr. Jennings were at a trial in Nashville all week and out of reach. So after stubbornly sitting in the reception area for two hours he finally got up and caught a bus to Arnold Air Force Base near the town of Normandy.

Stanley had never seen so many airplanes in his life. The air was abuzz with the sound of their engines as they crept slow and beetle-like in and out of hangars and down a cross-hatching of runways. Identical-looking men in identical uniforms moved purposefully about, the great sky above bestowing its cooperation, sending the occasional cloud scudding by in parallel with the busy mechanic walking the long expanse of a runway. The whole thing felt way out of scale to him, like a giant hand placed on the earth.

The screen door of the visitors' office slapped shut behind him. The small room had an ashtray on a stand and a few folding chairs lined against a wall that was papered with propaganda and recruitment posters. A model of the base laid out under Plexiglas reinforced the godlike sensation of having one's way with scale. In front of him was a counter staffed by a uniformed man with one sleeve pinned across his chest, still pressed and folded. His nametag read Jackson.

Stanley first asked if Nicholas Owens was employed by the base as a civilian. The one-armed man went into a back room, made some noise with a filing cabinet, and returned. "No, sir." Then he asked if a Sergeant Promise was stationed there. Another trip to the back room, more banging of metal filing cabinets, and another "No, sir." Stanley drummed his fingers on the countertop. Jackson stared blankly at him in the way soldiers often do, with the curtains pulled down behind his eyes. Stanley looked at his empty sleeve and asked, "North Korea?"

"Yes, sir. Got it blown clean off in the light of day." He shrugged. "Coulda been worse."

"My dad was in World War Two. MIA."

"MIA, sir?" He whistled. "Your dad was a great patriot."

"I don't think so. I think he's a fraud."

Jackson stared angrily at him with his hand flat on the countertop.

"Do you have a local telephone directory?" Stanley asked.

The man didn't move. He stared aggressively into Stanley's

face, then reached under the counter and slapped down the book. "Knock yourself out," he said. He turned and went into the back room.

Stanley flipped to the O's. Owens, Nicholas, 28 Montvale Lane, Normandy.

It was a small town, and Stanley easily found the squat little ranch house with 28 and a striped bass on the mailbox at the roadside, and a front garden filled with tulips in bloom. He rang the bell and heard a yappy dog come scampering up to the entrance. A woman's voice shushed it and the door opened. The screen door separating them added a canvas-like texture that had the effect of making her look like a painting. He was surprised to find that she was black. She was on the short side, with a pretty face and intelligent, shining eyes. She wore a dress of bold colors—enormous pink and blue flowers on a field of canary yellow. Her hair was the sort of elaborate construct that beauty parlors liked to put posters of in their windows. "What can I do for you, darling?" she asked. She cocked her head and studied him.

Stanley was about to say, "I'm with the Census Bureau. I'd like to ask you some questions." But then he remembered: *The Truth.* He looked her in the eyes and said, "I'm Stanley Owens. Nick's son."

He could see the surprise run through her but she was quick on her feet and steady. "I see." She smoothed her dress and swallowed hard. "I'm Sally, pleased to meet you. Can I ask you to wait here a moment?"

Pine. Oddly enough, that's the word that came to his mind when Nick filled the space behind the screen. There was something foursquare and serene about him. Seeing him in his white

T-shirt with his sharp features, straight mouth, and clear, kind eyes brought to mind the simple honesty of wood. Which was of course ironic, considering the immense deception he was guilty of. It was so odd to see a sort of amended mirror image of himself, a bit rougher looking, older of course, but recognizable all the same. Nick didn't say a word. He smiled gently and pushed open the door.

It was a modest place, cluttered with knickknacks. The TV was on, and Sally quickly snapped it off with a twist of the wrist. Nick and Sally sat on the couch and Stanley sat across from them in an armchair that apparently was the property of the dog. Sally tried in vain to shoo her away and then left to lock her in another room.

"So," said Nick. "Here we are at last."

Stanley just glared at his father, his anger burning within him beyond control.

"So," Nick said again, and rubbed his thighs. "I don't know where to begin..."

"Let's talk about Normandy," Stanley said.

"There's not much to say," Nick said in a small voice. "Little town, mostly military people, being so close to an Air Force base."

"I meant the other Normandy."

"I don't know much about that Normandy," Nick said quietly.

"Allow me to acquaint you with it. The name Normandy comes from the Northmen, the Vikings, who settled there in the ninth century. Normandy is a large geographical area situated on the northwest coast of France, at roughly 49° north latitude and 0° longitude, centered smack on the prime meridian. The Allied invasion of Normandy began in the early hours of June 6, 1944. Among the leaks of the invasion was a crossword puzzle that came out in the *Herald and Review* six days before. The puzzle's answers included Overlord, Neptune, Gold, and other terms and code words relevant to the invasions. It was declared a coincidence."

Stanley perched on the edge of his chair and delivered his monologue loud, fast and reckless, his voice rising as he spoke.

"The operation began with nighttime parachute and glider landings, air attacks, and naval bombardments. Amphibious landings on five beaches began by dawn. By June 11, over 300,000 troops and 54,000 vehicles had landed. Around 10,000 troops were killed in the invasion.

"You want to know how I know all this? You want to know how I spent my childhood? In a hotel room by myself, dreaming of my heroic dad and wondering how he died and who killed him and what he had been like and what was wrong with the world to keep a son from his father..." While he was speaking, Sally quietly reentered the room and slipped in beside Nick on the couch, putting her arm around him and clutching his hand.

"Allow me," Nick said when Stanley paused to collect himself. "Allow me to introduce you. This is Sally. Not at some latitude and longitude halfway around the world but right here. She's five foot five and a half in her stocking feet. I don't know how much she weighs because she won't tell me, but she says it's more than a loaf of bread and less than a bakery." At that she whispered, "Nicky!" "She's extremely ticklish, she can't stand polyester, and when she drives in to her job on the base she takes the long way around the lake because she loves spotting the deer. Every day when she comes home I sit at the table and we talk while she makes dinner. She's very close with her mother, Victoria, who lives in Smithville and still walks two miles every day at seventy-two. Sally makes one hell of a rib roast, and she makes me eat my vegetables. She won't go to see scary movies, but she's crazy for even the silliest comedy. Most of all she loves me. She's my angel, and she makes me happy."

"What's your point?" Stanley said.

"What's yours?"

Stanley wanted to drive the knife in farther, he wanted to make it hurt, he wanted to tell his dad about his unsatisfactory childhood, about how he obsessed over him and talked out loud to an imaginary version of him. Mailed letters that he fantasized being delivered in the world of the dead. He could have gone on for days, describing every miserable moment, and explaining how he lost himself in studying as a way of distracting his mind. But like Nick said, what was the point?

Stanley stood up and clenched his fists, trying to understand but failing to control his anger. "How could you?" he said. *"How could you?* You made a promise to her. You abandoned her, and you abandoned me. You're nothing but a scoundrel and a liar."

He turned away from them and wiped his eyes, then turned back. "You know, that was cowardly. The way you did it. Pretending to be enlisted. Sending a picture and writing 'Greetings from jolly old England' on it. You should have been honest with her and made a clean break, and saved us both a lot of pain."

Nick stood up too. "Stan. My son. In hindsight, you're right; I should have done things differently. I should have been honest with your mother. You want to not hurt people and then you end up hurting them more. I can't expect you to understand how I felt at that time. I was stubborn and probably not very bright, but the truth is simple and the truth is unavoidable: I fell in love with someone else. She gave me goose bumps. She gave me peace—

well, aside from both of us needing a thick skin because of all of the people we come across who don't like to see a white man and a black woman in love; aside from that, we've found peace together. She made me feel good about myself again when I had been feeling bad about myself for so long. Your mother and I had been having problems for some time. She became negative and critical and I wanted to live life. We were never a great match, in all honesty. I met Sally at the PX on the base, while I was going through basic training. She appeared like a gift to me and we fell in love at first sight. You don't want to hear that, but it's the truth. I don't know what you expected when you came here. I wish you hadn't suffered like you did. I wish things had been smoother for you. Like I said, I should have told the truth from day one, but I'm telling it now. I'm sorry."

Stanley threw himself into the chair so forcefully that it rocked back and fell forward again onto its front legs with a thump. "You fell in love with someone else? That's just wonderful. Fabulous. Fantastic!" He threw his arms in the air.

"What, you think you can pick and choose who you're going to be in love with? You think *you* get to decide the circumstances under which you're going to fall in love? Wake up, kid. You're all grown up now." Nick put a hand on his forehead and rubbed it in a pensive way that sent a shock through Stanley, recognizing the gesture in himself. "The fact is, you don't get to decide. Chance decides. Nature decides. I don't know who decides but I know one thing: It ain't you, son."

"I don't think I want you to call me that," Stanley said, and looked away.

Neither one of them said anything for a moment. Sally awkwardly straightened her dress over her thighs.

"Have you ever been in love?" Nick asked.

Stanley looked at his hands.

"I mean really in love?" Here Sally reached up and gave Nick's hand a squeeze.

"Yes. Yes, I have," Stanley said. He felt a hot wave of regret for having ruined things with Vera. It was an overwhelming sense of bitter futility.

"So what happened?" Sally asked brightly, leaning forward.

"Love wasn't meant for me."

Nick snorted and shook his head. "You're not very smart, are you?"

Stanley was stunned. He looked up at Nick. No one ever suggested that before. Of course he was smart. Wasn't he? On second thought, maybe his dad had something there. After all, would he be leading such a miserable life if he were?

Sally got up and returned with a little box. It was Nick's insulin shot, she explained.

"Yes," Nick said to Stanley. "I'm diabetic. It was diagnosed while I was in the service, and I was discharged before I even saw any action." Nick rolled up his sleeve as a matter of habit, without taking his eyes off his son, and as Sally administered the shot she reminded Stanley of Vera, the way she concentrated as she poured him a cup of tea, with the tip of her tongue just showing at the corner of her mouth.

"Here's what I think," Nick said as he rolled down his sleeve. "I certainly am not entitled to dispense fatherly wisdom, but for what it's worth, I think love is meant for you if you let it be. I also think some people are just meant for each other. Try as you might, there's nothing you can do about it."

"Well, that's one philosophy," Stanley said.

"Believe me, I tried."

"You tried? You couldn't have tried very hard. Mom was pregnant when you left."

"By the time I knew about it, I was already gone. Metaphorically speaking."

"Metaphorically?" Stanley stood up from the chair. "Well I'm not a metaphor. You want to know something? You were all I thought about as a boy. You want to know how I tried to distract myself? I read the fucking encyclopedia," he said, and let himself fall into the chair again.

"I'm sorry...Stanley. I really am. But I turned myself inside out during that time. I looked into my goddamn heart. And my heart only had one thing to say. I've thought about you. Believe me. I've thought about you a lot, all this time."

Sally delicately interjected. "He has, you know. He often talked about going to find you."

"I've sent money."

Stanley snorted. "Money," he said with derision.

"You are real. Very, very real." Nick got up and went to the chair Stanley was in and put a hand on his shoulder. "And I'm very, very sorry. I'm human. We make mistakes, you know, us humans." He knelt down and put his arms around him.

They stayed in that position for a drawn-out moment, Stanley sitting rigidly in the chair, his father kneeling with his arms around him. Sally quietly went off to check on the dog, and then Nick got up and paced the room. Stanley couldn't decide whether he should get up and leave and never come back, or if he should look into his own heart and seek a kinder resolution. Finally, Nick said, "You know what we should do? We should have a beer."

Stanley sat for a moment without moving, then rose to the

beckoning of Nick's outstretched arm and Sally's warm smile. The three of them went out to the back patio in time to catch the sunset, and together they began to go through all the beer in the house while the dog covered every inch of the patio with its restless paws. Nick grilled steaks and Sally made a big salad. Sally's laugh was a beautiful thing, full and heartfelt and always surprising even though you knew it was imminent, like lightning. And by the time he was shown to the tiny guest bedroom, Stanley was beginning to think about what at first seemed to be totally out of the question: forgiveness. Was it possible to forgive a father who had left his yet-to-be-born son? How could such a despicable act be pardoned? But then, what was the point in keeping anger on life support? He thought with deep regret about his own despicable acts. *Her* name kept announcing itself to him in a persistent whisper all throughout that day. He didn't know if he could forgive Nick, yet he hoped to be forgiven himself. He tossed in the bed thinking, Great, now I'm a hypocrite too. Stanley was searching for wisdom, and it felt as if the wise thing to do would be to add forgiveness to truth, and keep them both close for the rest of his life. He had exhausted his store of rage after all these years, and all that was left now was an emptied warehouse in his heart that longed to be of use again. In the morning, Nick and Sally invited him to stay the week, but he decided to leave because he didn't want Martha to worry and because his instincts told him a day was enough.

Nick took him for a drive, and at Stanley's request, he explained the messy details of his leaving—not being drafted when he thought he might be, then being encouraged to enlist by Greaper and the other hotel staff because, although Nick felt he had a responsibility to the hotel, it was more important for

him to do his duty for the country. Then it was on to basic training in Tennessee, and just as he was getting started came the
devastating discovery of the diabetes that chose then of all moments to reveal itself. Immediately after, in a state of despair, he
met Sally. Then came the decision to stay, the lies to Martha,
the move to Normandy. He told Stanley about his concierge job
in Nashville, and all the famous musicians he was acquainted
with. As Nick rambled on about the present, Stanley thought
about the big life decisions he made based on his father's deception, and that led to thoughts about the life decisions Vera made
based on his own deceptions. He wanted all to be forgiven; he
wanted the entire world to be one giant ball of happy forgiveness and contentment, but things were too complicated for that,
and for once, his mind felt small and inadequate to the task of
solving the puzzle before him.

When the car stopped in the driveway, something occurred to
him that he needed to know.

"Why MIA though?" Stanley asked. "Why didn't you have
Promise say you were dead, and spare her the anxiety?"

"That's a good question. Frankly, saying I was MIA felt right.
There was some honesty in it. Sorry if it upsets you, but it's the
truth. That's what this is all about, right?" He sighed and ran his
hand over the steering wheel of the parked car. "On a practical
level, if you die in battle the service starts paying death benefits
right away. Whereas if you're MIA, a period of time goes by where
they search for you. I needed time to get settled, find work, save a
little before I could start sending your mother checks."

Stanley just stared straight ahead.

"Promise knew an attorney," Nick began to explain. But then
stopped and said, "Was your mother ever skeptical? Did she...?"

"No. She's a trusting person. She trusted both of us."

Nick took his hand off the wheel and put it on Stanley's shoulder.

Stanley asked for the bus schedule, and after that they decided when they'd have to leave to get Stanley to the station. Nick peppered him with questions about his life. "How did you do in school? Did you go to college? What are you doing for a living?" Stanley didn't quite know how to answer these questions. But now, with The Truth as his mandate, at least there were no messy decisions to make. At first he held back, and only said that he messed up things. He could have gone to Harvard, as Martha wanted, but he chose to follow his own path, making crossword puzzles, working in libraries, tutoring, and teaching tennis. He wasn't a materialistic person; he preferred freedom. The next day, however, The Truth would not allow Vera to stay hidden. Tortured by the shame of it, he confessed what he had done. It started innocently enough, he said. It was part game, part desperate maneuver to launch himself into independence. It started out fun and flirtatious. He didn't know he was in love with her at the start. "Awfully oblivious for someone who's supposedly intelligent," Stanley said. "What an idiot I was."

"Beating yourself up won't do anyone any good," Nick said.

Gradually, Stanley continued, his feelings for her became obvious, but not until he had already pushed her too far to care anymore, and then—how?—she slipped away. He lost her.

He described the code she used to communicate with him. Vera was as good a constructor as he was, and more of a natural. He said he had just created some coded puzzles of his own to try to reach out to her. Sally, who slipped in beside Nick, was fascinated by this, and Nick suggested he keep trying with coded puzzles, but he also suggested, since Vera's goal was to get a PhD in math, that Stanley phone universities across the country asking for her. He could make a list and work his way through it over time, Nick said, contagious optimism in his expression. "What do you have to lose?"

"Well, Nick," he said. Despite whatever forgiveness might or might not come one day, he hadn't earned the right to be called Dad. "I suppose it's worth a try." But like his mother so many years before, he was closing the door on hope.

When Stanley got out of the car at the bus station, he stopped to buy all the papers from the boxes lined up at attention outside. Stanley had been publishing an enormous number of puzzles lately, and they were appearing scattershot all across the country, so just for kicks he flipped to the last page of the *Nashville Tennessean*. And there, next to an advertisement for Harvey's Department Store, was one of his very own puzzles, syndicated through the *Washington Post*. He turned quickly and found Nick still there in the idling car, smiling in his charismatic way with his arm hanging out the window. "Here," Stanley said, jogging back to the car. "Take this home and show it to Sally. It's one of mine."

CHAPTER FOURTEEN

August 1967

I'm sorry."
Stanley stood barefoot in the cold sand of Newport Beach with his shoes in his hand and his cuffs rolled up. It was uncharacteristically cold for August 1, dark rocky clouds looming overhead and the sand as glutinous as cold oatmeal. He had found Theodore Leviticus Wellington IV there, with his security retinue waiting by their cars along the roadside like mafiosi. Perhaps it wasn't necessary, but he had promised himself he would make amends with all the people he had lied to, and so, after a heartfelt letter of explanation and a phone call, Stanley finally convinced Mr. Wellington, through his secretary, to meet him there. He too was standing with his shoes in his hand and his cuffs rolled up. He stared out to sea with his back to Stanley.

"I want to apologize, man to man," Stanley called out over the wind.

Mr. Wellington said nothing, but half turned. He tilted his head, indicating that he was listening.

Stanley moved closer, until he was near enough to make

himself heard without shouting. "I was wrong to be dishonest with you. You were good to us—you and Mrs. Wellington both. I sent her a letter as well, saying that I'm sorry, but please convey my personal apology to her. I was wrong not to be straight with you from the beginning, especially considering the children."

Abruptly, Mr. Wellington said, "Yes, the children. How did you think this would affect them?"

After a moment's thought, Stanley replied, "I don't know."

I don't know. A laugh almost forced itself out of him. To not know, and to admit to not knowing! It felt as refreshing as if he had just jumped into the cold surf. The ocean didn't know and it went on being the ocean just the same. A quote about wisdom being the knowledge of one's own ignorance tried to step out onto the center stage of his thoughts, but that was just one more useless piece of knowing and he rejected it as he watched a seagull step across the sand. The seagull knew only how to be a seagull, but it was the world's expert on that one subject.

"That's what bothers me the most. Oh, I've been lied to," Mr. Wellington said with a cold laugh. "I can handle being deceived. I fight deception and thievery every day. Everyone wants a piece of what's mine. But to deceive my children? That I do not tolerate."

"You have every right to be angry about that." Stanley dug a foot into the sand. "It must have been confusing for them for Vera to suddenly be gone. It must have been difficult for you to explain. I thought about writing each of them a letter, but I wasn't sure if that would be appropriate."

"You don't have to bother with that," Mr. Wellington said. "You can try to fix this right now."

He turned and lifted his head in a gesture to the men at the cars. One of them opened a limousine door, and out sprang Theo and Thea, only a few months older than when Stanley last saw them but already looking different. They ran across the beach and threw their arms around him, smothering him and making it difficult for him to hold his balance in the sand. Mr. Wellington marched sternly back to his car, advancing the pudding-like bulk of his body across the beach with difficulty, as if dragging the chains of his holdings behind him, and as he passed by Stanley, he said, "Make things right with them, and you can consider yourself forgiven."

"Where's Vera?" Theo asked, and immediately his sister repeated the question.

"I don't know. Honestly, I wish I did."

"But we want to see her!" Thea said.

"Can we write to her?" Theo asked.

"You know, I want to see her even more than you do. But I haven't been able to find her."

"Oh," Theo said. "We miss her."

"Mrs. Olokoff is a meanie," Thea said.

"She's our new math teacher," Theo added.

Stanley took each of their hands in his. He looked them in the eyes one by one and said, "Theo. Thea. I have something to say to you. What I did was wrong."

Theo looked extremely grave. Thea said, "What did you do?"

"I lied. You see, a long time ago, I pretended to get married to Vera. For the gifts and ... well, it's complicated. You see, we had a wedding, but we didn't really get married ..."

"That's so silly!" Thea said, putting her hand over her mouth in the embarrassed way that young girls do.

Stanley knelt in the sand, to be on the same level with the children, and started over. "Do you know the story of Pinocchio?"

They nodded their heads.

"Okay. Tell me something. How does *my* nose look right now?"

Thea was puzzled. Theo said, "It looks fine."

"Really?" Stanley said. "Because to me it feels like it's about three feet long. Like this," he said, holding out his hand far from the end of his nose. The kids laughed.

Then he stopped and put on a serious expression and said, "Well, I was a big fat liar, just like Pinocchio. In the end, he became a real boy. And as for me, I'm trying to be a real man. And so that's why I'm here to say sorry. Even if you don't completely understand, that's okay."

The children looked at him with a mixture of sternness and puzzlement. They were unaccustomed to finding themselves on that side of an apology.

"I wish Vera was here too," Theo said.

Stanley looked up to the road and saw Mr. Wellington waiting by the side of the limousine.

"So do I, Theo."

Later that August, in Boston, Stanley spent a few days seeking a meeting with Chuck Reese, who proved to be a slippery man to pin down. He was either extremely busy or still angry about whatever fallout had come from the *Just Marrieds* episode. But when Stanley finally did get in to see him, Chuck was as jovial as ever. It turned out that he had no idea what Stanley was there to apologize for. No one had ever so much as glanced at the contracts Stanley and Vera signed using Socrates, and after Vera disappeared, everyone figured she did so out of sheer embarrassment from her taping of the television show. It turned out the network wasn't happy with the way it came out, the episode never even aired, and the check for their winnings had to be returned for lack of an addressee. Regardless, Stanley carried on with his mission of truth telling, laying out the whole sorry business for Chuck, who sat and listened with his hand on his chin, and when Stanley finished, went on about how they must make this into a "true crimes" special, or a game show about lies to give that CBS property *To Tell the Truth* a run for its money. Before Stanley left, he asked Chuck if he was forgiven, and Chuck threw up his hands and said, "I don't know what I'm forgiving, but, hey, all is forgiven!"

A few days later, in New York City, Stanley found the woman he was looking for, living in the wilds of SoHo under the name Abby Atherton. It took a little research in the newspaper archives at the New York Public Library and a bit of luck to hit upon her wedding announcement, but a quick look at the phone book revealed her address. Standing in front of the door of the old elevator that led up to her loft, Stanley expected—a slap in the face? A middle finger? He expected to meet a sour, disapproving person, the old Abby who hated everything. But this was a new Abby. Time's sleight of hand had worked its sorcery and produced a reverse image.

Abby Atherton loved cacti. She loved the windows of her loft and the strong morning light that poured in and helped her hundreds of plants big and small thrive. She loved the Rolling Stones. She loved Miles Davis. She loved big puffy bright-colored pillows.

She loved her husband, Tom, and all his good-natured friends who were always so much fun to have over. She loved painting. She loved sculpting even more, and couldn't stop talking about her work, showing Stanley every piece she came across in her happy bouncing tour, describing each one right down to individual brushstrokes. She told him she remembered how much she loved Vera. "How is Vera?"

As he was becoming accustomed to doing, Stanley described his whole sordid history, and apologized for hiding the truth and for breaking up her friendship with Vera. After he had gone on explaining so much that he was repeating himself, Abby waved him off. "I understand. I understand, believe me. In fact, you know what? I think it's fantastic. I love it!" She clapped her hands together, delighted with the subversion of it. They talked some more, and she told him she rarely drank wine anymore these days because she and Tom were going to have a baby. He gave her his warmest congratulations and a hug, and as he looked over her shoulder he noticed for the first time the monkey-themed wallpaper through an open door down the hall. He told her about his success with crosswords, and when he said he had dozens of puzzles published in the *Times*, she said, "Get outta town!" and gave him a shove that tipped him over. The conversation eventually came around to Vera again, and Stanley told her he thought Vera was working on a PhD in math, but he wasn't sure. When Abby asked him how he felt about her, it wasn't hard for him to speak The Truth. "The same as I ever have, only more so. If I could find her I would tell her."

When he finally got up to leave, he asked her, "So. Are we okay? Am I, you know?"

"Yeah, we're okay. It's good. It's cool."

"I think I need to hear a certain word that rhymes with 'driven.' "

"Okay," she laughed. "Right. You're forgiven."

When he returned to Washington, Stanley knew exactly where to find the last person on his list. Sitting in Greaper's office across the desk from him and delivering his confession, Stanley saw him as if for the first time. He realized that what he once sensed as coldness was merely the man's innate awkwardness. He was just that kind of man, perpetually confused and worrying his hands and forever trying to catch up with the present, which was always a few steps ahead of him, edging away around the next corner.

Surprisingly, Greaper couldn't keep from laughing at the details of the story, from the silliness of faking a wedding to the absurdity of his and Vera's pretending to be a married couple on a national television show. In fact, he got to laughing so hard that tears streamed down his cheeks. Stanley forged on, telling him of his plan to pay him back for the expense of the wedding and the cash gift he gave them, as soon as he could get the money together, which Greaper begged him not to do. Stanley insisted, but said he did have one favor to ask. Before granting Stanley his forgiveness, Greaper put on a serious expression for the first time and asked about Vera. Stanley told him exactly how he felt about her, and that he bitterly regretted what happened between them, and that it was too late to fix things now. Besides, he didn't know where she was.

"Nonsense," the man said. "I forgive you. Now go find Vera, if not for your sake then for mine."

*   *   *

Back in the suite, his mother was not in her chair as usual, but standing in front of the window looking down on Pennsylvania Avenue. "How did it go?" she asked. Of course, she now knew Stanley's story—with the exception of the part about Nick; they had agreed not to tell her for now—and closely followed his apologies.

"Fine. You know, I think he really is a very decent man after all," he said.

"It took you all these years to see that? And you call yourself smart. I ought to telephone the *New York Times* and tell them they have a fool for a puzzle maker."

Martha, despite the wreckage of her plans for his future, which now lay smashed and forgotten behind them, was actually quite thrilled with where he'd ended up. Chances are, the Lincoln Bedroom wasn't all that comfortable anyway. She did not ask him about Vera. She knew how he felt about her. She also knew he was searching for her and if there was any news he would tell her.

Having apologized to everyone on his list, Stanley sat down at his old desk in his old room in the suite where he had spent so many hours packing his head with knowledge, to take care of one more thing.

Dear Nick,

I want to set the record straight. I'm afraid when I left Tennessee, I left you with the impression that my wrongdoing was somehow connected to yours. That somehow your deception led to mine. But I want to say that I alone bear responsibility for my actions. You were as much a part of my mistakes as I was of yours. That is, no part.

I make my own decisions, and I accept the consequences for myself alone. That's all for now. Give my best to Sally.

  Love,

  Stanley

He wrote a real address on the envelope, affixed a real stamp, said good-bye for the time being to Martha, and left to go to the mailbox and then on to New York City.

CHAPTER FIFTEEN

Stanley cradled the receiver of his telephone under his chin while he waited to be connected.

"Good afternoon," said a woman's voice on the other end. "Tulane University, Department of Mathematics. How may I help you?"

"Good afternoon," Stanley said. "I'm looking for Professor Vera Baxter. Would you know if she's available?"

After a momentary silence, the voice answered, "I...I don't know of anyone by that name in this department. Are you sure..."

"I'm sorry, I was mistaken. Thank you," he said, and hung up the phone with a sigh, a sound that was very common with him these days.

In the six years after he discovered Nick living as comfortably as a cat with Sally in Normandy, Tennessee, Stanley set to work in earnest on making a career for himself in the crossword puzzle business. Over the years, he had created some of the most highly admired puzzles and introduced more creativity to the practice than was ever seen before. When the serious crossworders spread around the country got together to talk, his name always came up. And so, when the persnickety old editor of the *New York Times* puzzle page didn't show up to work one day, having collapsed on the linoleum floor of his Upper East Side kitchen beside a broken coffee cup, Stanley's was the name most frequently uttered as possible successor. He was young, he had worlds of potential, and the editorial board made a quick and easy decision. They wanted to infuse fun and creativity into the puzzles, which had been too sedate for too long, and he was the best man for the job.

The day he got the call might have been the best day of his life, if it hadn't been such a lonely one. He longed to share the news with Vera. It had been six years since he'd last seen her, walking out of the Wellingtons' kitchen, her dark hair fallen around her downcast eyes, her beautiful ivory face luminous as lamplight. He'd been taking Nick's advice and was making his way through a list of all the universities in America, calling their mathematics departments from his office in the *Times* building and asking if a Vera Baxter was on their staff. Every week, he crossed off another one from the list. So far, no luck. For all he knew, she could be teaching in Reykjavík. For all he knew, she might not be employed at all in mathematics. Maybe she had gone to France and become a translator. Where, who, and what was Vera today? All possible lives lay at the feet of his imagination.

Charlatan. C-H-A-R-L-A-T-A-N. Charlatan. There was a billboard Vera passed every morning on her way in to the university that advertised the sharp-edged '74 Chevrolets of an auto dealership on Charlotte Lane, with an aerial shot of shiny glazed rectangles like Chiclets, and in the doubting, hazy mindscape of her early mornings, when the thick, deep ruminations of night have not yet been cleared away, that old word kept making its footprints, letter by letter, through her thoughts. Was she really living, or was she only imitating life?

Vera had made a terrible mistake. Possibly to prove to herself that she was free to love whomever she pleased, or possibly because she was impulsive like that and goddamn it, it was her life after all, she had gotten married. His name was David Watson. She met him in a hardware store.

There wasn't anything wrong with David. In fact, he was tailor-made for her. He was a tenured professor of economics at the university, liked by the students for his entertaining lectures. He was six feet tall, a hundred and eighty pounds, and five mornings a week he jogged three miles at sunrise and then ate a bowl of oatmeal. He was pleasant enough, attractive enough, kind, sensible, and neat enough, and occasionally he made her laugh.

He gave her the biggest engagement ring she had ever seen, a genuine diamond, probably a very enviable prize to those who cared about that kind of thing. Vivian and Sonny came out for the ceremony. True to his word, Sonny never mentioned Stanley, and she didn't ask. There was absolutely nothing exceptional about the ceremony, which was the way she wanted it. The reception was held at the University Club, and Vera spent the evening dutifully making her way from table to table on David's arm while the whole time she spun out a very unlikely hypothesis involving hyperbolic 3-manifold groups. Neither of them wanted anything to do with the mundane details of the thing; they agreed on the silliness of wedding customs. The only thing she cared about was that their wedding song was not "I Love How You Love Me."

David moved into Vera's bungalow and they settled into a routine. Workaday life took command of everything. Dinner became a larger and larger entity. Often it was the only time they got to spend together during the day, so it always had to be something. Vera missed the way she used to putter through the evening hours in her own time, very often skipping dinner entirely or enjoying strange meals at strange times, like half a head of iceberg lettuce and a dish of cashews at ten p.m., or a late lunch at four o'clock and then a bowl of corn flakes with half and half in bed with her notepad. David flew to a conference in Montreal for a week, and when he came back he took her to see a movie, and when they came home at midnight he carefully folded his sweater and hung his pants on their hanger and fell into bed while she stayed up to watch *Bride of Frankenstein* on *The Late Late Show*. During that summer, when she didn't have to be at the university, she sat on the couch working problems in her notebook as the Watergate hearings droned on in the background, and occasionally when she looked up at the TV it felt for a moment as if committee chairman Sam Ervin was probing not John Dean's questionable actions and inactions, but her own.

In the fall, David installed storm windows for those half dozen or so that had none, and when he was away one Saturday she took them off again because she liked to have fresh air flowing even in the wintertime. For Christmas, they went to visit his family in Pennsylvania, a trip that felt to Vera like going to see some little-known civilization hidden in a shadowy nether region of the globe. She found his parents' house claustrophobic in the extreme and went for walks in the woods with her notepad. On the plane home they both worked in silence. His breath next to her was a little less than perfect. When she was unpacking her clothes and putting away things, and David was already in the den working up his next lecture, her hand went to the candy tin buried beneath her underwear and opened it and felt, only for a nervous moment, the cheap engagement ring and the pawnshop wedding band she kept there. She smiled to herself as she felt the minuscule diamond, remembering the moment in the empty conference room at the Marriott when Sss-paghetti gave it to her. The wedding band felt strangely warm, as if she had just taken it off. She didn't dare slip it onto a finger for fear of the power it may have over her.

They rang in 1974 at the University Club with a bunch of middle-aged, quizzical, and whiskery academics stuffed into formal wear, bringing to mind taxidermy. "You Are the Sunshine of My Life" played in the background and felt vaguely critical. Vera drank far too much champagne with the math people on one side of the room while David did the same with the economics people on the other.

Stanley knew it was an unhealthy obsession, yet he never gave up looking for Vera in the papers day after day, be it a Monday or a Sunday, Thursday or Tuesday, holidays, voting day, the Fourth of July or days of national crisis. He would get his newspapers delivered to his office and turn immediately to the puzzle page. And then over coffee, he would dispatch each puzzle in pen. If for some reason a paper didn't arrive, perhaps due to a smothering snowstorm, he would get it by any means necessary, putting on his coat and scarf and hat and gloves and setting out to track it down.

One particularly unremarkable morning of drizzle in the relentless march of the Vera-less days of his life, he had a stack of puzzles to go through and a decision to make for the next Sunday puzzle on the editorial calendar. As a small gift to himself, he allowed himself to choose his own puzzle. It was titled "Vacancy," and its theme was hotels. It was a call to her, one of his monthly coded messages out into the void for Vera Baxter. He would place it in the June 6 edition, and like all his puzzles, it would be syndicated out across the country. He forgot that day was the anniversary of D-day, something he never would have failed to remember before finding Nick. Millions of people would attempt to solve it. Perhaps it would find its way to her. Rather than bury a clue in the puzzle as to where she might find him, he did something this time that felt like cheating, and placed the word *inquiries* and his phone number directly below the puzzle in mouse type. The week after this coded puzzle came out, he was agitated, unable to focus. The phone on his desk was an impossible little savage that refused to jangle out with a call from her when he tried to entice it to do so by staring at it, and instead startled him at his most concentrated moments with useless calls from fact-checkers or bookkeeping or the like. And then of course it also began to ring mercilessly with inquiries from solvers from Anchorage to the Florida Keys wanting hints at some of the puzzle's answers. It turned out to be an unexpected joy to speak to his loyal solvers. But there was no call from the one person whom all those millions of sheets of newsprint were sent out to find. The spaces he created for Vera to occupy remained vacant.

In the spring, the weather in Nebraska changed quickly and new life emerged like in a pop-up book, and Vera and David began to snap at each other. Vera was at fault. She was the one who seemed to have reached the bottom of her patience, scraping at the last of what was once a very easygoing style. She began to secretly covet those nights when David had to stay late on campus for some meeting or other, traipsing around the house freely in her underwear and then retreating to bed, where she illicitly ate crackers and drank grape juice and at her leisure read a crime novel. Sometimes she pretended to be asleep when the lights of his car set fire to the window shade.

Sex with him had become a daunting proposition, like a game of croquet. It might be fun at some point in the game if she got to thwack her opponent across the lawn, but in general it required too much effort to put the whole thing in gear and she began to grow bored with his style of play, aggressively gunning for her wicket, and with the way he almost seemed to gloat over her when he achieved victory. She began to see that not only did she not love him, she didn't even like him very much. He was, upon further reflection, not all that easy on the eyes. He was as useful and reliable as a butter knife, and just as dull.

The divorce was quick and painless. It went as smoothly as she imagined those things could possibly go. He remained stone-faced throughout, but cordial, as if a stranger had spilled something on his best clothes and he was pretending not to mind. She remained matter-of-fact. There were no children to consider and money matters were simple. She kept her house, they split the few things they had bought together, and they ended all financial ties with neither side owing the other anything. It felt to Vera a bit like she was going to court to evict a guest who had come to stay at her bed and breakfast and refused to leave. It was 1974, she was twenty-nine years old, and this was what her life had come to. When the movers finally packed the last of his things and he walked out holding a lamp in his hand, and they exchanged goodbyes as friends, she closed the door with a sense of relief that the squatter who had tried to presume to make himself at home in her heart had finally taken his things and gone. She threw the bolt on the door.

A few days later, she stopped by his office and returned the engagement ring to him, and on another day, as she was hurrying to campus, where her students were waiting for her in a lecture hall, she reached into her pocket, took out the silver wedding band David slipped on her finger a year earlier, and tossed it into a stream.

After weeks went by with no miracle resulting from Stanley's message to the universe, he took one of his frequent weekend trips on Amtrak to visit his mother in DC. She brought up his job in conversation all the time, so much so that it became something of an embarrassment. She told every last soul in the hotel. She told waitresses at restaurants. Yes, she had begun to visit restaurants. She had begun to leave the suite. She purchased an outfit via mail order from the Sears catalogue, so she could leave the building in something other than pajamas and a robe, and after Stanley found out about that, he took her to Garfinckel's and in one long and exhausting Saturday bought her a starter wardrobe of dresses, skirts, tops, pants, shoes, a hat, stockings, a sweater, and a camel hair coat.

As he was about to leave the suite to return to New York, she straightened his collar for him and said, "You know, I've been thinking. I'm going to move."

"You're leaving the Hawthorne?" Impossible. She had lived there her whole adult life. She had become so entrenched in the suite, like a gastropod in its shell, that it seemed almost against the laws of nature for her to change location.

"Yes. I was thinking of coming up to New York. You're all I've got, you know. And Sonny's there too now."

Of course. It made perfect sense, now that she seemed to be emerging from her anthropophobia at long last. "Well," he said. "Sure. Definitely. Mom, I'll find you a place and I'll take care of the rent." He was doing well now, making reasonable money not only in his job but also from his book of puzzles on the market. Besides, he lived frugally and was uncomfortable spending money on himself, so he could afford to take care of his mother.

"Those checks from the military won't be coming forever, you know," he said to her. Since first discussing it with Nick down in Tennessee, Stanley had a couple more discussions with him about whether to tell Martha about his existence. It still seemed un-necessarily cruel to both of them to tell her, but yet it seemed equally cruel to remain silent. Although Stanley was a convert to The Truth, and initially was inclined to tell her, he realized that it would be more mature not to. It would only hurt her and cre-ate pain in her life, which was only just getting healthy. One day when the moment was right perhaps she would find out that Nick had not gone missing in World War II but had in fact gone miss-ing in a very different kind of conflict. But let it be at a later date when she could better handle it.

In the quiet of the suite at the Hawthorne, Stanley and his mother talked over the idea of moving—they would find her a nice one-bedroom near Riverside Park, where she could take the walks that were invigorating her recently. Stanley looked around wistfully at the surroundings that had been the theater of their lives for so many years. The kitchenette; the little round table at which Stanley had fed himself both physically and intellec-tually; the moss-colored armchair with its hollowed-out cushion and threadbare arms, which had picked the pocket of Martha's years and which he would be so glad to see her leave behind that he rather wished he could throw it out the window. On his way back to New York, bumped about by the movements of the train, his thoughts of his mother eventually led him to Vivian. He looked at the note on which Martha had written Sonny and Vivian's New York address, and he resolved that as soon as he got back to the city he would pay them a visit too.

Vivian and Sonny lived in a beautiful apartment on Twenty-Second Street on the West Side. It was an expensive place in an intricately detailed old building, but they could afford it. Vivian had done well in her career, once she finally attained her well-earned role on the sales force, bringing in a good salary and commission, and now that she had achieved what she had set out to achieve, she threw over all the caution by which she had governed her life. She stopped living as if she were paying down the principle that occupying an existence required, and was now enjoying her life as if she had only just taken ownership of it. Sonny, indulging in an early retirement from the Hawthorne, had also managed to build up a strong savings account over his years of dedicated service to the hotel. The apartment was a place of good cheer and elegant design. Spending time there, one felt optimistic and pleased with one's general outlook on life. The feeling of visiting there reminded him of Nick and Sally's place, different though the two homes were. Vivian and Sonny's apartment was done with incredible taste and forethought, while his father's house in Tennessee, a mismatched slapdash place of happy existence, had as interior designer the momentary impulses of daily life.

For good measure, Stanley apologized to Vivian and Sonny for making a mess of things and for lying to them all for so long. He had already done so with incredible thoroughness before, over the phone, begging their pardon as if his life depended on it. There in the apartment on Twenty-Second Street, Vivian waved him off, having long ago forgiven him and come to terms with it. "Please, not that old sad song again," she said. Sonny said, "Oh for goodness' sake, stop." He had not only quit smoking but had quit cursing too, for the most part.

"I would like to ask you a favor, although I don't deserve it," Stanley said.

"I'm not going to tell you where Vera is, if that's what you want," Vivian said. "You know that I made a promise."

Stanley put his hands in his pockets and looked at the floor. He looked up at her and smiled. "A hint? One hint couldn't hurt."

Vivian looked into the distance, as if she were contemplating an entirely different subject. "How's your father?" she asked. She knew, from Sonny, that he had found Nick and that they saw each other from time to time.

"My father is well. I visited him this past Thanksgiving."

"Funny that all those years you thought he died in Normandy," she said.

"Yeah. Funny," Stanley replied ironically.

"What was the code name of that beach they attacked again? The one with the American name?"

"Omaha."

"Omaha, right. Well, I have one or two more deals to finish— conquests, Sonny calls them," she said, wrapping her arm around him, "and then I'm going to take an early retirement as well. I'm looking forward to just sitting around the house with this character."

Sonny gave her a playful squeeze, and it struck Stanley that just as his mother was emerging from her domestic retreat, Vivian was doing just the opposite.

On his way back uptown, with the subway car tossing him side to side, he tried to figure out what it was in the conversation they just had that was pricking him. He recalled Vivian's mention of the Normandy invasion. He saw her mouth making a circle and pronouncing "Omaha." It was an odd thing for her to bring up. Of course. That's what it was: She gave him a clue.

He arrived at work early Monday morning and went straight to the shelf for the directory of American colleges and universities he had purchased. Omaha. The University of Nebraska at Omaha. That had to be the one. In his weekly calls to mathematics departments, he was working his way west and had only just gotten across the Mississippi.

Nevertheless, he didn't call right away. He waited. He was nervous. What would he say to her? How would she respond? He puttered around his Upper West Side apartment instead of calling. At work, he discovered all sorts of reasons to make his way around the *Times* building to see various people with whom he had unfinished business. He made puzzles. He solved puzzles. He corresponded with his contributors, writing some of them peculiarly long letters of encouragement and congeniality. At last, at his desk at work, he picked up the black telephone receiver, heavy in his hand, and with trembling fingers, dialed the number. He was told there was no Vera Baxter working there. He put down the phone. He was sure it had been a clue. It had to have been. Perhaps... He took out an atlas and saw that Lincoln was roughly thirty miles away. She could be living in Omaha and commuting to Lincoln. He looked up the university there and was reassured by the sense that, from the larger entry in his directory of universities, it seemed to be a more prominent school. He dialed the number and was transferred to the department secretary.

"University of Nebraska School of Mathematics, please hold," the secretary said.

His throat was dry and he felt like a fool. He was on hold for several minutes, and toyed with a puzzle as he waited, although he couldn't concentrate and everywhere he looked in the grid he imagined he saw her name filling the squares.

"Hello, how can I help you?" the secretary asked when she finally returned.

He stumbled through the lines he had planned out. "Yes. I'm Stan...My name is Stanley and I'm looking for a friend. Is there...Do you happen to have a Vera Baxter in your department?"

"Vera..." she repeated absentmindedly. It sounded as if she was occupied with some other task at the same time.

"Any Vera at all...?"

"Oh, Vera! Yes, we have a Vera. Professor Baxter."

"Can you connect me to her?"

"I'm sorry, sir, it's the end of the semester, and I'm sad to say that as of today she no longer works here. In fact, we just had her going-away party a few days ago."

"Can you tell me where she's going? Is there a forwarding address?" he asked rather frantically.

"I'm sorry, sir, I'm not at liberty to divulge that information."

"*Please.*"

"I'm sorry, sir, rules are rules."

Desperate for some way to keep her on the line, some way to

dig out the essential information he *must have*, he thought quickly for a moment and blurted out, "But you must tell me. I'm in love with her."

With a laugh, the secretary replied, "Isn't everyone?" and hung up.

CHAPTER SIXTEEN

Vera sat in her raven-black '67 Ford Mustang with the radio off, silent and thoughtful, tearing down I-80 with the engine making a constant steady tone of complaint that coincided with her frame of mind. She had had more than enough of Nebraska. The day the primitive movers came and roughly stuffed everything of hers into their truck was ferociously windy. The wind blasted from the west, combing down the treetops and tearing out garden beds and, with a laugh, chucking garbage bins across the state. It plucked letters out of the hands of mail carriers, and sent cans and bottles into Iowa and plastic bags into outer space. It felt to Vera as if the forces of nature and the very will of the universe wanted her out of there too, and she gladly acquiesced, muscling herself into her car and revving the engine and following the wind in the direction of New York City, where a job at Columbia University would be waiting for her in the coming fall.

"So that's it then," Stanley said to himself, reluctant to set down the telephone receiver. She was gone. He had come so close, the distance between them nothing more than a string of ragged electrons buzzing through a telephone line. She had been teaching in Lincoln and now, once again, she could be anywhere. He almost had a hold on her and then she slipped away again, as if her life was inked by her magic pen, Socrates. He saw her disappearing: translucent, a fog, cellophane, gone. He went through the day mechanically. There was no joy in it. And then again the next day. And the next. Each damn day an inferior copy of the one before. His job felt suddenly preposterous. Cobbling together inconsequential little quizzes for desperately bored people was a simpleton's game. What an embarrassing occupation for a grown man. On his way out of his office for a lunch he didn't feel hungry for, on the third day after the phone call, he passed an open puzzle from the *Los Angeles Times* and as a matter of course stopped to dispatch it standing up. Nothing.

He went to the disgusting little diner on Forty-Fifth and Ninth and sat in the humid corner booth that felt like a world apart, with its steamed-up window and waitress who left you with the same look of indifference whether you ordered food and didn't touch it or tore mechanically through crossword puzzles over a bowl of tomato soup. He went on an adventure of the imagination, seeing himself and Vera as a shrunken old couple under the dominion of a deep weathered love, happily playing cribbage on the porch of a Victorian house in a small town as the Fourth of July parade passed by. It was a bitter vision that he blinked away. The *Times* lay on the table in front of him, open to an item about a girl who just won the forty-seventh annual bee spelling *hydrophyte*, a plant that grows in water. Feeling entirely underwater himself, he ordered a bowl of soup, and while he waited for it to cool he took a dollar from his wallet and put it on the table and got up and walked back to the office, where the rest of the day passed just as emptily.

Oh God, he thought, here comes the night. When he felt crushed by the night and at his most desperate, alone in the isolating hours, when life itself with its people and activity seemed to be celestially remote from him and at its most forbidden, he tried to treat the condition by reducing his experience of life to the simplest of things: Lemons are tart. Salt is good on food. An old cotton shirt feels nice. If you're cold, put on a sweater. He moved slowly and deliberately. Every night at eleven p.m. he brushed his teeth. Looking in the mirror he repeated what he often said to himself: Fate will never intervene on your behalf. The universe will not come to your rescue. You are yours and yours alone to save. The work is yours to do.

Still the exhaustive power of the night made his limbs feel heavy and his head cloudy. He found himself most comfortable in the aisles of 24-hour grocery stores, the Gristedes on Sixty-Eighth and Broadway, with its mechanical noises and the benedictive issuance of the fluorescent lights. Looking into the windows of the freezer section, he saw the little frozen toastlets that mothers are meant to heat up for their children. The quick frozen meals. The veggies in bags. Things one person might make for another. He would cook for Vera if she lived in his home with him. He would take classes at the culinary institute. He would learn to flip the contents of a sauté pan into the air without a care in the world while he laughed with her and she sipped from a goblet of wine.

Those ghostly midnight aisles fed his imagination with the poison of yearning. He could peer into wonderful little scenes of domesticity rich with activity. The focus was so clear that he could even see the small white thread that he would pull off her

black cardigan for her. He heard ridiculously trivial bits of talk—
Where did I put my keys? Oh, not again, why are you always losing your keys?—followed by laughter. Paradoxically, it was the
mundane things that formed the richness of existence, if you existed, which he felt he didn't, an insubstantial reflection in the
freezer windows and nothing more. He watched her come to life
as if she too were reflected in the glass doors of the frozen section.
He could half believe that if he turned to the side, there she would
be, reaching for his hand.

On his way home, he passed a record shop that was open late.
His eye scanned the window display, and just as he was almost
beyond the shop window and on to the next one, he stopped and
walked a few steps back. There, in a corner of the window, was
that 45 from the past with the red-and-black label that was so familiar. He let down his guard and allowed himself to enter the
shop, knowing full well it was an invitation to wallow in self-pity,
something he normally was strong enough to stop himself from
doing.

Back in his apartment, the 45 popped and sputtered on his
turntable. The cupcake voice of Priscilla Paris was a ghost from
his past life, a sinister sound of undoing that snaked into his head
as he stared at the hypnotic adapter in the center of the record.
But he didn't allow it to go very far. When he heard the lyric
And when I'm away from you, it was too much to bear and he tore
the needle off the record, poured a quick glass of Scotch, drank it
down, and went to bed.

The next day was a Saturday, so he had the whole expanse of
the day before him to waste away as he pleased. He would go
someplace where there were people, he decided. Maybe he'd call a
friend and go have lunch. He showered and got dressed and then

opened the door and retrieved the papers. He had arranged for the large news vendor down on Broadway and Fifty-Eighth to deliver him all the various papers he needed on the weekends, when he wasn't in the office to receive them. The *Times*, the *Globe*, the *Inquirer*, the *Journal*, the *LA Times* and the *Tribune*. Those were the only papers with original crosswords anymore. All the others were now running only syndicated ones. Like he always did on Saturdays, he drank his coffee and dispatched the puzzles one by one before heading out for a walk in the park or down Columbus Avenue to the café that had good croissants.

First he had a quick look at his own page in the *Times*, giving it a once-over to make sure everything was okay. Then he picked up the *Globe*. The headline read, "Judge Hints Nixon Risks Being Cited for Contempt." He looked out the window as he flipped to the puzzle page. It was a warm June morning, the eighth to be precise, and he got up to open the window while he glanced over the grid. One across: First first lady. MARTHA. Two across: Beer or bearer. PORTER. He sat back in his chair and wondered if maybe he should occupy himself by walking Broadway from the northern tip of Manhattan all the way down its entire length to Battery Park. He would be sure to encounter lots of humanity if he did that. How long would it take? Twenty minutes a mile times, oh, maybe seven miles? He scribbled in the answer to 11 across, DIAMOND. He looked at 12 down: Aloe ____. Seven times twenty, so about two and a half hours, but longer than that because he would take his time and stop often. He looked at the clues for the words crossing VERA. Nine across: Toolmaker. The answer had seven letters. Instantly he thought, Mankind, of course, the only animal that makes tools. But the third letter, not the second one, had to be an "A" to cross the "A" in Vera. Then it hit him. STANLEY. He launched himself out of the chair.

Vera stood near the information booth in the main concourse of Grand Central Station and looked up again at the clock. Had she made the meeting time too early? Was he a late sleeper on the weekends? Perhaps he did the puzzles in the afternoon. Or had he stopped doing the *Boston Globe* puzzle every day? It saddened her to realize how little she knew about his life. The sign next to her read INFORMATION. That was what she wanted. What if she were to go to the woman behind the counter and ask her what his habits were. "Excuse me. At what time does Stanley Owens of New York City do his crossword puzzles on Saturday mornings, if indeed he does still do them?" And she pictured the lady responding most politely, as if it were a perfectly normal question to ask, "I'm afraid I don't have that information at hand. You'll have to ask the universe." But the universe wouldn't come to her rescue. It was up to her. She looked up at the clock again and waited, checking each of the arched entryways through which people were hurrying who were not Stanley.

He had never done a crossword faster in his life. His mind was lucid and articulate and his fingers were nimble enough to carry out its commands. He did it standing up. The pen was a blur. All the hints were there filling the empty spaces, empty spaces he felt as if he had been carrying around with him all his life. STUDY, HAWTHORNE, SONNY, HARVARD, BEE, WASHINGTON, NEWPORT, NUPTIALS... He discovered the theme: three-word phrases in which the first and last words were replaced with homonyms.

TEEFORTOO
WONFORAWL
HEARANDTHEIR
WHOLEINWON

And finally, there was a message running boldly across the center of the puzzle, wearing the clothes of that familiar voice as if
it were coming directly from Vera's lips: EYEFORGIVEYEW. At
this he paused for a moment while the world came to a stop, and
blinked at the puzzle, and blinked again while the seconds ticked
away, and he stored away the feeling that he would go back to
later again and again to take full pleasure in.

Also near the center of the puzzle he found the critical in-
tersection of time and place, GRANDCENTRAL crossing
HIGHNOON. He didn't know what day she might have intended but it would make sense for it to be the day the puzzle
came out. He looked at his watch. It had stopped. He ran to
the kitchen and checked the little lime-green stove clock. Eleven
forty-five. He lunged for his clothes and threw them on. The zip-
per of his pants got stuck. A button jumped off his shirt. One of
his shoelaces knotted itself fiercely so he threw aside the shoe and
shoved that foot into a loafer. The knob on his front door refused
to work properly and he had to slam it several times to get it to
stay shut. He lived on the fifth floor but rather than mess with the
ancient elevator he gambled on the stairs being quicker. On the
fourth-floor landing was a very old neighbor, Mrs. Kupke, fussing with her little dog, and the two of them were blocking the
way down. She glanced up at him and explained that she had just
come from the veterinarian and the wrapping and splint on her
dog's leg had come loose. She held the pieces in her small hand

with its skin as thin as tissue paper. Stanley stopped to rewrap the leg and said to come see him if she needed any more help.

Just as he finished, the elevator came down from above and the doors opened with their catastrophic clatter. He lunged for it and squeezed himself in between two other people. It was one of those sometimes charming, sometimes not so charming old accordion metal gate numbers, as small and rickety and slow as Mrs. Kupke herself, and equally determined. It took forever to begin to move, and then when it did, it shrieked. Ever so slowly it began to carry him down.

Just as Stanley was about to ask the young woman next to him the time, the elevator let out a soft, exhausted groan, lurched, and bounced a bit before coming to a full stop. Stanley and the young woman and the third passenger, a dapper elderly gent, looked at each other. The young woman pressed the buttons to no effect. There was no super in the building and the landlord was rarely to be found; it could be a long time before help came. When Stanley tried to flip the emergency switch, it broke off, leaving a tiny puff of red Bakelite dust. The young woman said, "Maybe this is something," tugged at a metal panel, and it sprang off. She leaned forward and peered at the jerry-rigged wires and what-not inside. Stanley knew the landlord to be a do-it-yourself type with a dangerous interest in chemistry and mechanical engineering. She poked around. "There's a tab here that says 'emergency access,'" she said over her shoulder. She read aloud: "Enter the passcode." She squinted at the handwriting penciled on a sticker, while Stanley and the other gentleman looked over her shoulder. "It says here, 'restart passcode.' There's a question that seems to be a hint, or a reminder. Does anyone..." She squinted again at what was written there. "Does anyone know..."—she looked up at the two of them, already smirking at the futility of it—"Does anyone know the atomic mass of boron?"

Out in front of his building, Stanley waved frantically for a cab. "Grand Central," he said to the driver, "as fast as you can go, please." The clock in the taxi read 12:05. He told himself that Vera was a patient person. Certainly she would wait. Wouldn't she? He drummed on the seat with his fingers. "Get out of the way!" he said under his breath to an oblivious jaywalker.

Vera looked up at the four-faced clock on top of the information booth. Twelve fifteen. He wasn't going to show after all. If he saw her message, and if he still loved her—and she thought he did because she had been doing the *Times* puzzle every day, she knew he was the editor, and she had seen and let pass some coded messages from him as recently as three months ago—he would not arrive late to such an important rendezvous. But perhaps he had given up. Or found another interest. Another woman. Or stopped caring. In the past it was easy for her to believe what she wanted to believe, but no more. She was cured of that. Not only the lessons of her life but also her mathematical study had imposed a rigorous pragmatism upon her. But far within, in the closet of her heart, was the girl she used to be, who once stood bravely on a stage and dreamed of being a champion. She had to believe that there was still a championship that was hers for the taking.

Then she saw him. Dashing into the great hall wearing two different shoes, with his shirttails flying and a frantic set of emotions playing across his face. When he saw her he smiled, stopped, and walked over to her, the sea of bodies parting for them as if every last bystander were in collusion with the forces that brought them together. There was his easygoing self again, the Stanley she met at the Hawthorne Hotel in 1960 who was nervous but possessed of himself and smart beyond his years. He stopped in front of her and looked at her with the innocence of a boy.

In Stanley's eyes, Vera was still an apparition. A spectral reconstitution of a dream that had once been real. She wore a black dress cut like a thunderbolt and her long black hair framed her supernaturally pale face. An impossible beauty. Catching sight of all those features again in one real, touchable place was the greatest relief he could possibly imagine.

"Hi, my name's Stanley," he said, somewhat out of breath and as nervous as if he were asking her to the prom.

"I'm Vera," she replied, with a smile that illuminated the rest of his life.

"A pleasure to make your acquaintance," he said.

She looked down at the ground beneath his feet while she got control of a burst of giddiness that spread across her face. She took her time. There was nothing but time now. She took a deep breath and let the import of the moment fill her. Then she looked up, caught hold of his eyes with hers, and said, "Tell me something good and true."

*   *   *

They lived together in a beautifully restored, turn-of-the-century West Village apartment, on the top floor, with a picturesque artist's skylight angling overhead. The kind of apartment everyone is aware exists, but no one has ever actually lived in. There under the skylight, or in front of the fireplace burning its bodega-bought logs, they read the paper and did the crosswords together, year after year, Stanley on the love seat with Vera's head in his lap, or Vera on the Eames chair and Stanley on the floor with his head between her knees and his toes hot in front of the fire. He read the arts section; she read the international news. Then he picked up the book review and she took the arts section from his other hand, and it went like that in a circular fashion.

They made up all sorts of terms of endearment for each other. She called him Mr. Know-It-All. He called her Fruitcake. They called each other the names of a wide variety of baked goods. She called him Baby. He called her Beautiful. They took classes together at the culinary institute and his specialty became bouillabaisse, which became her favorite dish, and her specialty became risotto, which became his. Every time he opened his mouth to spout out his knowledge of some esoteric tidbit they came across in the priceless humdrum of their daily living, she put her forefinger to his lips and stopped him by planting a kiss there. From time to time he slipped into his old con-artist persona, at an electronics store, say, scratching his chin and raising an eyebrow and testing the limits of a salesperson's bullshit, and then Vera would slip in beside him and there they would be again, just for a moment in time, Bonnie and Clyde. Two oranges in a world of apples. Two renegades living peacefully and happily together in the West Village.

They saw their mothers and Sonny nearly every week for Sunday dinners until, one morning, Martha didn't wake up, and then it was just the four of them. They took the subway uptown together on weekday mornings, he to Midtown and the Times building, she to 116th Street and Columbia University. And sometimes, standing side by side as the train rocked and bumped, they saw someone working a crossword puzzle that they made together, and they glanced at each other with conspiratorial smiles.

Of course, life is never perfect. When something as precious as lifelong true love is gained, something of comparable value is likely to be lost. And so it came to pass one day not too long ago, after decades of all-too-perfect happiness, that Stanley was shocked to find himself slurring his words, and Vera took him in to see his doctor. After some fussing about, and referrals to specialists, a brain scan and then a biopsy revealed a malignant tumor the size of a mouse living near his brain stem. There was no point in operating. It was stage IV. Everything that they could do absolutely nothing about was explained to them in detail. It was too late. The little rodent had taken hold. "Well," he joked to Vera after he got the verdict, "that's what you get for overcooking your brain, I suppose."

And it wasn't long—to Vera, it felt like only a day—before the pulsing red light of the ambulance invaded the windows of their home and its thieves in uniform gently took away her world.

At the hospital, standing over the bed where the silly young doctor was trying to make the unacceptable official, Vera made things as difficult as possible for him until it could be avoided no longer. He took up the clipboard with the death certificate clenched in its jaw, and patted his pocket in search of a pen. Vera reached into her bag. "Here, use mine," she said. The doctor took Socrates without hesitation, and Vera knew that from the moment the form was filed away, the ink would begin to fade, and within twenty-four hours, the official certification of his death would be completely blank. And she knew that if she tried, it wouldn't be very difficult for her to believe, that day, and all of the days that remained to her, that he was still alive somewhere, living in a hotel in some eastern city, writing crossword puzzles, coded in a way that called out to her and signaled that she should come to him, and that he would be waiting for her there.

IN GRATITUDE

I'm happy to have this opportunity to express my deep, sincere thanks to: Laney Katz Becker, my wonderfully wise and honest agent, whose decision to take a chance on me I hope to prove a good one beyond any shadow of a doubt; Emily Griffin, the kindest and smartest editor I could have wished for; and Pamela Topper, without whose encouragement I never would have returned to early, failed drafts of this book. Occasionally in life, a small miracle happens whereby some angel swoops down and rigs the machinery in your favor. Kerri Kolen is one of those angels, and her help was beyond measure. Several people read and critiqued early iterations of this book. In that regard, thanks to Jens Birk, Richard Kamm, Nalani Clark, Wendy Amstutz, Jonann Brady, and the insightful Susie Mee—I'll always be learning from those nights I spent in your workshop. Rick Ball deserves thanks for the excellent work he did copyediting the manuscript. Zoe, though you're small now, you fill my life, and without your love, laughter, and spark, I would be lost.

Several books and films were helpful in my research: *American*

Bee by James Maguire; *The Crossword Obsession* by Coral Amende; *Cruciverbalism* by Stanley Newman with Mark Lasswell; *Wordplay*, both the book, with foreword by Will Shortz, and the documentary itself, directed by Patrick Creadon; and the documentary film *Spellbound*, directed by Jeffrey Blitz.

ABOUT THE AUTHOR

Jeff Bartsch is an award-winning copywriter who has worked on campaigns for many major brands. He studied creative writing at the University of Wisconsin and held the Katey Lehman Fellowship in the MFA program at Penn State University. He lives in New York. *Two Across* is his first novel.